BLACKOU

JOHN BOYNTON PRIESTLEY was b
schoolmaster. After leaving Belle
in a wool office but was already
writer. He volunteered for the arm. __ ₁₉₁₄ during the First World War
and served five years; on his return home, he attended university and
wrote articles for the *Yorkshire Observer*. After graduating, he established
himself in London, writing essays, reviews, and other nonfiction, and
publishing several miscellaneous volumes. In 1927 his first two novels
appeared, *Adam in Moonshine* and *Benighted*, which was the basis for
James Whale's film *The Old Dark House* (1932). In 1929 Priestley scored
his first major critical success as a novelist, winning the James Tait Black
Memorial Prize for *The Good Companions*. *Angel Pavement* (1930) followed
and was also extremely well received. Throughout the next several dec-
ades, Priestley published numerous novels, many of them very popular
and successful, including *Bright Day* (1946) and *Lost Empires* (1965), and
was also a prolific and highly regarded playwright.

Priestley died in 1984, and though his plays have continued to be
published and performed since his death, much of his fiction has unfor-
tunately fallen into obscurity. Valancourt Books is in the process of
reprinting many of J. B. Priestley's best works of fiction with the aim of
allowing a new generation of readers to discover this unjustly neglected
author's books.

FICTION BY J.B. PRIESTLEY

Adam in Moonshine (1927)

Benighted (1927)★

Farthing Hall (with Hugh Walpole) (1929)

The Good Companions (1929)

Angel Pavement (1930)

Faraway (1932)

Wonder Hero (1933)

I'll Tell You Everything (with Gerald Bullett) (1933)

They Walk in the City (1936)

The Doomsday Men (1938)★

Let the People Sing (1939)

Blackout in Gretley (1942)★

Daylight on Saturday (1943)

Three Men in New Suits (1945)

Bright Day (1946)★

Jenny Villiers (1947)★

Festival at Farbridge (1951)

The Other Place (1953)★

The Magicians (1954)★

Low Notes on a High Level (1954)

Saturn Over the Water (1961)★

The Thirty-First of June (1961)★

The Shapes of Sleep (1962)★

Sir Michael and Sir George (1964)

Lost Empires (1965)

Salt is Leaving (1966)★

It's an Old Country (1967)

The Image Men: Out of Town (vol. 1), *London End* (vol. 2) (1968)

The Carfitt Crisis (1975)

Found Lost Found (1976)

★ Available from Valancourt Books

BLACKOUT IN GRETLEY

A Story of—and for—Wartime

by

J. B. PRIESTLEY

VALANCOURT BOOKS

Blackout in Gretley by J. B. Priestley
Originally published in Great Britain by Heinemann in 1942
First American edition published by Harper & Brothers in 1942
First Valancourt Books edition 2021

Published by Valancourt Books, Richmond, Virginia
http://www.valancourtbooks.com

ISBN 978-1-954321-08-3 (trade paperback)
ISBN 978-1-954321-09-0 (trade hardcover)

Also available as an electronic book.

Set in Dante MT

I

BEFORE we start out for Gretley, here are the essential facts. My name is Humphrey Neyland. I am forty-three, just old enough to have had a little packet of the last war. I call myself a Canadian, though I was born in England, but my parents took me out to Canada when I was ten, so I went to school there and, after the last war, I went to McGill. After that I did various civil engineering jobs between Winnipeg and Vancouver, and then was taken on by the big Seely and Worbeck outfit and spent most of the Nineteen-Thirties working in Peru and Chile. I'm five feet eleven, run to large bones and turn the scale at about a hundred and eighty-five, am dark and rather sallow and long-faced and inclined to be sour. No doubt there are various reasons why I'm inclined to be sour, and one of them was that in 1932 I married a lovely girl called Maraquita in Santiago, Chile, and in 1936, driving like a madman between Talca and Linares, I had a smash that killed both her and our little boy and left me, there in the hospital, wishing it had killed me too. What with that, and what happened to my friends the Rosentals, and what was happening to the world in general, I was inclined to be sour all right, and it's a long long time since Humphrey Neyland was the life and soul of the party. So anybody who must have Blue Birds Over the White Cliffs of Dover had better turn elsewhere.

Now I'll explain briefly how I came to be working for the department on counter-espionage. Paul Rosental, who was a German Jew, worked with me for Seely and Worbeck, both in Peru and Chile, and he and his pretty little Viennese wife, Mitzi, were my best friends. The Nazis down there murdered them. I got all but one of those rats put away, but that one was the head man. He went to Canada, and I followed him. There I missed him, and now the war came and I sailed at once for England, to try for a commission in the Sappers. While I was hanging about in London, waiting for my application to go through, I caught

sight of the man I'd followed from Chile. He was now calling
himself a Dutchman. I passed on my information, was asked
to see old Austwick of the department, and then found myself
roped in for a temporary counter-espionage job. The War House
still refused to give me that commission—I know now that the
department had a hand in that—so I agreed to take on several
more spy-catching jobs, mostly abroad. I came back to England
in the winter of 1940 a regular member of the department, which
kept me fairly busy going between London and Liverpool and
Glasgow. And if you think I spent most of my evenings in these
places in luxurious flats, double-crossing girls who looked like
Marlene Dietrich, and Hedy Lamarr, take it from me that you're
reading the wrong yarn.

Actually, I didn't like the job much—it's boring most of the
time, though I see now that I'd have been worse bored in the
army—but I couldn't forget Paul and Mitzi Rosental, and what
I'd seen for myself here and there of Himmler's methods, and
I hated the Nazis like hell, so this kept me going through some
long dingy stretches. And anyhow I hadn't a dog's chance of
working now at my own profession, doing sensible civilized
work in a sensible civilized world. But I was particularly sour
about this Gretley job. To begin with, I'd just missed going out to
the Pacific Coast, and I was very anxious to get out there again.
I was beginning to feel I was suffering from claustrophobia in
this island of Britain, doing the same monotonous journeys in
crowded trains, hearing the same talk everywhere, and stifled
by the black nights. I wanted space and light again. But the new
policy of the department was to send men to any particular
territory who were strangers there. I was to go to Gretley just
because I didn't know Gretley and it didn't know me. The idea
was that it was easier this way to assume a character without
having to tell too many lies, and that you brought a fresh eye and
mind to the job.

All I knew about Gretley was that it was an industrial town in
the North Midlands, with a pre-war population of about forty
thousand, that there'd been serious leakages of information from
it, which suggested the presence there of one or two genuine
Nazi agents as well as the usual Fifth Columnists, and that it was

a bad place for any enemy organization to be successfully working in, because the big Charters Electrical Company was there and also, just outside the town, the huge new Belton-Smith Aircraft factory, now turning out the new super-Cyclones. In addition there were several squadrons of heavy bombers not very far away. If you knew how to dispose of your information, you could do the Axis quite a bit of good by keeping your eyes and ears open in Gretley. I knew that both M.I.5 and the Special Branch had their own men in the town, and they were dealing with the routine stuff. But there was some evidence that Gretley or its neighbourhood was one of the Nazi agents' clearing-houses, a minor espionage H.Q. I knew what that evidence was, of course, and it was all right as far as it went, but you couldn't have shot a cat on it. What it amounted to really was that there was the haystack and all we knew for certain was that there were a few needles somewhere inside it. I said as much to old Austwick, just before I left London.

"Yes, but though you're not particularly clever, Neyland," he said, grinning and showing me his yellow stumps, "you're impudent and you're lucky. There's a lot of luck in this game and so far you've attracted it."

"If I really was lucky," I told him, "I'd be on my way to the Pacific Coast now and not booked for any stinking Gretley."

He gave me a letter of introduction to the works manager of the Charters Electrical Company there. It was a good letter, and needless to say, it didn't mention the department. Also it didn't attempt to explain what a civil engineer could do in a big electrical works. But the idea was that I should present this letter soon after arriving, and, if they looked like taking me on, which wasn't very likely, I should ask for better pay and prospects than I was worth, and so be kept hanging about while the Board made up its mind.

This was in January, 1942, and you know what the weather was like and what the war news was like and what life in general was like just about then, so you can imagine that when I slumped into that Gretley coach at St. Pancras I was feeling as sour as vinegar. I was travelling first-class, and soon the other five seats in my carriage were filled. Opposite me, in the other corner away from the corridor, was a handsome woman with a long neck, who wore expensive fur-lined boots and gloves and had enough rugs for a trip to Labrador. Next to her was a pink-cheeked oldish fellow, who was probably on several boards of directors and quietly helping to slow up the war effort. Next to him was a squadron-leader, lost in a sixpenny thriller. Opposite him, on my side, was a subaltern who looked, as so many of them do, as if he were wearing a borrowed moustache. (I wonder if all these fierce moustaches grown to order are a bad sign? I suspect they are.) He was putting in some heavy studious work on an evening paper. Next to him, and therefore in the middle, next to me too was a swarthy fat man, sporting most of his jewellery and reeking of luxurious hair-dressing. He might have been in a foreign government or making British films. The carriage was icy, and we took it in turns to tap our feet or clap and rub our hands. The train pulled out through the cold dusk.

Nobody said anything for an hour or so, by which time the blinds were drawn and the dim top-lights were making us all look sick and mysterious. The woman opposite closed her eyes but didn't give the impression of having gone to sleep. I closed my eyes but couldn't get to sleep. The pink-cheeked oldish fellow began to talk to the other three men. Without being asked, he told them what the military spokesman and B.B.C. announcers had been telling him, and for all the sense there was in anything he said he would have done better to tell them the story of the Three Bears. The Japs would never take Singapore. Big reinforcements were on their way. The American Fleet was about to do something terrific. The two service boys were polite. The shorn Assyrian emperor next to me was obviously sceptical but had too much sense, as a visiting alien, to contradict any of these nice fairy tales. I listened, as I always do because you never know when or where you might pick up something useful, and God knows I needed everything I could possibly pick up to start me off on this Gretley job. Also, it soon appeared that our pink-cheeked friend had something to do with the Charters Electrical Company, though he did not say so in so many words. What the alien gentleman was up to never came out. Probably his handsome luggage was crammed with forged clothing coupons and orders for a few hundred thousand eggs. But I knew in my bones that he was altogether too obviously foreign to be of any interest to me. Any fancy double-bluff of that kind would fail, simply because the ordinary police here are impervious to anything subtle, and therefore would soon have under lock and key any too-clever Nazi agent who hoped to get away with it by giving an obvious performance as a sinister foreigner. But now it was about time I joined in the conversation, for I have always found it useful to explain what I want people to think I am doing. In this way you can help to build up the character you want to sustain in a place even before you have arrived there.

So after slipping in a remark or two here and there, I let it be known that I had recently arrived from Canada and had an appointment to see about a job at a big concern in Gretley. I made it all a bit pompous and hush-hush, because that is the line most fellows like to take now. I asked a few questions about Gretley—was there a decent hotel?—would it be possible to take a house later?—that sort of thing—and pink-cheeks and the subaltern, who tore himself away from his evening paper to hand out information about his native town, gave me the necessary replies. The Air Force lad preferred his thriller—and I don't blame him. But then I noticed that the woman opposite no longer had her eyes closed but was sitting erect, her long neck rising out of her furs almost as if she were a bird, and was staring hard at me. She kept this up for a minute or two, then talked with old pink-cheeks at her side about various people they knew, mostly, I gathered, the local Gretley big-wigs; but now and then she shot another puzzled glance or two in my direction.

At the end of another hour, both the older men in the middle had nodded off and the service lads were deep in their reading. I was beginning to doze myself when suddenly the woman opposite opened her eyes very wide, smiled, leaned forward and said softly: "Did you say you had just come from Canada?"

"I did," I told her. "Why?" Probably I would now have to hear all about her two wonderful children who were in Canada. I might even be asked if I'd seen them.

"Because," she said very softly, "I happened to notice you, about six months ago, dining one night in the French Restaurant of the Central Hotel, Glasgow. In fact, you were dining with a man I know slightly."

Well, of course, there were a good many answers to that, but I had to choose the safest, and to choose it quickly. But I had time to notice that none of the others was listening. The woman was still leaning forward and smiling, with her eyes fixed on mine, but now she had put on a special look of wide innocence, which I could have cheerfully smacked off her face.

"You're sure you're not mistaken?"

"Quite sure," she said, and added, with a hint of parody about it that I didn't like: "I'm awfully good at faces."

I was trying to remember who the fellow was she had seen me with in Glasgow, though it wasn't likely to be anybody important. In the meantime, I stalled again. "I said I'd just come back. I didn't say when I went to Canada. Ships still sail from Glasgow, y'know."

"Of course. You might have been sailing then."

"Exactly." It didn't matter now who the fellow was.

She leaned forward another inch or two, now more like a silky scented cat than a bird, and whispered: "But, you see, I noticed you again—I simply can't help noticing faces—dining in London at the *Mirabelle*—oh, less than three months ago. You couldn't have been in Canada then, could you?"

I shook my head. "Sorry! You were right the first time, but not this time." But of course she was right, and she knew I knew she was right. I was handling this very badly, though it was probably all something and nothing.

She arched that long neck now and leaned back, still regarding me with amusement. I looked at her steadily. Nothing was said for a minute or two. Then she asked: "Are you staying long in Gretley?"

I told her I didn't know, that it depended on whether I got the job I was after or not. And I made it sound as sincere as, in its real meaning, it undoubtedly was.

She nodded, then took out a visiting card and handed it across. "I apologize for being so curious. But I find it so puzzling, and so unlike me, noticing you in Glasgow and then mistaking some-body else for you in London. I can't ever remember it happening to me before. So—if you should ever hit on an explanation, perhaps you'll give me a ring and come out for a drink or a cup of tea—I live not far from Gretley, quite near the Belton-Smith aircraft works, in fact."

That was that. She closed her eyes, with the mocking ghost of a smile still there, while I slipped the card, still unread, into my waistcoat pocket, and shrugged down into my heavy overcoat, feeling that I had made a bad start on this Gretley assignment, and that possibly I was feeling so sour about being given the job, and stale over my work and depressed at the rotten war news into the bargain, that I was slipping. It is all right building up a character even before you arrive in a place, but to this woman, who was no fool, knew everybody round the town, and probably talked twelve hours a day, I was already known as a clumsy liar so, what was worse, a mystery man. Had any of the other men followed this talk? The two boys were still reading hard; pink-cheeks was blowing gently somewhere at the bottom of the sea; but when I looked round at the swarthy gentleman on my left I was just in time to see a heavy yellow lid close over his right eye, which might have been swimming in oil. So he had listened in. That probably meant nothing but it didn't make a bad start look any better. At this rate, by the end of the week I'd be parading the main street of Gretley wearing a gamboge false beard and a placard to announce that I'd been sent by the department. Nice work, Neyland!

I pretended to go to sleep, and after half an hour or so I saw the woman opposite obviously exchanging a knowing glance or two with the fat foreigner on my left. I couldn't see him, of course, because I was still pretending to be asleep, but what I saw of her convinced me that they knew each other, that probably later on somewhere they were due to meet, but that they didn't want the rest of us to know they were acquainted. And whatever it was they were up to, it certainly wasn't a love affair, for she wasn't giving him that kind of glance. It looked more like some kind of business partnership. Black market? More likely that than anything in my way, I concluded, but also decided that before the week was out I would accept the lady's invitation.

We rolled into Gretley, which seemed to have one of those miserable little stations that so many of these smaller industrial

towns have. I could just find my way to the exit, but beyond there
was a terrific blackout. Now I hate the blackout anywhere. It's
been one of the mistakes of this war. There's something timid,
bewildered, Munich-minded about it. If I'd my way, I'd take
a chance right up to the moment the bombers were overhead
rather than endure this daily misery of darkened streets and blind
walls. There's something degrading about it. We never should
have allowed those black-hearted outcasts to darken half the
world. It's a kind of tribute, an acknowledgment, of their power.
We can almost hear those madmen chuckling as they think of us
groping in the gloom they wished upon us. We make a darkness
to fit the darkness deep in their rotten hearts. I tell you, I hate
the blackout. But this blackout in Gretley was the worst I've ever
seen. That station might have been wrapped in indigo blankets.
You could have been stepping from it into far outer space.

Three cars—and I think I saw the woman with the long neck
hop into one—went rattling off, presumably over a bridge; and
then there was nothing. Not a taxi in the place. I had written for
a room for a night or two to the *Lamb and Pole* Hotel, Market
Street, and now that had to be found in this pitch darkness. I
turned back and collared a porter, who was helpful but would
keep on pointing, as if we were looking over the Bay of Naples
on a July noon. Trying to remember his directions, I trudged off,
carrying my heavy bag. There was snow about, but even that
looked black. There was more snow to come. The air was heavy
and raw. Twice I took the wrong turning, wandering into blind
alleys, but finally a policeman put me right.

We don't face this war all the time. In fact, most of the time
we really dodge the stupendous terrifying reality of it, and
merely try to come to terms with its various inconveniences and
restrictions. But now and again, when we're tired and dispirited,
the whole weight of it suddenly comes down on us. Then it's as
if you woke up to find yourself walking at the bottom of the sea.
I had one of the worst of those moments on my way to the hotel
in Gretley that night. The fact of the war came down on me like
a falling tower. Somebody inside me—not Humphrey Neyland
afraid of his skin, nor one of the British tribe doubtful about his
possessions—shook and screamed, seeing in front of him a great

and ever-widening black pit into which men, women, houses, whole cities, went slithering. It was a vision of Evil triumphant. It was the idea of Hell let loose. Strings were being pulled on some underside of the universe we had never even dreamt of once, and we danced and then slithered, everything toppling with us. The wretched Nazis hadn't started it—I hated those backroom gang-sters but wasn't going to pretend they were a hundred times their real size—but had merely been hooked on to the strings first. They could push you into that widening pit, that steaming dark gulf which went down to Hell, but they couldn't have created it. Either we all created it together, or there were giant powers of darkness no longer chained. But there it was, and now I felt on the edge of it. All Gretley was on the edge of it. And a few of its citizens—and that fellow I bumped into at the corner might have been one of them—were working hard to push us all over the brink. Here, behind the dark curtain of the blackout, was deeper evil within evil. But where?

2

THE *Lamb and Pole* Hotel was recommended by the R.A.C. and the A.A. and, I imagine, by nobody else. But it was full, and the woman at the reception desk told me I could only have my room there for a couple of nights. When I saw the room, which had managed to make itself both cold and stuffy, I thought two nights would be long enough. After that I could try for some human digs. I was just in time for the last of the dinner, which seemed to have been concocted entirely out of flour paste: there was flour paste soup, boiled flour paste fish and vegetables and potatoes; and a flour paste pudding. Don't think I'm grumbling about war rations. I'll bet the food at the *Lamb and Pole* wasn't much better in peace-time. The trouble there was the proprietor, Major Brember, who had probably retired from the police in Penang not to keep the hotel but to let the hotel keep him I saw him and his wife, both starched and pop-eyed, sitting like sahibs in the dining-room, pretending that this was their country house, when they ought to have been in the kitchen, with their sleeves rolled up, cooking us a real dinner. But I mustn't get going on the Major Brembers of this island. I don't like them and I wish they wouldn't pretend to keep hotels.

After dinner I went into the private bar, which didn't open until eight, because of the shortage of drink, but was now in full swing. There was no whisky, and people were drinking port, gin and beer. There were some Air Force and Army officers and their girls, mostly in quartets at tables, a few quiet middle-aged citizens ruminating over their beer, and then, with a corner of the bar to themselves, what I recognized at once to be a Regular Gang, a Bunch, a Set. I anchored myself, with a beer, on the edge of this group, and took note of its members. Two of them were officers, and one of them, a red-faced captain, was already rather tight. Then there was a small oldish civilian, who had a high mincing voice and a giggle like a girl's. He seemed to be the entertainer of the party. One of the two women was a plump dull creature who looked rather embarrassed. The other was younger, smarter and quite good-looking. She had a rather long impudent nose and full lips, which even when she wasn't talking and laughing were eagerly parted, ready for the next explosion. I felt sure I had seen her before somewhere, and under very different circumstances too, but I couldn't think where it was. This worried me and I kept staring at her. She noticed this, and I thought that for a second, before she turned away and laughed again, I caught sight of a flicker of alarm in her bold eyes. The red-faced captain noticed me staring too, and didn't like it.

At first the conversation of this bunch centred about a party that one or two of them, notably the handsome lively girl, had attended at what sounded like the *Queen of Clubs,* and was probably some sort of road-house. There were the usual jokes about various people being tight or showing signs of having affairs. There was also some reference to a certain Mrs. Jesmond, who, I gathered, "must be rolling", was very smart, and rather a mystery woman. So I made a note of Mrs. Jesmond. Then the talk degenerated even further into that silly badinage, always with a sexual undercurrent, typical of these sets in hotel bars. The only wit there was the elderly pansy, whose cheeks, I noticed, had been rouged. I noticed too that his line, beneath his obvious clowning, was a continual disparagement of the whole war effort. He made it pretty clear that to him our attempt to fight Nazism was funny, though his favourite word for it was "pathetic." He had plenty of money to spend too. And he was no fool, this Mr. Perigo, as I heard them call him. I began to wonder if I hadn't struck lucky right away. And where had I seen that girl before?

"Look here," said the red-faced captain, suddenly turning and leaning on my table, "we're not the B.B.C., y'know."

"I didn't think you were," I told him, taking an instant dislike to his bloodshot pig's eye.

"Now, Frank!" said the plump woman, warning him. She made a gesture towards the other officer, obviously her husband.

"You've embarrassed this lady already—staring," the captain went on.

"No, he hasn't, Frank," said the girl. And to me: "It's quite all right."

"No, it isn't, Sheila. Let me handle this."

"What is it you want to handle?" I asked him, and I've no doubt looked as contemptuous as I felt. "I happen to be staying in this hotel, and if you don't like my sitting here, then go somewhere else."

"And why the devil should we?" And he banged the table, spilling some of my beer. I felt like throwing the rest of it into his idiotic face.

The fantastic Mr. Perigo had been busy ordering some complicated round of drinks. Now he saw what was happening. He smiled at me, showing a set of teeth that looked as if they had been made out of porcelain, and patted Frank on the shoulder. "Now, now, now! Frank, you're not to be naughty or no more drinkies. Now don't mind him, my dear sir. He'll feel better when he's had another little drink."

It was up to me now. So I smiled back at Mr. Perigo and told him no harm had been done. He insisted on my joining them, and as he was paying for this round, the others could hardly object, though friend Frank still looked surly. This move suited me, of course, and I found myself at the bar, next to the girl with the impudent nose. One of her eyes, which were a flashing dark blue, was a shade darker than the other, which only made me more convinced than ever that I had seen her before somewhere. Her name was Sheila Castleside, and she was the wife of a major who had left that morning for a course.

"What are you doing here?" she asked me. She kept up her saucy manner but I thought I noticed a wary look in her eye when she turned to me.

I told her the usual story. "So I'm going to see the works manager at the Charters Electrical Company to-morrow afternoon," I concluded.

"Now who's that? I ought to know," she cried.

Mr. Perigo knew. "At Charters? Why, my dear, it's Mr. Heacham, you remember, that worried little man. And of course he might well be worried, when he can never get a reply from the Ministry of Supply. The poor man's got all kinds of hush-hush things rusting away at the back of his factory, while they try to make up their minds whether they want him to make some more or not. Pathetic, isn't it?"

And the little monster gave us his porcelain grin, as if we were all in a badly organized bridge tournament and not fighting for our lives.

"Perry," cried the girl, "you're awful. And I heard Colonel Tarlington tell Lionel the other day that he thought you were a Fifth Columnist."

"Sheila!" said the other woman. "Really!" That's about all she ever did, these warnings.

Mr. Perigo looked serious for once. "Now I object to that. No, dear, I mean it. I really *object.*"

"Quite right," said the other officer. Frank was somewhere at the other end of the room.

"Just because I try to be *amused,*" Mr. Perigo continued plaintively, "and don't pretend to be *patriotic* the whole time—really, it's too bad. And I shall tell Colonel Tarlington so. We can't all go about behaving as if we were Britannia's brother. We can't all even *look* like Tarlington—he looks red-white-and-blue."

This amused Sheila quite a lot. She was probably a bit tight and anyhow she was the kind of girl who must have the party going in top gear all the time. Or was she? And where had I seen her before?

I ordered a round. Then I asked who Tarlington was.

"One of the local big-wigs," said Sheila carelessly, no longer interested.

"He's on the board of the Charters Company," said Mr. Perigo, who, as I had guessed, knew all about everybody. "And he's a great gun in the local Conservative Party, and never misses a chance to tell us all to Go To It and that sort of thing. And I think he carries a pike or banner in the local Home Guard. But I ask you—just because I like to make a few little jokes—calling me a Fifth Columnist!"

I told them I thought people over here had stopped talking about Fifth Columnists.

"Yes, they have really," said the officer, who was an ass. "Got 'em all under lock and key now, I'd say."

"I wouldn't." And Sheila shook her head, with that ultra-profound look of the pretty featherhead who suddenly turns serious. "Dozens of 'em about."

"How d'you know, Sheila?"

"Never mind, but I do."

I lifted my eyebrows at Mr. Perigo, who promptly winked. He had very pale eyes, and very odd they looked set in that leathery rouged face. The hair just above his ears was grey, but the toupee he wore was downright auburn.

"There's Derek and Kitty over there," cried Sheila, and bounced across to them. I watched her go, still worrying about her.

"A charming girl," said Mr. Perigo, with a porcelain and leather leer that contradicted his words. "We're all very fond of Sheila, aren't we, Mrs. Forrest? So full of life and fun! One of our Civil Servants exiled here told me the other day that there were days when only the occasional sight of her exquisite legs stood between him and suicide."

Mrs. Forrest did her warning again.

"Had quite a tough time of it, though, before she married Lionel Castleside," said Major Forrest pompously. "Married very young in India—poor kid—and then her husband died suddenly. Never forgets it."

"No," said Mrs. Forrest, who was ready for a bit of sentiment after several gins-and-limes, "I've often seen her eyes suddenly fill with tears, and then she's said she couldn't help remembering those last terrible days in India. Not that she isn't very happy now, of course."

"And she did very well to marry Major Castleside," said Mr. Perigo solemnly. "He's very well off, and of course he's the nephew of old Sir Francis Castleside. You know," he added, to me, "the Gloucester Castlesides."

I told him I'd never heard of them. The fame of the Gloucester Castlesides just hadn't reached as far as the prairie. The Forrest pair stiffened at this colonial crack, but I thought Mr. Perigo twinkled in my direction. "I've seen her before somewhere," I added.

"Is that," asked Mr. Perigo gently, "why you were staring so hard at her?"

"Yes. It doesn't matter, but you know how these things worry you."

Mrs. Forrest worried for days and days if she couldn't remember just when and where it was she had seen a person before. She appealed to her husband, who told us he had seen her doing it, days and days. It must have been an impressive sight. Then Mrs. Forrest announced that they ought to be going. I think it was her husband's turn for a round. They left.

I was wondering how Mr. Perigo would behave when left alone with me. And as I expected, he now turned serious.

"Now and then, Mr. Neyland," he began, "I've caught a look in your eye that asked what I was doing here. You're an intelligent man yourself—oh, I knew that at once—and you could see that I was intelligent too—um?"

"Yes, I could."

"And so you wondered why I was playing the fool with these people, who of course aren't my kind of people at all. But the truth is, Mr. Neyland, I must have a little relaxation, no matter how foolish it is, to try to escape from this terrible war. I used to have a little art gallery in London, but it was badly bombed, so I came down here because an old friend lent me his cottage, just outside the town—a miserable place now, of course, but what can one expect? And now and again I sell a picture—or do a little deal with a piece of antique furniture—but really, of course, my world has gone." He sighed. People are always sighing in books but they rarely do it in real life. However, Mr. Perigo sighed. "So now and then I come in here—or go along to the *Queen of Clubs,* which is much more amusing, and much better food and drink— and talk nonsense for an hour or two. It's a frightful place, Gretley, really one of the foulest little towns you ever saw—you don't know it at all?"

"No, I haven't seen it yet. But it'll do me."

"Yes, of course—engineering and all that sort of thing. But to me, who've always tried to live among *beautiful* things, it's just death—like this terrible war. Tell me frankly, Mr. Neyland, do you think we've the *slightest* chance of winning?"

I did a big surprised act at him. "Slightest chance? You surprise me, Mr. Perigo. Why, we can't lose. Look at all our resources and man-power—the Empire, the States, Russia, China."

"Yes. I know, that's what they all say. But sometimes it seems to me—of course I don't know anything about it—that we forget that resources don't mean anything until they're turned into the munitions of war, and even then they don't mean much unless they're used properly. And the Axis powers do seem to know what to do with their war machines, don't they? And they can organize. We don't seem to be able to organize any longer."

"Oh, we're getting better all the time."

"Are we? I'm glad to hear you say so. But——" and Mr. Perigo dropped his voice—"here or up at the *Queen of Clubs,* I meet so many Air Force and Army officers, and men who are in war production too, and I hear so many awful stories of inefficiency and stupidity and red-tape, that really—I get quite depressed sometimes. And now *you're* going to say I'm a Fifth Columnist too, just because I've been frank."

"No, that's all right, Mr. Perigo," I told him, in a bluff, hearty manner, suggesting I had a skin a foot thick, "no need to apologize. I guess we all feel like that sometimes."

"Now you sound quite American," he said, smiling. He wasn't missing anything and was nobody's fool, this little man. "Will you have dinner with me one night, and then we can talk over these things properly?"

"I'd like to, Mr. Perigo. Many thanks. Don't think much of the dinner here, by the way."

"No, it's much better up at the *Queen of Clubs.* We'll go there. In a day or two, if that suits you. Now here's Sheila again, full of mischief."

Sheila insisted upon standing a round, but Mr. Perigo said he had to meet a friend and went off nodding and smiling.

After talking nonsense with a gang, people nearly always want to be serious when they are left alone with a person they don't know very well. But of course they are more on their guard than when they are rattling away with a crowd. Now it was Sheila's turn.

"The boys think he's an awful old fool, but really he's not."

"No, I know he isn't."

She looked hard at me. I couldn't tell whether she was a bit tight or not. She had that kind of manner which makes it difficult to tell. "I thought you might have noticed it," she said slowly. "But most of these boys are so silly. And—my God—so dull. Are you dull?"

"Yes, I'm dull."

She put a hot hand on my wrist. "No, you're not or you wouldn't say you were. It's just the stifling bores who think they're driving you mad with excitement. Why were you staring at me so hard?"

"I was wondering where I'd seen you before."

"That's what I thought. I mean, it was that kind of puzzled stare. Well, let's see, shall we? I was in India for several years, you know. My first husband died out there, quite suddenly."

"When was that?"

"Just before the war. In Mysore. But I don't want to talk about it. Were you out there?"

"No," I said, "I've never been to India."

There was a pause. "Well?" she asked, with sudden irritation.

I looked at her solemnly. "Well what?"

"Why are you looking at me like that? What's the matter with you?" she demanded, her voice rising.

"What's this?" Frank was back with us, full of fight too.

She shrugged her shoulders very elaborately, then turned

away from both of us. That seemed to decide Frank, who apparently thought nothing of the fact that he was about ten years younger than I am. But then I didn't think much of it myself.

"Come outside," said Frank, almost purple in the face.

I could see the gentle Sheila watching us in the mirror behind the bar. Those odd eyes of hers fairly glittered. Here was fun and games. I felt that when I'd finished with Frank, I'd like to come back here and slap her so hard that she would stay at home for the rest of the week. "Certainly," I told Frank. "Lead the way."

We went through a back door into the yard where people had parked their cars. There was a certain amount of light out there. "Now listen to me," I said to him severely, "you've made your gesture, so let it go at that. Besides, you're tight."

"You insulted a lady in my company," he announced, "and anyhow I don't like Canadians—or whatever you are."

Well, I'd had a long day and felt as sour as forgotten milk, so when he charged in I side-stepped him, then let him have everything I've got. I was lucky in that light to catch him on the point of the chin, but I did, and down he went. I heard a gasp behind me. That nice girl, Sheila.

"I'm glad," she said. "I've wanted somebody to do that to him for weeks."

"Better write and tell your friends in India all about it," I told her, and pushed my way past her, marching straight up to my bedroom.

There I got into a dressing-gown and slippers, lit a pipe, and tried to do some thinking. Then I remembered the visiting card that the long-necked inquisitive woman in the train had handed me, and fished it out. It said *Mrs. G. D. Jesmond,* and the printed address had been crossed out and above it was written *At The Queen of Clubs.* That was where the boys and girls and Mr. Perigo liked to go and play. And somewhere on the premises was Mrs. Jesmond, known locally as rich, smart, and rather a mystery woman, and already known to me as a woman who sometimes travelled about and certainly didn't miss much. And then what about Mr. Perigo, whose account of himself to me hadn't been worth the breath he'd used on it? If he was here as an evacuated art dealer and aesthete, who liked to relax by standing round

after round of drinks, then I was here as a champion female tight-
rope walker. So far I didn't know very much—and I hadn't even
seen Gretley yet—but already I knew enough to realize that the
department had not sent me down here on any fool's errand. I
smoked three pipes before I went to bed.

3

MY APPOINTMENT to see Heacham of the Charters Electrical
Company wasn't until afternoon, so I spent the morning wandering round the town. There was a lot of dirty snow and slush
about, and the sky was grey and sagging with another load of
the stuff, but the morning was fine enough for a walk. Gretley in
daylight provided no surprises. It was one of those English towns
that seem to have been built simply to make money for people
who don't even condescend to live in them. On one side there
was the misty bulk of the Charters works, about thirty acres of
them, with various railway sidings and a canal, the whole outfit
being surrounded by long dingy streets of little brick houses; and
then at the other side of the town were some wider roads, with
a few pathetic attempts at tree-planting, and a mess of gimcrack
bungalows. In the centre were Market Street and High Street,
and a square where they intersected. If you ask me, these towns
give the whole cynical industrial game away. They were run up
as cheaply as possible as money-making machines to provide
people who never came near the places, with country man-
sions, grouse moors, deer forests, yachts, and winters in Cannes
and Monte Carlo. In most other countries the people simply
wouldn't live in a town that offered them so little of what a town
can offer. But the British can take it. I hoped they'd go on taking
it until the day Hitler screamed for the last time, and that then
they'd pull these damned places down and throw the bricks at the
greedy old fakers who'd pop up to tell them they were now all
poor again. I go where the department tells me to go, and every
time I catch a Nazi agent or anybody who sells out to one, then
I'm delighted, for you don't have to tell me what sort of a world
Hitler and Himmler would leave us with; but that doesn't mean

I haven't my own ideas or that I don't know what I'd do to the idiotic old noodles who come to these places and ask the people to fight and sweat for "our traditional way of life." Holy Moses!

I spent most of the morning in or near the square, where the shops are. I've found you get ideas now and then as you watch people going in and out of shops. As a matter of fact, a shop doesn't make a bad post office, and nine-tenths of espionage work isn't getting the right information but passing it on, often along a chain of these improvised post offices. Perhaps I ought to explain here that the department was now sitting pretty in one of the big clearing-houses, the gentleman in charge having recently been picked up, and that so far the rest of the agents and their stooges didn't know this, but kept passing their information down the line for us to examine at the other end. Sometimes of course we supplied the information ourselves, and then when it arrived at the other end we had some idea how it might have got there. This deliberate planting and subsequent checking of information, though cumbersome, was one of our most successful methods. I had done plenty of it myself, and it looked as if here in Gretley I would have plenty more to do. Meanwhile I walked round and looked at the shops.

I was thinking how, these people having been cheated out of having a real town, a good profit was being made by selling them dreams and dope. There were druggists, with windows advertising and offering miraculous cures. There were grocers, who had boxes of patent bran and sawdust that apparently turned your hair into pure gold and gave you muscles like Sandow. There were tobacconists and wine merchants –but they were sold out. There were twopenny libraries, bright with book jackets showing South Sea maidens and shop-girls marrying dukes, pure opium without a hangover at about a farthing an hour. There were two cinemas, which would demonstrate for a shilling what fun it was to be young and handsome, and rich and have funny quarrels with your wife or husband in Long Island or Santa Catarina. Cold as it was, and early as it was, the women of Gretley were already peering and nibbling.

Down a side street I noticed there was a little variety theatre called the Hippodrome, which twice-nightly was offering its patrons what it called the *Great Musical Hit Show of 1942* entitled *Thank You, Playmates,* featuring "Your Favourite Comic, Gus Gimble", "Radio's Songstress, Marjorie Grosvenor", "Leonard and Larry—Always Fooling", and the "Sensational Act of Two Continents—Mam'zelle Fifine." In the photograph-frames in front of the theatre, which was obviously very small, Mam'zelle Fifine claimed most of the space, in a liberal display of herself in various acrobatic poses. She was a hefty young woman with a broad face and prominent cheek-bones, and suggested a product of the French travelling circus. She invited you "To Count My Twists and Turns", and I decided to accept her invitation before the week was out. I like these hard-working little troupes, who always seem to me on better terms with their simple audiences than their superiors are in London and the big cities. Moreover, there have been times when the department has asked me to run an eye over one of these obscure travelling revue companies.

Going back to the square I came across a shop that I had overlooked earlier. It looked newer and brighter than the others, and rather out of place. In bold buttercup lettering against its apple-green paint was *Prue's Gift Shop,* and the windows on each side of the door were filled with little bunches of imitation flowers cut out of soft leather and cloth, art pottery, beaten copper work, and whimsy calendars and the like. It was a familiar type of shop, but I didn't expect to see such a bright new specimen here in Gretley. I saw through the window that at the back of the shop there was a small lending library, and this gave me an excuse to go in and look round.

A young girl, who had a yellow smock and a cold in the head that did not get on too well together, was helping an old lady to choose some tiny wooden toys. I lounged across to the books at the back, and found them not a bad selection of fairly recent stuff. There are times, even on this job, when a man likes to read, and I soon spotted two books that I'd been meaning to read for some months. I didn't take them down, however, but pretended I hadn't yet found anything I wanted. This was because I felt rather curious about a tall green-smocked woman who had now entered through a small back door. This one was Prue to me, because she looked and behaved as if she owned the place. And after a minute or two helping out the girl in the yellow smock, who wasn't too bright, Prue came over to me.

"Can I help you?" she asked.

I looked at her curiously. At first I had thought her little more than a girl, but an unusually tall, stately, handsome young woman, but now I saw that she might easily be somewhere about my own age. She was a natural blonde who looked as if she had been packed in preservative for a long time. The phrase "well preserved" really meant something when applied to her. She looked like a young beauty of the last war who'd only just been taken out of cold storage. She wore her hair in thick heavy golden plaits across her head and round her ears. She had a broad white neck untouched by age. Her eyes were the palest blue, and cold and wary. Close to her, you could see plenty of tiny lines on her face, as if now she might be rapidly thawing out into her proper age. Her voice was very clear and cool.

I told her I was looking for a book or two, and asked about terms. She explained them, and asked if I was staying long in the town.

"I don't know," I said, glad to do my act. "I'm an engineer of sorts, from Canada, and this afternoon I'm trying for a job up at the Charters Electrical Company."

"And if you get it, then you will be staying?"

"Yes, but I doubt if I'll get it." I smiled at her. "So if you don't mind, I'd better not take out any subscription. But of course I'll leave a deposit on the books."

She nodded, and asked me where I was staying. As I told her I watched her rather large white hands writing out a receipt. Then I gave her the two books I had chosen, and she entered their titles into some sort of record. I also told her my name.

"By the way," I said, "if you don't mind my asking—are you Prue?"

"No," she replied, with a faint smile, "because there isn't a Prue."

"But if there was, you'd be she, eh?"

"Yes, it's my shop, if that's what you mean."

"New, isn't it?"

"Yes," she said, opening her eyes a little, "I've only been here about four months. And so far we haven't done badly at all. Even these people, if they're given the chance, can appreciate charming little things. I came here rather as a forlorn hope—but the shop itself was quite a bargain—and it didn't cost much to do it up—and really we've done very well so far. Only of course it's more and more difficult to obtain the kind of things we want."

"That's the war, of course."

"Yes, the war."

I looked hard at her and lowered my voice. "Between you and me and those bookshelves, I hate the damned war. Doesn't make any sense to me."

"And yet you came here from Canada to help in it?" She was almost reproachful.

"I came here from Canada," I told her, "because there wasn't anything doing in my profession out there—I'm a civil engineer, really—and I thought I'd better see if there was any money to be picked out of this war machine over here. And that's a fact, Miss—er——"

"Axton. Miss Axton. But not Prudence, thank you."

"Thank *you*, Miss Axton." I grinned at her, then did a little gentlemanly hesitation. "Now I know this is all very informal—but this is war-time—and after all I'm a Canadian—an——"

"Well, Mr. Neyland?"

"Well, Miss Axton, I was wondering if you'd take pity on me—I don't know a soul here yet—one of these evenings, and come and have dinner with me. I can't recommend dinner at the *Lamb and Pole,* but I hear there's another place just outside Gretley, the *Queen of Clubs,* where the food and drink aren't bad. Do you know it?"

"I've heard of it," she said slowly.

"And what d'you think of my suggestion?"

Now she smiled, with an odd sudden warmth. "I like it. And please don't apologize for making it. I'm still almost a stranger here myself. But to-night and to-morrow I'm engaged."

"Then we'll leave it until later," I said very heartily, "and I'll look in again and we'll fix it up. But perhaps you're on the telephone?" She was, and I took down the number. It seemed that she lived above the shop. We exchanged a few idle remarks and then I left.

Two doors farther down there was a tobacconist's, and I went in to ask for a packet of cigarettes that I knew he wouldn't have and that, anyhow, I didn't particularly want. But shopkeepers who can't sell you something you want generally are glad to talk a little, if only by way of apology.

"Oh, it's cruel," said the tobacconist, after I had prompted him. "There's many a day, as I've said to the wife, when I feel I might just as well shut up shop."

"Still, I don't suppose your overheads are much here. These shops ought to be cheap enough."

"These!" He nearly screamed. "Why, we have to pay a terrible rent for these—yes, a terrible rent. And as fast as one's empty it's snapped up, so if you don't like it, you can lump it."

"No bargains in shop premises, then, eh?"

"Not here there isn't, I give you *my* word. So if that's what you're looking for, you can look somewhere else." He wasn't being rude, only emphatic. We parted friends.

It was possible, of course, that Miss Axton was one of those hopeful, muddle-headed, inexperienced females who imagined that a terrible rent was quite a bargain. That kind of woman frequently opened just that kind of artsy-craftsy shop. And that is why I found Miss Axton so interesting, for she was clearly not that kind of woman at all. But she would keep.

The department, which always looked after these details very well, had forwarded on my behalf another perfectly good letter of introduction to Heacham, the works manager of the Charters Electrical Company, so I was able to see him after only a very short wait that afternoon. I handed him the second letter, which I carried with me. There was, of course, not a word about my connection with the department in these letters. But apart from that, they gave the facts—my right name, age, qualifications, experience in Canada and South America, etc. The great thing— and half the people we caught never realized it—is never to tell unnecessary lies, but to let the truth work for you as far as it will go. So I felt quite easy in my mind as I watched Heacham, who, as they said the night before, was a worried little man, reading my letters. I was a lot easier than he was, poor chap. He had the grey brittle look of a man who works too late and never gets any air.

"D'you know what I was thinking, Mr. Heacham?" I asked him, if only to make it easier for him.

"No. Tell me."

"I was thinking that this production mess is terribly hard on you fellows on the management side. You're all working like blacks——"

"Some of us are doing fourteen hours a day, Mr. Neyland," he cried. "I've never known anything like it, I can tell you. And, you see, the devil of it is that the very things that hold up and cut down production are the very things that make so much of our work. If I began to tell you——" And he rubbed what the war had left of his hair in deep exasperation.

This did what I hoped it would do, broke the ice.

"Now, Mr. Neyland," he said, glancing at the two letters again, "I'm not going to say we couldn't do here with one or two good men who are used to handling labour. And if you'd had any electrical engineering experience, I wouldn't hesitate to say we could find room for you. But of course you haven't."

"No, I haven't." This was going just the right way.

"I believe myself that purely technical experience isn't as important now," he went on, "as experience in organizing big jobs, handling labour, all that sort of thing—and that you've had, evidently. But whether the Board would agree is another matter."

This was my cue. "Mr. Heacham, there's no hurry, and I don't want to worry you at all. If you'll put my name and qualifications before your Board, and say a good word for me, that's all I ask. Meanwhile I'll stick around in Gretley."

This was just what he wanted too, and I could see that the way I'd made it easy for him impressed him greatly in my favour. So I took the opportunity of asking him for a letter of introduction to the manager of the Belton-Smith aircraft works, saying that I might as well see if there was anything in my line up there, while I was in the neighbourhood. He agreed without hesitation and at once dictated the letter to his secretary. Which only confirmed what I'd told the department more than once, that anybody who spoke English and didn't wear the Iron Cross too conspicuously only needed one phony letter of introduction to be able to see everything we'd got in ease and comfort.

"I usually go round the works at this time," said Heacham, after he had dictated the letter to the Belton-Smith people. "Would you like to see what we're doing?"

He was very proud of what they were doing, and he trotted me through shed after shed for the next hour and a half, explaining the processes and enlarging on some of his difficulties. Everybody seemed to be very busy. It's funny but although I'm always reading about war factories where half the men have nothing to do but make model airplanes or arrange football sweeps, I've never yet managed to walk into one of them. And if they're faking it just to deceive the manager, surely the manager ought to know he's being deceived or he's not fit to be a manager. All the time I kept my eyes open for a glimpse of somebody who might be there from M.I.5 or the Special Branch, for it might be somebody I'd met before or who would recognize me, having worked with the department at some time or other, but nothing happened. Somehow when we reached the end of our long walk, I couldn't help feeling sorry I was still engaged in this odd, intangible counter-espionage work and not doing a solid and sensible job at production. I'd always liked handling decent men and creating a team loyalty. There was none of that in working for the department. You were nearly always on your own, hanging about and sniffing about, and listening to the lies people tell. It has a fascination, of course. But that afternoon it wasn't working for me. As I told you, I was sour on that Gretley job.

Heacham was having my two letters copied for me, so when we had finished walking round the works we crossed the yard to return to his office. But one of his foremen came running out after Heacham, so I walked forward towards the office. Then I waited for him, not far from the entrance to the office block. A police-sergeant, who'd been talking to the man at the factory gate, now came across. He was a youngish fellow, probably only recently promoted, and an officious type. He had that kind of jutting chin which in magazine stories always stands for character, intelligence, grit, but which in real life has always seemed to me to mean nothing but downright damned stupidity.

"Just a minute," said this sergeant, as if he'd caught me hurry ing off instead of standing stock still. "I'd like to see your pass."

"I haven't got one," I told him, pleasantly enough.

"You've no business to be inside these works without a pass," he said.

Well, I couldn't quarrel with that, could I? But I explained that I'd had an appointment with the works manager and was still, so to speak, in his company, only waiting for him to catch me up.

"What's all this about, sergeant?"

This fellow had just come out of the office entrance. He was a stiff, well-brushed man of about sixty, who had a face like a slab of sirloin, bushy eyebrows and a neat grey moustache, and reminded me of our generals in the last war. But he wasn't in uniform, though you felt he'd only just got out of uniform and might be back in it again any minute now. He had, of course, the clipped authoritative voice. The sergeant saluted him like a shot, and I felt that these two belonged to the same series.

"Just asking about a pass here, sir," said the sergeant.

"Quite right," snapped the other. "Told the Superintendent myself to send somebody along to check up. Getting altogether too damned slack here."

"Yessir!" Then they both looked severely at me. These fellows have to have a stooge. What's the use of cultivating that manner if you've nobody to boss about and dress down?

"I've already explained that I've been seeing Mr. Heacham. In fact, I've just been round the works with him. Here he is. He'll tell you."

"All right, sergeant. Carry on!"

The sergeant saluted again, but before he went, feeling that somehow I'd put him in wrong with the great, he gave me a long and nasty look. Heacham now came up and introduced me. This was the Colonel Tarlington I'd heard them mention last night in the bar. I wasn't surprised.

"Look here, Heacham," the colonel began, after barely acknowledging our introduction, "I see this fellow Stopford's on the Canteen Committee here."

"Yes, I believe he is," said Heacham, not much interested.

"Well, we can't have that, y'know. Fellow's always been on our dangerous list. He's a Communist."

"I know he is," said Heacham, looking more worried than ever, "but the men elect the members of the Canteen Committee, and if they want Stopford, I can't prevent them."

"Of course you can," said the colonel angrily. "Easiest thing in the world. I shall bring the matter up at the Board meeting to-morrow. You know my views, Heacham. Here we are—doing all kind of hush-hush jobs—and we've communists being elected to this, that and the other in the works, and German refugees roaming about the town, until we don't know where we are. And I warn you. I'm going to take a strong line. Both here and in the town—a strong line." And he gave us both a sharp nod and went marching off.

"I've heard of him already," I told Heacham as we climbed his office stairs.

"Who? Tarlington?"

"Yes. Tell me about him."

"Well," said Heacham, almost apologetically, "he's rather a big noise round here. Landed man really, but has a seat on our Board, and a local J.P. and all the rest of it. Very keen, of course, makes a good speech in Warships Week and all that, but overdoes it. Got a bee in his bonnet now about German refugees. Thinks they're all spies and Fifth Columnists, and got one of 'em, a very good metallurgical chemist from Austria, kicked out of here. Couldn't stop him."

"Backbone of the country," I suggested.

"That's about it," he sighed. Then, feeling he might have gone too far, he became brisk and business-like again. "Well, here are your two letters, Mr. Neyland, and I have copies for the Board. And you have that note for Robson of Belton-Smith? Good! But don't take anything there without letting me know first. God knows we need a few men here."

That sergeant was still hanging about when I went through the gate, and though he'd seen me with the heads I knew he was still suspicious and was wishing he had some excuse for taking me to the station. I gave him a bright smile and a nice wave of the hand, and then afterwards wished I hadn't. We never work with the local police unless it's unavoidable, but there was no sense in my going out of my way to feed this sergeant's little grudge

against me. But that's what I felt like, and I was in the mood to
indulge myself a bit.

I had a pot of tea in the lounge of the *Lamb and Pole* and saw
Major Brember strutting about in a canary pullover and ginger
plus-fours. I bet myself any odds that he and Colonel Tarlington talked the same language, though I knew very well that
there was much more in Tarlington than in Brember. (It was a
pleasure to strip them of their ranks. I am always rather wary of
civilians who can't stop calling themselves majors and colonels.)
There were a few odds and ends of folk in the lounge, drinking
tea and whispering, but nobody I'd noticed before. Over a pipe
or two I turned over in my mind, rather lazily, the few items of
information I had picked up during the day, but as yet nothing
made a pattern or even began to link on to the miserable bit of
stuff, mere hints and winks of information, that the department
had given me. I began to feel that even the little the department
knew about espionage activities in this district was all wrong. I
was still idly fumbling with these inadequate bits of the jig-saw
puzzle when the six o'clock news burst into the lounge, with the
announcer trying to pretend that what were obviously the begin-
nings of huge calamities in the Far East were somehow counter-
balanced by our bringing down a couple of German fighters or
machine-gunning a few trucks in Libya. After ten minutes of this
drivel, the radio was still on at full blast, and we were threatened
with some good advice by some minor official, so I decided to
clear out. The bar didn't open until much later, so there was no
point in staying in the hotel.

Already the blackout looked as bad as it had done the night
before, and I was just beginning to curse myself for leaving the
hotel when I remembered the little variety show down the side-
street not far away. So I groped my way round there, and found
that the first performance had just begun. For two shillings I was
given a stall that must have been designed for a midget, for there
was no space for any grown man's legs. It was a square little box
of a place with a single balcony. A tiny orchestra, in which stout
middle-aged women were prominent, rumbled and squeaked.
Six chorus ladies, all platinum blondes with Jewish noses, were
giving what might charitably be called an enthusiastic sketch of

a dancing team. You felt that somebody had described to them roughly what a revue chorus was like, and that now they were doing their best. Gus Gimble, Our Favourite Comic, was a little hoarse elderly trouper, who worked like a nigger, dashing on and off with a variety of comic hats and props, carefully bringing in references to Gretley and district, and dishing out bits of dirt that made the women in the balcony scream with laughter. There was nothing wrong with Gus except that he just wasn't funny. But I preferred him to Leonard and Larry, a couple of dreary playboys who seemed to be going through their routine in a melancholy delirium; or to Radio's Songstress, a very severe, excessively lady-like soprano, wearing half a hundred-weight of beads and bangles, who was pretty intimidating even when she was serious and simply terrifying when she turned domestic and coy. The six platinum Jewesses kept returning, their grins more fixed and their thighs more mottled each time. But up to the interval there was no sign of Mam'zelle Fifine, that sensation of two continents, the hefty, broad-faced young woman whose photographs took up so much space outside. Fifine was being kept in reserve for the second part of the show, which would badly need her.

When the lights went up I saw to my right, two rows in front, quite a party in which were several people I knew. There was Mr. Perigo, who was the nearest to me, and then wedged between two young officers my friend of last night, Sheila Castleside, and then next but one to her was the long-necked woman who had sat opposite to me in the train, Mrs. Jesmond. The sight of her reminded me of the swarthy fat foreign gentleman who had pretended not to know her in the train, but had yet exchanged a knowing glance or two with her, and as I began to wonder what had become of him and looked away from Mrs. Jesmond's party, there of course he was, leaning against the wall near the first *Exit* and only a few paces behind Mrs. Jesmond. I crammed my hat down over my eyes and turned up my overcoat collar, then watched the whole party rise, presumably to go out to the bar, with Mrs. Jesmond well ahead. When she reached our foreign friend, she hesitated a moment, and I was certain that they exchanged a quick low word or two. Then she went out, followed by the rest of the gang.

When half a minute later I passed the foreign gentleman I glanced quickly at him and was just in time to see a flicker of recognition in those sad swimming eyes of his. Just a flicker, that's all. He wasn't definitely recognizing me, as we often do a recent fellow-traveller. The next moment he was lost in a reverie again. No doubt an old admirer of Mam'zelle Fifine, a fan from both continents.

The stalls bar was fairly large but not very crowded. I was recognized and hailed at once by Mr. Perigo, who this time was not buying the drinks. I had a notion this was Mrs. Jesmond's party. Mr. Perigo was delighted to see me, and you would have thought we were old friends.

"My dear boy," he said, patting me on the shoulder, "we meet again. And I've just heard you had to take very drastic measures with our friend Frank last night after I'd gone. No, no, I don't blame you, don't blame you in the least. Now, let me get you a drink, and then I'll introduce you to Mrs. Jesmond. A charming woman. I don't know what we'd do without her here. What's it to be? I may be able to get you a little whisky."

He went bustling through, in his own mincing fashion, to the bar, while I remained standing where he'd found me. But the next moment Sheila caught sight of me and steered that impudent nose of hers in my direction. She seemed in exactly the same excited goggly state that she'd been in late the night before, and as she couldn't be tight already I saw that this must be her usual state when there were people and lights around.

"Now listen," she said, not smiling at all, "if you think I'm going to forgive you for last night until you've apologized, you're mistaken. So please yourself."

"Okay," I said.

"Well, go on."

But I didn't go on. I began filling a pipe, almost as if she weren't there.

"I don't say that Frank didn't behave badly or that I wasn't rather glad. He had it coming to him, though he was ages coming round, and he swears he'll half-murder you next time he sees you. But that's all right. I happen to know he's on duty for several nights now."

"Thanks," I said, "but I'm not worrying."

"Say you're sorry."

"Sorry for what?"

She put a hand on my arm. "For the damned rotten way you behaved to me. You know you did, didn't you?" She was quite serious too, almost as if we'd been intimate for months and I'd suddenly treated her badly. She didn't know why she was taking this line, but I thought that I did.

But Mr. Perigo was weaving his way towards us now, carrying a whisky, and smiling his huge porcelain smile. "Here you are, my dear boy, and they swear it's the very last drop. What's the matter with Sheila? Being tiresome again, Sheila? You're a sweet child, but sometimes very, very tiresome."

"Oh——" And Sheila just stopped herself from saying something very coarse and unlady-like indeed. And I had a notion then that Mr. Perigo, at that moment, gave me a quick understanding look. He was no fool.

"Now you must meet Mrs. Jesmond," he said. "This is really her party."

"As a matter of fact, I've already met Mrs. Jesmond," I said.

"I'll bet you have," cried Sheila crossly. "All the mystery men and mystery women together."

But when I followed Mr. Perigo, as he moved towards the bar, Sheila came close behind and kept pinching my elbow. Married to one soldier, and surrounded by dozens more, with whom she seemed to be on easy terms, Sheila ought not to have been worrying about her sex life, and perhaps she wasn't, but she certainly gave out some pretty powerful radiations. I was thankful that she wasn't the type of young woman that attracted me.

"Well now," cried Mrs. Jesmond, after I had said Hello and had been introduced to the Air Force boy and the subaltern who were entertaining her, "isn't this absurd? I hope you were going to ring me up, as I suggested, um?"

I told her, quite truthfully, that I had made up my mind to telephone her the very next day. Then I asked her how she liked the show.

"It's dreadful, isn't it?" she exclaimed, smiling at her two young men. "I've never been to this horrible little place before, but Mr. Perigo insisted and these boys backed him up. They say there's a woman acrobat who's quite marvellous."

"Cracking!" said the Air Force.

"I've heard of Mam'zelle Fifine before," said Mr. Perigo, with mock gravity, "and believe I may have seen her at the Medrano in Paris. Apparently you count her twists and turns."

"Good show!" said the Army.

"Then we ought to be wedging ourselves into those ghastly seats again," said Mrs. Jesmond, smiling at us all. "Mr. Neyland, I'm celebrating—I don't quite know why—and all these nice people are dining with me at the *Queen of Clubs*. Will you join us?"

I said I'd be delighted to, and now we all returned to our stalls, but this time I found myself sitting with the bunch, jammed between Sheila and Mr. Perigo. The fat foreigner was still leaning against the wall, but now there wasn't the flicker of an eyelash between him and Mrs. Jesmond. I found myself thinking about Mrs. Jesmond instead of attending to the huge lolloping of the six platinum Jewesses. In the train I had never been able to see her clearly, and had only been able to discover that she was long-necked, expensive and quite good-looking. Now I had a very clear image of her. She wasn't young, but at least my age, but she had a good figure, rather full peachy cheeks, and experienced handsome eyes. Like many women who seem to be successfully defying their years, she didn't look quite real. You felt that if you shook her hard she would fall to pieces. For my part I didn't want to set a finger on her, yet there was something disturbing and rather fascinating about her. She was rather like an exotic fruit that had been too long on the way and was now probably dead rotten inside and yet still gave out an air of faint musty sweetness.

"You be careful," whispered Sheila, so close that she tickled my ear, "that woman's dangerous. I don't know how, but she is."

I nodded, and pretended to be attentive to Leonard and Larry, whose routine was even worse than before. I didn't mind Sheila talking about Mrs. Jesmond, and could have done with some more, but I knew that Mr. Perigo had sharp ears and missed nothing.

He was shaking his head over Leonard and Larry. "Pathetic!" he exclaimed. I didn't tell him that one of them rather reminded me of him. But a sharp nudge from Sheila suggested that she might have had that idea too.

Gus, Our Favourite Comic, returned to work harder than ever, to the delight of the audience, including our officer friends and Sheila, who laughed at his blue old chestnuts until she was nearly in hysterics. She laughed in exactly the same places and in exactly the same way as the factory lasses in the balcony. It was very revealing. I was quick enough to notice that once Mr. Perigo turned to give her a speculative glance that was dead cold. I couldn't see Mrs. Jesmond very well, for she was three seats away, but I never heard her voice ringing out and I had the impression that she was bored. I wasn't.

I was still less bored when the curtain went up on Mam'zelle Fifine, who performed with rings and trapezes. She looked as powerful as a young horse, but was extraordinarily flexible too, so that she was able to contort herself in the most amazing fashion. As advertised, she invited us to count the number of times she could achieve every particular fantastic twist and turn, so that you could hear everybody murmuring *One—two—three—four— five*—and so on. There would be seven of one, eleven of the next, nine of the next, fifteen of the next, and always she repeated the total herself. She didn't talk much, but I fancied that she was an Alsatian. Her act, which she had obviously been doing for years, was a good mixture of acrobatics and showmanship, and she was a huge success.

"Look at Mr. Perigo," whispered Sheila. "Now we know what he likes."

He heard her, and turned at once, creasing his leathery cheeks and showing us the usual white grin. That didn't matter, however, because I'd already seen quite a different Mr. Perigo. The woman hadn't been on the stage two minutes before I seemed to feel him go all rigid in concentrated attention, and peeping at him without turning my head I saw that he was staring, fixedly with narrowed eyes, at the gleaming twisting figure. I heard him counting too, quite seriously, almost as if he were her manager.

"You were fascinated—admit it," Sheila shrieked at him, as Mam'zelle Fifine acknowledged, with no great amiability, our enthusiastic applause.

But Mr. Perigo was back in ordinary circulation again now. "Of course I was, darling," he replied, at the top of his shrill voice. "She made me feel so exquisitely small and weak. I adore the creature. What arms! What thighs! And then, you see, I amused myself making little bets about the number of times she'd go round, and won thirty-two and sixpence from myself. You see?" he added, specially for me.

"Yes, I see," I told him. But of course I didn't quite, then, though there were certain things I did already see.

By this time the full company, led very solemnly now by Gus, was telling us in no wild spirit of optimism that There'll Always Be A Ningland, and Mrs. Jesmond and party were preparing to leave the theatre. Somehow we found two cars in the sootbag outside, and I shared one with Sheila, Mr. Perigo, and the sub-altern, who drove. As we went rattling and groaning through the sleety darkness, Mr. Perigo was strangely silent and detached and I had nothing to say, but Sheila and the subaltern kept up a running bellow of nonsense. I felt depressed, as I often do after that sort of utterly brainless entertainment, but probably I was also hungry and in need of a drink. I said as much.

"Don't worry, sweetie," screamed Sheila over her shoulder, "there'll be marvellous food and drink, you'll see. I don't know how Mrs. Jesmond does it, but she does."

We had arrived somewhere, but I couldn't see where. Now that the car had stopped, however, I could hear dance music.

"And let us remember," said Mr. Perigo softly, "that from the Arctic to the Black Sea, thousands of men are now freezing to death. In Greece and Poland, millions are starving to death. In the Far East, other people—perhaps friends of ours among them—are probably being bayoneted and raped to death——"

"Oh, for God's sake!" cried Sheila, overhanging some of it.

"Quite, darling, quite, quite!" said Mr. Perigo, chuckling, as he climbed out. "But I wasn't talking to you but to our friend Neyland, who is, I can see, a man of sense. And being a man of sense, he's beginning to wonder why we go on with this elabo-rate self-destruction."

"To beat Hitler," muttered the subaltern, who was a decent lad.

"No doubt," said Mr. Perigo, with a kind of malicious relish, "but can we beat Hitler?"

"Oh, I say—look here," said the subaltern, who didn't like this at all.

"Oh, stop arguing and let's enjoy ourselves for once," said Sheila. She always took this line, as if she'd just finished a twelve-hour spell of duty in an operating theatre, whereas she'd probably done nothing but powder her nose and ring up her pals since she got up that morning. But mind you, it was all a performance on her part. She was taking the line that she thought was expected of her. I knew that, and she knew I knew it.

The great thing at the *Queen of Clubs* apparently was to make straight for the cocktail bar, not only because you wanted a drink, but also because this bar was in the hands of Joe. I heard a lot about Joe during the next ten minutes. He seemed to be the great man at the *Queen of Clubs*. He was a daring and precious importation from London, where he used to shake the cocktails at Borani's, and it was felt on all sides that it was very good of him to condescend to Gretley. I had to admit that Joe knew his stuff and also knew where to find it, for the two dry martinis he made me were the best I had had for months. He was a smooth, broad fellow, very clean and trim in his white jacket, and he was quick and obliging and told good stories in a rather American accent. There was a touch of the naval man about him. I enjoyed watching him at work.

There were eight of us at dinner, in a combined dining-and-dance-room that had been laid out in much better style than you would expect to find in a provincial road-house. Sheila had been quite right about Mrs. Jesmond. She did us very well. The dinner was as good as the cocktails. There was lobster, roast duck, a cheese soufflé, and some first-rate claret and liqueur brandy. I sat between Mrs. Jesmond, who had the Air Force lad on her other side, and Sheila, who had the subaltern as her other neighbour; and then, of course, there was Mr. Perigo, who ate and drank with obvious enjoyment and chattered away to two rather dull women who completed the party. I couldn't make out why Mrs. Jesmond was making such a fuss of me, because I certainly wasn't her type and anybody could see that she was putting in some heavy work with the Air Force lad, who was a bit embarrassed about it.

I had one surprise. There, dancing with a burly wing-commander, was my friend of the fancy gift shop, Miss Axton. She was looking pretty good too. I remembered that when I had mentioned this place she had replied that she had heard of it and had said nothing about coming here to-night herself. Of course, she may not have known then she was coming here. Sheila noticed that I was looking at her. Sheila didn't miss much.

"That's the woman from the awful arts and crafts shop, isn't it?" said Sheila.

"Is it?" I asked. "I was wondering who she was."

"Yes," said Sheila, narrowing her eyes. "And she's a lot older than she looks at a distance, I can tell you. And I don't like her."

I laughed. "What's the matter with her?"

"For one thing, she's a snob. And another thing is she's a liar."

I knew she was a liar, and the snob angle didn't interest me. Half the people in England condemn the other half as snobs, and generally they're right. "Is that all?" I asked, trying to appear not too curious.

"No." Sheila thought for a moment. "She's also a bit sinister somehow. Notice the look in her eye when you get close to her." She turned and now looked me in the eye. "I'm not a fool, y'know. I don't mean I haven't behaved like a fool, but I'm not one really. I've seen a lot of life, more than most of these people."

"Yes," I told her, "I know you have." And now I looked her in the eye too.

That wiped the smiling ripe impudence off her face and left it white. She drank what was left of her wine and said: "Let's dance."

I didn't want to dance, but it was easier talking on the dance floor than it was at the table. "Well?" I said, once we'd settled into a steady rhythm.

"Are you going to give me away?" she whispered, her fingers moving inside my grasp.

I looked surprised, though I didn't feel surprised. "What is there to give away?"

"There's plenty, and you know it. And I knew you knew it last night. I've seen you before too, but I can't remember where. It worried me all last night."

"I can't see that it matters," I said. "And as for giving you away, I wouldn't know what to give away or who ought to have it when it's given away. So let's drop the subject, shall we?"

She gave me a long sideways look, then nodded and began to smile again. The band stopped, but there was some clapping, so it started again. We kept on dancing.

"I didn't know there were places like this tucked away outside English manufacturing towns," I said.

"There aren't," she replied promptly. "This is just a bit of luck for us here in Gretley. God knows if it'll be able to carry on like this long."

"Whose place is it?"

"Oh, haven't you met the proprietor yet? There he is—that little man standing over there. Yes, he's the proprietor—Mr. Settle. You'd never imagine it, would you?"

"No, not in a thousand years." We were nearer the man now, and I wanted to make sure. "You do mean this little man, don't you?"

"Yes. Mr. Settle," she repeated. He saw her now and nodded and smiled. Then he saw me, and he stopped smiling. His name wasn't Settle, and I was willing to bet the rest of my year's pay that though he might be the manager here he certainly wasn't the proprietor. When I'd met him in Glasgow—at the time when Mrs. Jesmond noticed me there—his name had been Fencrest and he hadn't had enough in the world to pay for the knives and forks in this place, to say nothing of the rest of it. He didn't know I was connected with the department, probably didn't even know it existed, but he'd met me with one of the police officers in Glasgow, may have seen me with one or two more, and probably thought I'd something to do with the police. Meanwhile he'd vanished only a second or two after his smile had vanished. Even apart from its roast ducks and drinks, this looked like being a very interesting place.

"You look quite pleased," said Sheila.

"Yes, I'm glad I came out here. Nice of Mrs. Jesmond to ask me."

"She likes to celebrate, as she calls it, now and then, and then most of us don't see her for days. And when I say *us* I don't mean these Air Force and army boys she gets hold of. God knows when and how they see her."

"That, Sheila, isn't a nice thing to say about your hostess," I told her. "I see our party seem to have left the table. What do we do now?"

"Go back to Joe and ask him to find us a couple of nice whiskies and sodas," said Sheila. And as we went across, she told me how lucky the *Queen of Clubs* had been to find Joe, how amusing and useful he was, and how fond all her set was of him. Joe was wonderful.

"I think I could learn to love him too," I said, wondering what had become of Mrs. Jesmond and Mr. Perigo. They weren't in this cocktail bar. Probably there was a lounge somewhere.

Joe was telling the boys at the bar the story of the air-raid warden and the widow. It was going well. When it was over and I'd got our drinks, I was glad to see that two of the service lads were talking hard to Sheila. I gave her the drink, swallowed mine quickly, then marched out, though I wasn't sure what the next move ought to be.

Along the corridor at the other side of the dining-room was a door marked Private. I opened it quickly, shouted "Sorry!" and shut it again. I thought Fencrest might have been there, for it looked like a manager's office, but he wasn't. Somebody else was, though, and it was the fat dark foreigner I'd already seen that night in the theatre.

At the end of this corridor, to the left, was the entrance to a large gaudy lounge, where people were sitting at little tables, drinking and listening to the radio. I stood at the entrance for a moment, just long enough to notice that Mr. Perigo and the two dull women and the subaltern were safely in there. Opposite this entrance, to the right of the corridor, were the stairs, rather narrow and poorly lit. But there was just light enough for me to see that the man coming downstairs so carefully was Fencrest, now Settle. And this time there was no escape for him.

"Hello!" I said, grinning.

"Oh—hello! Mr. Neyland, isn't it?"

"It is. But what do I call you these days——"

"Come into my office," he said hastily, "and have a drink."

It was the same room I'd looked into only a couple of minutes before, but now the fat dark foreigner wasn't there. And I noticed that this office had another door.

"The fact is, Mr. Neyland," said Fencrest, not making a very good job of it, "I'd been having trouble with my wife that time we met before—where was it?——"

"It was Glasgow, and you'd also been having trouble with the police." It was a Board of Trade affair, something to do with an export licence, and had been no business of mine, except that he might have been running round with some people who would interest the department. But he was a shifty little man and I didn't like him. He was one of those fellows who are always on the edge of something very crooked, not because they're born crooks themselves, but simply because they like easy money and easy living and no hard work. There are thousands of them, and the sooner they're taken out of their hole-in-the-corner private offices and set to felling trees and mending roads, the better it'll be for the rest of us.

"That was just a mistake," he said quickly. "But as I was saying, I'd been having trouble with my wife, so when I got this job I changed my name to Settle, hoping she wouldn't find out where I was. And that's all there is to it. Have a drink, Mr. Neyland?"

"No, thanks. Why do they think you're the proprietor?"

"How do you know I'm not the proprietor?"

"How do I know you're not heavy-weight champion of the Navy?"

"That's different. You've only got to look at me——"

"That's what I am doing." And did for half a minute. He was very uneasy, and fussed about with his drink and a cigarette-box. "Who does own this place?"

He looked to one side of me and then to the other. He wriggled his shoulders a little and rubbed the bald patch above his forehead in the centre. He was very uncomfortable indeed, and I was delighted to see it.

"Well, who does own it?"

"I don't think you've any right to ask that question, and I'm not in a position to answer it."

"You're in a very good position to answer it, Fencrest," I said, "and I propose to repeat the question, and never mind about my having no right to ask it. Come on."

He gave in. "Mrs. Jesmond owns this place," he muttered, "but nobody's supposed to know, so don't say I told you. You were dining with her to-night, weren't you?"

"Yes. Very good dinner too. Who is she?"

"Don't know much about her myself, and that's a fact, Mr. Neyland," he replied, a bit heartier now. "She's a widow, I think, and she used to live in style on the Riviera and then just got away before France collapsed. But she must have had plenty of money in this country. She bought this place for fun, and runs it as a kind of hobby. Some of the people who are working here are people she knew before and wanted to help, such as the chef. And Joe."

"She knew Joe at Borani's, eh?"

"Yes," said Fencrest, "and then after Borani's was bombed, Joe didn't know what to do and his nerve went and he wanted to get out of London, so she brought him up here."

There was only one thing wrong with this story, and that was that the dates didn't fit. I happened to know that Borani's was bombed in October, 1940, which meant that Joe must have spent about a year watching his nerve go and travelling up here.

"Well," I said, "you were lucky to get him. He's obviously a great draw. You must be making money here."

"We are," he admitted. "But chiefly because we happen to have had some good stocks of tinned stuff and wines and liqueurs."

"Some time, Fencrest," I said, "you must tell me where I can buy a few tins of that lobster and roast duck I ate here to-night."

"Excuse me," he said, for there was a knock. One of the waiters had a message for him. I knew by the fine easy way he left me alone in that private office of his that there couldn't be anything worth looking at in it, so as soon as he had gone I tried the other door, through which I thought the fat dark foreigner must have gone. It was unlocked and led directly to a narrow dark flight of stairs. I closed the door behind me, and, using my torch, crept quietly up the stairs.

There was another door at the top, also unlocked, and this

opened into a small landing that seemed to serve as the hall of a separate suite or flat. Standing in this hall, I could hear voices coming from the room on my right, which I took to be the sitting-room of the suite. But though I put my ear close to the door, I couldn't catch a single word nor even recognize the voices.

This little hallway was quite dark, except for a thin strip of light coming under the farther door that opened into the main corridor. I heard a faint sound from that door, and then saw a sudden vertical strip of light that soon widened. Somebody was very quietly opening that door. I stepped back, flattening myself against the bedroom door, where the light from the corridor wouldn't fall upon me, but from which I could see who was opening that door.

It was Mr. Perigo. I had only just time to recognize him before he slipped through and quietly closed the door behind him. It was a very quick neat job, and if he had learned how to do things like that in his art-dealing he must have pulled off some very queer deals. Well, there we were, the two of us, in this small dark space. I had to hold my breath. But I knew he was doing what I'd been doing only half a minute before. He was trying to listen in to the talk in the sitting-room, which meant that he was very close to that door and the width of the hall from where I was. But obviously this couldn't last.

Without anything happening to warn us, that sitting-room door was pulled wide open and the little hallway flooded with light. And there was Mr. Perigo, upright in a flash, and there was I, standing just behind him, and looking, of course, as if I'd just arrived with him. In the sitting-room doorway was the fat dark foreigner, carrying a small leather case, and behind him, looking very much at home in her own apartment, was Mrs. Jesmond. It was a very nice little situation.

But somebody had to talk fast. "Oh, I say, Mrs. Jesmond," I began, over Mr. Perigo's shoulder, "is this all right? Mr. Settle told us we'd find you up here, but of course if you're busy——"

"We were just wondering whether we oughtn't to go away again," said Mr. Perigo smoothly.

"No, no, of course not," said Mrs. Jesmond, smiling. "Do come in. And, Mr. Timon, now you really must stay a little longer. You can't be in such a tremendous hurry. Though he's always such a busy man," she told us. She was giving Mr. Timon the chance to pull himself together, for it was clear that he had been badly rattled by discovering us there. Making a big effort, he muttered something I didn't catch, tried to smile, and moved back into the room, and we followed him.

When I first described the fat dark foreigner in the train, I said he was altogether too obviously foreign to be of any interest to me, because I'm not looking for men who have Alien written all over them. But in the train I'd never heard him speak. Now when I did hear him, I had a surprise. This Mr. Timon had a broad Lancashire accent.

"An' Ah can't stay long 'cos Ah'm getting night train back to Manchester," he told us.

"Ah, you live in Manchester, Mr. Timon," said Mr. Perigo.

"'Ave done ever since Ah was a boy," he replied heartily. "Ah know a lot o' people don't like Manchester, but it suits me all right."

Even as he was talking now, he still looked as if he had been picked up anywhere between Salonica and Basra and dropped on us by parachute. I never saw anybody who looked less Lancashire. Yet nobody who hadn't lived most of his life there could have acquired that accent.

Mrs. Jesmond was busy giving us drinks, with a little tonic water for Mr. Timon, who announced to us proudly that he'd been teetotal all his life. "Never touched a drop, nor me father before me," he added, keeping an eye on that small leather case, which was probably filled with dirty pound notes.

The sitting-room was as surprising as Mr. Timon or the superb dinner we'd had downstairs. It wasn't at all the kind of apartment you'd expect to find in a place like the *Queen of Clubs*. The furniture was good, and the pictures were even better. If Mr. Perigo had really been an art-dealer, he'd have been nosing round those walls like a bloodhound after a raw steak. After I'd been given my drink, and Mr. Perigo was chattering away to Mrs. Jesmond, and Mr. Timon was trying to look interested and obviously longing to go, I moved round the room looking at the pictures. I like pictures, though I'm no expert. But Mrs. Jesmond hadn't wasted all her time and money in France. She'd picked up some good stuff. There was one of the best Utrillo street scenes I'd ever set eyes on; a Bonnard of an orchard that was like a glimpse of a lost world; two or three Derain drawings; and a rose Picasso that must have been worth all the rest of the *Queen of Clubs*. That wasn't all, of course, but I hadn't time to do more than give a quick glance at the rest.

"You've got some grand pictures here," I said to Mrs. Jesmond.

"Hasn't she?" cried Mr. Perigo, quick as lightning. "I've spent hours up here looking at them—by special permission—haven't I?"

Mrs. Jesmond said he had, and then Mr. Perigo nodded and smiled at me, as if he'd known what I'd been thinking.

Mr. Timon, clutching his case, told us he really must go, and Mrs. Jesmond walked out into the corridor with him.

"So much better our arriving together like that," Mr. Perigo whispered, "wasn't it? Though before that I'd been looking for you."

"I'd been talking to Mr. Settle."

"Oh—yes. Rather a commonplace little man, I always think, Mr. Settle. You'd never imagine such a fellow having the enterprise to start and run a place like this, would you?"

"No. I found that quite impossible to imagine," I said, grinning.

"So did I. Quite impossible. Now a woman like Mrs. Jesmond," said Mr. Perigo enthusiastically, "well, I believe she'd run a place like this—just as a hobby, mind you—very successfully."

"Perhaps she would. But then I don't know her as well as you do."

"I don't know her very well," Mr. Perigo whispered, with an air of being very confidential. "I really don't know anybody round here very well. I'm clean out of my element, of course. No, no," he added quickly, "that's not quite true. Because I feel that with Mrs. Jesmond—as you see for yourself just by glancing round this delightful room—I get a glimpse again of my own element. So I can forget this horrible war sometimes when she's about, and that makes me very grateful. That's why I was hesitating outside the door, wondering whether I ought to disturb her,

You see, I knew our friend Timon of Manchester—and I must confess he looked far more like Timon of Athens—was with her, perhaps doing a little business."

"What kind of business?" I asked.

He smiled and shook his head. "I've no idea at all. Do you like Rouault's work? Because if you do, there's a very good Rouault over there."

Mrs. Jesmond was back now, smiling sweetly at us. I could not help admiring her. She must have known by this time, even if she didn't before, that her Mr. Settle hadn't suggested our coming up here and that we'd coolly broken in on her, but she gave no sign.

"I was just telling Mr. Neyland about your Rouault," said Mr. Perigo.

"He'd also been telling me that he could forget this horrible war when you're about, Mrs. Jesmond," said I, looking admiringly at that long neck and those downy cheeks of hers.

"Do sit down and let's be cosy," she said, moving delicately into a high-backed chair. She was a good mover, and sometimes I felt that in her earlier days she might have had some ballet training. "Mr. Perigo doesn't like the war. Do you, Mr. Neyland?"

I did a big dumb act. "Well, I don't suppose anybody likes it, if it comes to that," I spluttered.

"Mr. Neyland has a disconcerting trick of pretending at times to be much less intelligent than he really is," said Mr. Perigo gently.

I didn't like this but I kept right on with the act. "The way I feel is this," I told them. "Here I am, a Canadian, coming here to get a job, and until I've been around a bit, I don't think it's up to me to say too much."

"Oh yes, the job," said Mrs. Jesmond. "I hear you were out at the Charters Electrical Company this afternoon."

I stared at her. "Now how did you know that?" This fitted in nicely with the act.

"Mrs. Jesmond knows *everything* that happens in Gretley, my dear boy," said Mr. Perigo.

"Not quite everything," she said, smiling at us, "but I've generally found that what I don't know, Mr. Perigo does. But then, you see, we've neither of us much else to do but to listen to gossip.

You know, Mr. Perigo, we don't do much for this famous war effort, do we?"

"I think you do more than I do," he remarked, as smooth as cream. "Here, for instance. I mean, the way you so often entertain these splendid young men of ours. Whereas I do nothing but gad about the place. But then I don't believe in this war effort."

"Now, now, you'll shock Mr. Neyland."

"Go ahead. I have my own views."

"Naturally," said Mr. Perigo, "and I'd very much like to hear them."

"No, your turn first. Besides—well, if I'm trying for a job round here, I'd better be careful what I say."

"You can say anything here," said Mrs. Jesmond. "Can't he, Mr. Perigo."

"He can, but of course he doesn't know that," said Mr. Perigo. "But I make no secret of my views, except of course in front of fire-eating patriots like Colonel Tarlington. I admit that in some ways it's a selfish point of view, but then I've never pretended to be anything but selfish. I know the kind of world I like, and I believe there isn't a hope of such a world surviving if we go on with this war. Even supposing we can beat Hitler—and we've shown no signs of beating him yet—we can only do it by bleeding ourselves white, with the result that even in the event of a so-called victory, one half the world will be completely dominated by America, and the other half by Soviet Russia. And that, to me, is a hopeless prospect. Therefore—in strict confidence, of course, Mr. Neyland—I see no point in continuing this war, and I consider we'd do better to come to reasonable terms with the Germans—not necessarily Hitler himself, but at least with the German General Staff."

"And I thought so even before Russia came into the war," said Mrs. Jesmond, not smiling now. "And now I'm certain."

"Certain of what?" I asked.

"Certain that it's stupid to go on fighting, chiefly on behalf of the Bolsheviks. We've nothing to gain and still a great deal to lose."

I looked at her and then let my glance wander idly round the room, and I was thinking how, during the first winter of the war, when it refused to get started, in rooms very like this in Paris there must have been a lot of women not unlike Mrs. Jesmond, beautiful women, clever women, cultured women, exquisite, long-necked, sweet-smelling, downy rats.

But out of the tail-end of my eye I saw her exchange a quick meaning glance with Mr. Perigo. It was up to me to say something.

"Well," I mumbled, making it obvious I was playing the act again, "I see what you both mean, but it isn't a point of view I'm used to, and—well—what with the U.S.A. coming in——"

"America, I understand," said Mr. Perigo, "has an astonishing armaments programme. But it's mostly still a programme."

"But with their resources," I began.

He wouldn't let me finish, and for once dropped his easy smooth manner. "We talk a lot of nonsense about resources, as if aeroplanes grew on trees and you could dig tanks out of fields. It not only takes time to turn these resources into the materials of war but it also demands great organization, national energy, supreme will-power. Have the democracies got that organization, energy and will-power? If so, they've given few signs of it yet."

There wasn't much of the gadabout art-dealer in that speech. I looked across to see Mrs. Jesmond smiling at me. Then she glanced at her watch, pretending to do it too quickly for me to notice but taking care I did notice, and I took the hint. It was almost time for one of the boys downstairs to find his way up here.

"Well, thanks very much, Mrs. Jesmond," I said, keeping up the act in the same clumsy style. "I've had a swell time, and if I do get this job I hope you'll let me come round here again pretty soon."

"Oh—but you must," she said, and gave my hand a nice meaning little squeeze. There was something fascinating about those peachy downy cheeks of hers. She was probably in the Black Market for blood transfusions too.

Mr. Perigo left at the same time. "I'm afraid I talked too much in there," he said softly, as we went down the corridor. "Mrs. Jesmond and that room and all those pictures—well, they excite me, and I'm apt to say more than I ought to say. But I knew I was among friends, of course. If you went round Gretley repeating one or two of those remarks of mine, you might get me into trouble, but I'm sure you don't want to do that."

"Wouldn't dream of it. I like to speak my mind, and I don't care if other people speak theirs." My God, I sounded idiotic.

He squeezed my arm as we went down the main stairs. "I had that impression of you when we first met, my dear fellow, and that's why I said I hoped we'd soon meet again. Going home?"

"Yes, I've had quite a day, and I have to go out to the Belton-Smith works to-morrow—got quite a nice letter of introduction to them—so I'll turn in and keep fresh. How do I get back to the town without using anybody's car?"

There was just time, he told me, to catch a late bus at the corner, and he was right, for I just managed to catch it as it was moving away. And I had plenty to think about on that bus.

4

THE next afternoon I went out to the Belton-Smith works, and a rotten bad afternoon that would have been if it hadn't been for something that happened towards the end of it. To begin with, they didn't like me much out there. Robson, the general manager, to whom Heacham had written his letter of introduction, was away, and after a lot of waiting about I was handed over to a thin young man called Pearson. He wasn't interested in me, and I couldn't blame him for that, but he might have tried a bit harder to disguise his complete lack of interest. After he'd yawned several times he did explain that he'd been up late for the last two or three nights getting a new shed into operation. He pointed it out to me through his window, for the huge office block was several hundred yards away from the sheds, which were on a gigantic scale and seemed to stretch for about half a mile. Nobody has ever explained to me yet how it is that after putting up these giant aircraft factories all over the place we still never seem to have enough aircraft anywhere.

When he wasn't yawning, this fellow Pearson made it as plain as his face that I hadn't a dog's chance of a job with this Belton-Smith outfit, and he seemed to think it was a pretty low trick for Heacham to encourage me even by giving me this letter. I didn't care for Pearson. He was one of those Englishmen who give you the idea that this is a very private exclusive sort of war, something like the Royal Enclosure at Ascot or the members' pavilion at Lords. If I hadn't had strong reasons for wanting to look round the works, I wouldn't have asked a favour of him. But asking favours of people I don't like seems to be part of my job. So I had to try it. "Any objection to my looking around the works?"

"I wouldn't mind," he replied, "but our people have cracked down rather severely on it just lately. Lot of hush hush stuff, y'know."

"I see." These boys with their "hush-hush" always annoy me. It's such a dough-headed phrase anyhow, and it always attracts attention instead of avoiding it. More than once the only thing I've clearly heard of a man's conversation has been that "hush-hush" idiocy. You can hear it clean across a room. However, I didn't say any of this, and tried hard not to look it.

"But if you think it worth it," said Pearson, "I can let you have a quick peep inside our main shed, just to give you an idea of the scale we're working on here. If you'll hang on, I'll find you a guide."

I thanked him heartily, not because I wanted a quick peep into his shed but because I was only too anxious to see this guide. Unless we were all going crazy, this guide ought to be worth seeing. So I hung on.

The guide was good. He wore overalls that reeked of the dope they spray on planes, and he had steel-rimmed spectacles on the end of his nose and an untidy moustache, and was in his fifties and looked as if he wished he hadn't to work so hard. You could see somebody just like him in any builder's yard. And he had a worrying little Cockney voice.

"Don't come from these parts, do yer, sir?" he inquired, as we left the offices.

"No," I said to him carefully. "I've just come down from London, but I'm a Canadian really. I was sent down to the Charters Electrical Company to see if I could get a job there, and while they're making up their mind, I thought I might see if there was anything doing here."

"Is that so," he said, not even looking at me, but trotting along. "Always wanted to see Canada. South America too, I've always fancied."

"I worked for some years in South America," I told him. "Chile and Peru. Wonderful country, if you're young and healthy."

"Well, I'm not young an' I'm anything but 'ealthy. The old pump's not so good these days. Yes, 'eart trouble—thet's me."

We were now crossing the wide space between the office block and the enormous camouflaged sheds. Way over to the right, looking as if it went on for ever, was the flying field where they tested the new super-Cyclones. I could hear the roar of their big screws. For once there was a little sunshine, and a high wind had cleared the sky, so that now it was one of those winter afternoons when everything looks part of a sharp tinted drawing. The guide stopped, and touched my arm. By this time we seemed a long way from anybody or anywhere.

"'Eart or no 'eart," he said, pulling out a packet of cigarettes, "this is where I like to 'ave a quick draw."

After he had given me a cigarette too, he produced a lighter. As soon as I saw it I knew that now the Gretley job had really begun.

"Won't work," he said, not even giving me a look. "You got a light?"

I pulled out my own special lighter and we used it for our cigarettes. "I'd give you this one," I said carefully, "only it's a present from an old friend."

"Don't think of it," he said. "I'll take care my lighter works to-morrow."

Satisfied now, we looked at each other and nodded. He didn't seem the same man. The tired look was still there, for he wasn't any younger than the age he pretended to me, but any suggestion of the Cockney artisan had vanished. They had put a good man in here.

"I came out here specially for this," I told him.

"It was the best way," he said. "They put me on to everybody of course, but I guessed it was you. That's why I mentioned

Canada and South America first. They sent me a few particulars
about you. Let's keep moving slowly. We don't know who's
watching us."

"Not much chance of talking now, is there?" I asked.

"No, not a hope. But we've got to talk as soon as possible.
Now listen, Neyland. I have a bed-sitting room at Fifteen, Raglan
Street—that's the second turning to the left off Mill Lane, which
is off Upper Market Street. Got that? Right! My room's on the
first floor—and I don't mean the American first floor, which is
our ground floor, don't forget—and my name here is Olney, and
my landlord's name is Wilkinson. Right? Well, come and see me
there to-night at half-past nine. I can't make it earlier because we
don't finish here until seven, and there are one or two things I
want to check before I give you my line to-night." He stopped to
throw down his cigarette and stamp on it. I did the same. It gave
us an excuse to linger for a minute.

"You have a line then?" I asked.

"Yes. I haven't been wasting my time, though it's not easy
when I'm tied up here all day. Any ideas yourself?"

"One or two, but it's too early yet to make much sense out of
'em. I'll tell you to-night—at half-past nine."

"All right," he said. "And now you're going to take a quick peep
inside the shed and be treated as a rather suspicious character. I
shall tell Pearson I don't feel too easy about you, and that may
help because information like that travels fast here in Gretley.
You'd be surprised."

In a quarter of an hour I was being shown out of the front
gate, trying to look not too pleased. This had been a good afternoon's work. I liked the look and the sound of this little man,
Olney. And I felt it would be wiser not to do anything more
myself, though there were now several angles that seemed to
me to ask for investigation, until I'd heard what Olney had to say.
But I spent most of the early part of the evening up in my room,
trying to assess the value of the bits and pieces of information I'd
already picked up in Gretley. Some of these, I felt, were useless
until I'd compared notes with a man who'd spent some time in
the town. I was looking forward very keenly to this meeting with
Olney, I can tell you. Not only did I need all the pointers he could

give me, but also I was looking forward to being myself for an hour or two and talking easily and freely about the job. It was a depressing time, and, as I said before, I was feeling sour, and what I wanted was some real companionship, which was only possible with somebody who knew the real reason why I was in Gretley. Practically all the talk I'd had so far with people, as I hope you've noticed already, was heavily baited and about as friendly as the fish-hooks in the bait. So when I left the hotel at about quarter-past nine, I felt pretty good.

The blackout seemed worse than ever. It was like groping about in a vault. Upper Market Street was easy enough to find, but after that my troubles began. As usual, two of the men I hurried after and then nearly knocked down, told me when I asked them where Mill Lane was, that they were strangers in the town. For a moment I imagined the streets of this blacked-out Gretley being paraded by nobody but strangers. Perhaps there wasn't anybody left in the town but strangers. Then finally a policeman showed me, almost by sticking my nose into it, the narrow entrance to Mill Lane. I missed Raglan Street once by thinking that a genuine turn to the left was nothing but a garage entrance or something of that sort, which meant that I overshot the mark. But at last, probably ten minutes late, I found Raglan Street, and was soon ringing the bell at Number Fifteen, which was a smallish terrace house.

A grey mouse of a woman answered the door, and looked terrified until I made it plain that I had an appointment with her boarder, Mr. Olney.

"Mr. Olney's room is straight up the stairs and to the right," she said timidly. "But he isn't back yet."

We were now in the little hall, which had that stuffy woolly smell you get in so many small English houses, as if there were too many old blankets about. I could hear a couple of noisy comedians on the wireless in the front room.

"I expect it'll be all right if you go up," she went on. "He sent a message to say a gentleman would be calling, just in case he was a bit late."

"Yes," I said, "he knows I'm coming."

"That's right. But he didn't say anything about the lady,"

"What lady?"

"Well," and she dropped her voice, "there's a lady waiting to see him too. A Doctor Somebody—I didn't catch the name."

This was a nuisance, unless of course this woman turned out to be a colleague of his. Nothing had been said about a woman joining us, and for my part I hoped no woman was. "Well, never mind," I said. "I'll go up and wait for him."

There are advantages sometimes in a sudden entrance. I went quickly and quietly upstairs and charged straight into Olney's room. And I was just in time to see the woman in there cram the piece of paper she'd been holding into the pocket of her fur coat. The move was instinctive, but there it was. And she looked badly startled.

"I'm sorry if I startled you," I said, "but I was late for an appointment I had here with Mr. Olney——"

"He's not here," she said, still breathless and playing for time. "I've—been waiting for him."

She was a woman about thirty-five, with a thin and rather severe face and bright greeny-brown eyes. She looked intelligent, but harassed and uncertain of herself. And she hated my finding her there.

"I'll take off my overcoat," I said. "It's warm in here." And it was, for there was a good fire burning, and it was clear that Olney made good use of the place as a sitting-room. It was rather a big room, shabbily furnished but comfortable. I remember thinking that I must find a similar place for myself, if there was one still to be had in Gretley.

The woman looked at her watch and frowned. "I only wanted to see him for a minute or two," she began.

"That's all right. I can wait until you've finished."

"You say you were late for your appointment with him?"

"Yes," I said. "He told me half-past nine. Have a cigarette?"

"No, thank you. I don't smoke."

That brought the preliminary polite conversation to an end. I lit a cigarette, stared about the room idly, and occasionally took a peep at my companion. Dr. Somebody, eh? And a badly startled and rattled doctor too, whose first move was to get rid of the paper she was holding.

"By the way," I said, with an easy air, "my name's Neyland. I'm a Canadian, just arrived in this town. Come about a job. Engineer. Saw Mr. Olney out at the aircraft factory this afternoon."

"I see." And now she smiled, and looked quite different. "Age? Married or single? Hobbies?"

"All right, no objection. Age—forty-three. Widower. Hobbies fly-fishing, history and travel books, pictures and not too difficult music. There you are."

She smiled again, and very nicely too, but it didn't last long. The next moment she looked as if she wanted to be quiet, but I grinned at her expectantly. I hadn't given her all that information—and all of it except that bit about the engineering job quite truthful too—to sit there learning nothing about her.

"I have a practice here in Gretley," she announced solemnly. And then, with a touch of defiance she couldn't suppress: "I'm Dr. Bauernstern."

There it stopped. No little jokes about marriage and hobbies. Dr. Bauernstern. But not the least trace of any foreign accent. She might not be English, might easily be a Scot, but with that accent she certainly wasn't German. I've read and heard about these Germans with faultless English accents but I've yet to meet one. They belong to the same imaginary series as the super-spies with ten different personalities and the master criminals with vast organizations.

"I don't think I ought to wait much longer," she said, not looking at me. She was sitting now on the edge of a large old armchair, and I was lounging in another one at the other side of the hearth-rug. I was trying to make her feel a bit more comfortable and confidential but I wasn't succeeding.

"Can I give him a message?" I asked. "I've got to wait for him."

"Well," she hesitated, still looking away. Then she stared straight at me, with those bright alarmed eyes, as people so often do when they propose to tell you some thumping lie. "Mr. Olney happens to be a patient of mine, and I gave him a prescription yesterday that I think—well, I'm sure—wasn't quite right—or anyhow that I could improve upon. So—I called in, on my way home—to tell him so. That's all."

"I see." Then I chanced a long shot. "And was that the wrong prescription, then, that you hid in your pocket just as I came in?"

She hadn't much colour anyhow, and now her face might have been paper. But that didn't last long. The next moment she was pretending to be insulted and therefore angry. It's their favourite move, whether they've had an expensive medical education or not. She got up, of course, and began fastening her coat. I got up too, and was careful not to smile.

"When you came bouncing in here," she said, speaking as from an immense distance, "I happened to be reading a letter, and—naturally—you startled me——"

"I know. And I said I was sorry. I'm also sorry to have asked a question that was none of my business. I'm afraid I'm a rude and inquisitive man."

"Yes," she said, ready to go. "I noticed how very curious you were. No, I don't mean because of what you said. Your eyes give you away. They're very restless, very inquisitive, and as unhappy as they deserve to be. Good night."

And she was out before I'd thought of any reply or begun to consider my next move. Caught off her guard this Dr. Bauernstern might look like a startled hare, but once she was herself again she was nobody's fool. Well, Olney could tell me about her, because whether he was one of her patients or not (and I could imagine several good reasons why he should choose her particular surgery), he must know something about her. All I knew was that she was a woman living under a desperate sense of strain, that she was intelligent, and that I didn't like her.

But what had happened to Olney? It was now ten o'clock. I found it hard to sit still and I kept wandering round the room, which was just as much in character as Olney himself had been when I first met him that afternoon. There wasn't a book or a sheet of paper that suggested anything but a factory foreman. Once again I told myself that Olney was a very smart little man, and this only made me all the more eager to get down to some real talk with him.

Some time round about quarter past ten I heard a ring below and then voices. Somebody had arrived. I peeped down the stairs and saw that it was a policeman. Then I recognized him. It was that mule of a sergeant, the fellow with the chin, who'd taken such a dislike to me at the Charters works. And he was coming upstairs.

I'd less than two seconds in which to make up my mind. There was no staying there and dodging him. Either I'd to face him or clear out. If I faced him then either he'd be so suspicious that I'd have the police following me round for days or I'd be compelled to tell him who I was and what I was doing in Gretley, and I didn't want to do that because although somebody in the local police might have to know about me soon, the less this officious jackass knew about me the better it would be for the department, the British war effort, and the United Nations. The only thing to do was to clear out. I shot over to the window, which was blacked out with long heavy curtains, dived between the curtains, spilling the light into the dark world, pushed up the bottom half of the window, held on to the sill while the rest of me swung down into the darkness, and then when I was fully stretched I let myself go. If there had been some sort of basement at the back I'd probably have dropped into hospital and a few months in plaster-of-paris, but I took a reasonable chance on there being no basement but only a backyard or garden. And I was right, though at that I went down with a most unpleasant thump. But it was a back garden of sorts and there was still quite a lot of snow piled up there, which broke my fall.

As I landed I could hear the sergeant shouting in the room above, which was still spilling some light. I also heard a voice, probably belonging to some air-raid warden on the prowl, which seemed to come from the back street way over to my left. I picked myself up as fast as I could, found the back gate easily in the light that was escaping from the upstairs window, and turned sharply to the right down the lane. Somebody was blowing a police whistle, and I had a notion that the sergeant was now preparing to jump after me, and then I heard the sound of somebody moving fast towards me up the lane. It was very slippery under foot and I didn't propose to go slithering any further with the police on my heels, so I darted in through an open gateway about three or four houses farther down, ran up the little path, found that the back door wasn't locked, and landed inside what seemed to me in the dark a little kitchen.

I didn't know what was happening outside but I felt it would
be dangerous to go near that back lane for some time. My best
plan was either to stay in this strange house as long as I could or
try to sneak through it to the front door. It was then I had time to
remember that I'd left my hat and overcoat up in Olney's room
and that my chances of seeing them again, except at the police
station, were very small. There was, however, nothing in either
the hat or the overcoat to identify me, not even a maker's name,
for I had learnt a trick of two after working for nearly two years
for the department. But it was a nuisance, and I cursed myself for
not contriving to bring them away.

Fortunately I'd put my torch, which was a small one, in my
inside coat pocket, and now I used it to find my way out of this
kitchen, which was a dirty little hole and stank of cats and cabbage water. I now realized that this house was exactly like the
one where Olney lodged. The little hall was just the same. As I
crept forward I could hear voices coming from the front room,
just as I'd heard the wireless comedians when I was talking to
Mrs. Wilkinson. Outside the door I listened to these voices, and
after a moment easily recognized one of them. Inside that room,
no doubt refreshing himself and taking his ease after the night's
hard work, was no other than Our Favourite Comic, Mr. Gus
Gimble.

I knocked and walked in. Yes, there was Gus, still with some
traces of make-up on his battered face, and dispensing with a
collar and tie at this late hour. At the table with him were a stout
motherly woman, one of the six chorus girls, and either Leonard
or Larry. They'd just finished supper and were now lighting cigarettes and pouring out more beer. The room was very warm and
smelled as if nobody had stopped eating, drinking and smoking
in it for the last twenty years.

"Mr. Gimble?" I said, hastily closing the door behind me.

"That's me," he replied, not very much surprised. And here
I was lucky because I'd struck probably the one set of people
in Gretley who wouldn't be very much surprised if a stranger
marched in on them at this hour.

"Excuse me coming in like this," I began.

"Quite all right, old man, quite all right," he said cheerfully.

Perhaps he wasn't sorry to see a new face just when he felt relaxed and expansive after the show was over. "This is Mrs. Gimble. And this is my daughter and her husband, Larry Douglas. Both in my show. Have you seen the show?"

"Saw it last night," I said, pulling out all the enthusiasm I could, "and enjoyed it enormously. That's why I'm here, in a way. My name's Robinson, and I was visiting some friends down the street here, and they said you were lodging here, so as there was something I wanted to ask you, I came along. But I couldn't make anybody hear me at the front door, and as I was feeling a bit cold standing out there and I could hear your voices I came in. I hope you don't mind." I said this to Mrs. Gimble, very politely, feeling that she'd be flattered.

"It's quite all right, quite all right," she said. "Pleased to meet you, I'm sure, Mr. Robinson." And she gave her daughter a stately glance, as if to say that here was true politeness and that for once she was being properly treated.

"Just goin' to say you look cold, old man," said Gus, getting up and pulling back his chair. "Here, Mother, let's shove the table back. Come on, Larry, Dot."

"The landlady 'ere," said Mrs. Gimble, as we re-arranged ourselves, "goes to bed very early, an' she's deaf too, so that's why you couldn't make yourself 'eard. She never 'ears me, whatever I say."

"She hears when she wants to all right," said Dot, who seemed in a bad temper. "Trust 'em!"

"Now that's better," cried Gus, as we all crowded round the fire. "You'll 'ave a glass o' beer, Mr. Robinson? Of course you will. Pour one out, Larry. We've been lucky this date with beer, Mr. Robinson, I can tell you. Some of our dates just lately 'ave been dry as a bone—not a drop o' beer to be 'ad, at least not for us pros. So you liked the show, eh, Mr. Robinson?"

"I did, and so did the rest of the audience."

"Oh yes," said Gus. "Well, they'll always be kind to me 'ere in Gretley, can't grumble at all, can't grumble. Of course, as you can imagine, I've got an interest in this show. And the 'Ippodrome 'ere's one of our smaller dates. I won't call it a fill-in," he added carefully, "'cos that wouldn't be fair. No, it wouldn't be fair to

Gretley to call it a fill-in. But, any'ow, one of our smaller dates. Mind yew, Mr. Robinson, this may not be a *big* show—I'm not sayin' it *is* a big show—but you'd be surprised the money we're payin' out in salaries. Take our vocalist, Marjorie Grosvenor——"

"Never worth the money," his wife interrupted, with great decision, "never worth the money. I said it from the first. Didn't I, Dot?"

"Yes, Ma, and you've been saying it ever since twice-nightly," said Dot.

"Your health, Mr. Gimble!" I cried, lifting my beer.

"All the best, old man! Now, did you say you wanted to see me about something?"

"Well, it's nothing very much," I said apologetically, "but I couldn't help being interested in one of your acts last night, and that's why I thought I'd slip round and have a word with you. You see, a friend of mine, a French Canadian, had a sister who was a great gymnast, and I know she came over here a few years ago to go into vaudeville or something of that sort, and so, last night, when I was watching your Mam'zelle Fifine, I wondered if she mightn't be my friend's sister."

"Ah, I see," said Gus. "It's a funny thing but we were just talking about 'er when you came in."

"Nothing very funny about that seeing we're always talking about her," said Dot.

"Oh you shut up—or go to bed," said her husband, Larry.

"What do you mean?" shouted Dot, turning on him at once.

"Now then, now then, now then," bawled Gus, glaring at them both, and showing more authority than I'd have credited him with, "we want a bit o' quiet conversation. And anybody who doesn't can go upstairs and shout it out. So that'll do. He turned to me, and gave me a quick wink. I liked Gus much better in private life than I did on the stage. "What was your friend's sister's name?"

"Helene Malvoix," I replied promptly, remembering the name of a dear old maiden lady I'd met years ago in Quebec.

"No, that's not it," said Gus, who was now looking very official and solemn and grand, and enjoying himself. "I 'appen to know that Fifine's real name is Suzanne Schindler." He spelt it for me carefully. "And she came originally from Strasburg. That I *do* know."

"Then it can't be the same," I said, "but it happened that your acrobat had rather the look of my French-Canadian friend. A good act too, that."

"A good act certainly," said Gus, as the other three exchanged quite knowing glances. "Very clever, and put over with some real showmanship. But—well, a most peculiar artiste, most peculiar."

"Peculiar? She's bats," cried Dot. "Already she's frightened the life out of two of our girls in the chorus, just because they happened to go into her dressing-room that time in Sunderland."

"I said it from the first," said Mrs. Gimble, who seemed to have a rather monotonous line. "Didn't I, Gus? I said she'd only make trouble in the company 'cos she's not a nice woman. I don't mean drinkin' an' I don't mean men——"

"I'm not so sure about the men," said Larry, "though if it is men she's got a funny taste by the look of the few I've seen asking for her."

"It isn't men," said Dot decidedly. "You ask Rose and Phyllis, and they'll tell you."

"That'll do," said Gus, "else you'll be giving Mr. Robinson some wrong ideas about the company. No, she's a most peculiar artiste, an' when I say peculiar I mean peculiar, 'cos I've seen all sorts, after forty years touring. To begin with, she makes no friends. You might go a month an' never exchange ten words with 'er, unless of course she thinks there's something wrong with 'er props or band parts."

"Perhaps that's because she doesn't speak English very well," I suggested.

"These foreign 'acks," cried Mrs. Gus, with the most passionate disgust, "I wouldn't 'ave 'em. I wouldn't. Dirty."

"Half a minute," said Larry, "you can't call Fifine dirty."

"If they're not dirty in body, then they're dirty in mind," said Mrs. Gus, with an air of finality.

"Mother, you don't know what you're talking about," said Gus good-humouredly, giving her immense thigh a slap. "Now shut up an' let me talk. 'Er English isn't so good, of course, but I've known 'em much worse when they talked your 'ead off. But there's no friendliness about 'er. She doesn't want to be one o' the company. An' doesn't seem to really care about the show either. Mind yew, Mr. Robinson, I can't really complain because she always gets a big hand—you saw for yourself, last night. An' yet, believe it or not, she could go much bigger if she wanted to."

"How's that?" I asked, and not simply out of politeness, believe me.

"Well, you saw the act. She makes 'em count the twists and turns, an' of course that's always good showmanship, like making 'em sing a chorus. An' standin' in the wings as I do night after night, hearin' 'em count in front, that's 'ow I began to notice. You see, she could go much bigger if she went all out every time, but some nights she'll do a certain twist over the trapeze per'aps only four or five times when I know for a fact she could 'ave just as easily done it fifteen or twenty times. I know she could 'cos on another night she'd *do* that very same twist fifteen, eighteen or twenty times. Well then, why not do it every performance? See what I mean, Mr. Robinson?"

I told him very earnestly that I did see what he meant.

Now Dot gave us a surprise. "I know why she does it all different every time," she began.

"She doesn't do it different every time," said Larry. "Sometimes it'll be just the same for several nights running. I know 'cos I've noticed the counting."

"You mean you've been staring at her big fat legs," said Dot, giving him a sour look. "But she keeps changing it because she's superstitious. She told Phyllis and me that, one night. And I know she's terribly superstitious. She sits in her dressing-room telling her fortune by cards, though she won't tell ours. I think she's bats, and let's stop talking about her."

"Now the very idea!" cried Mrs. Gus, frowning upon her daughter. "What mightn't interest you might interest some other people."

"What sort of men come round and see her?" I asked.

"Well, I only remember one or two," said Gus. "Ordinary sort o' chaps. Oldish, I seem to remember. Nobody special."

"The ones I remember," said Larry, who had seemed to me one of the worst comics I've ever seen but now gave me the impression of being a rather shrewd young man, "weren't at all the sort who might be chasing her—y'know, the usual line. And I've seen her once or twice in pubs and cafes talking to chaps, and they weren't holding hands either."

"Everybody hasn't got your ideas," said Dot, who was clearly one of those wives who feel it's their duty to insult their husbands every few minutes in public.

"You know what I mean," cried Larry angrily. "I mean there was no boy-friend stuff about it. They looked to me as if they were there on business, though what the business could be, God knows."

Mrs. Gimble suddenly began to yawn gigantically. I finished my beer. "Well, thanks very much," I said. "It's been very interesting. And thanks again for the show last night, Mr. Gimble." I shook hands.

"I'll see you out," said Larry. And then when we were out in the hall and he'd closed the door behind him, he said quietly, "You're a detective, aren't you?"

"Good lord, no! What gave you that idea?"

"All right, I don't suppose you want to tell me anything. But I guessed you weren't asking those questions about Fifine for fun. And if I were you, I'd keep on asking more questions. And if there's anything I can do, let me know. I got my discharge out of the army a year ago, and I'd gone and married Dot, so I came into the show, though I don't like it much and I know I'm stinkingly bad. But I'm no fool."

"I know you're not," I told him. Away from the stage, that bad act, and the terrible Leonard, he was a lad not hard to like, and I felt sorry for him.

"Besides," he added, with one hand on the front door now, "you owe me something for not giving you away in there. You see, you told us you let yourself in through this door. But I came in last, and I knew I'd locked and bolted it and that nobody had touched it since. So I knew you hadn't come in this way, see?"

"All right, Larry," I said, "I'm not going to argue about that. But I'd be obliged it you'd keep it to yourself. And I may see you again before you leave."

"You've only three more nights," said Larry, "but come round

any time. The room I dress in—I can't call it mine because there
are three of us in it—is next door to Fifine's, and she has to do her
act twice nightly—see?"

I slipped out into what now seemed a particularly cold night,
for I missed that hat and that overcoat. It was still as dark as ever,
and nobody saw me on my way back to the hotel. It was a nuisance having missed Olney, and I felt vaguely depressed about it,
as if things somehow were going badly wrong. But I didn't feel
I'd wasted my evening. Fifine would stand thinking about. And
so would this Dr. Bauernstern, who called so late on her patients
when they weren't ill, who looked so strained and was so terrified
inside, and who was such an irritating type of woman. I could
still see those bright fearful eyes. Doctors shouldn't look like that.
While I was having a last smoke, up in my room, I told myself
that there were too many women popping up in this Gretley job,
for I could now count five who all needed watching. It was high
time I had that talk with Olney.

5

THE next day began badly. It was a cold sleety morning. The
headlines in the papers were as black with bad news as mourning
cards. Coming out from breakfast I was reminded by the woman
at the reception desk that my two nights were up and that my
room would now be required again by "one of our regular
residents." I told her I had no objection to giving up my room,
though I hadn't yet found another one, but that the few hotels
we have left should now be used by travellers and not by regular
residents. She put me on to Major Brember, and I told him the
same thing. He informed me briefly that this was his business
and not mine. I said I didn't agree and left him, knowing that he
was so busy being a country gentleman (in the main street of an
industrial town too) and keeping an hotel in his spare time that
it would be useless to try to explain to him any demands the war
might make. The papers were beginning to ask what was wrong
with us. Well, one of the things wrong with us was the idiotic
genteel tradition of Major Brember and his kind, which was

hanging round our necks like the heavy rotting carcase of the albatross. They were all pretending to themselves that it was still about 1904, and then wondering why no good seemed to come of it. They would neither decently die nor come to life. Yes, I was feeling very sour that morning.

Round about ten o'clock I rang up the Belton-Smith factory and asked for Olney, saying that I was a close friend and it was urgent. I didn't like doing this, but it was better than trying to get into the factory again so soon or asking for him at the gates. After a long wait, the girl told me that he hadn't arrived yet, and that probably he wasn't very well as he'd had several days off before. I had to take a chance now or waste a lot more valuable time, so, minus hat and overcoat, I took a taxi through the sleet to 15, Raglan Street, and asked the man to wait for me.

Mrs. Wilkinson was in, luckily, and looked even more alarmed when she saw me this morning.

"I only want to do what's right," she said dubiously, as I followed her into the hall.

"I'm sure you do," I told her, and meant it, because she was that kind of hard-working little woman. They seem to get nothing worth having out of life, these worn, timid little women, and yet on the other hand they are speaking no more than the plain truth when they say, as they always are saying, that they only want to do what's right. "But what do you mean, Mrs. Wilkinson?"

She looked at me doubtfully for another moment. Then she said: "You're to go upstairs to his room."

I thought, of course, that Olney had told her I might be calling, although that doubtful manner of hers seemed queer, so I marched straight upstairs without another word.

Sitting in Olney's room, and almost appearing to fill it, was a massive reddish man, ruminating there like a buffalo. And on the table, not to be ignored, were my hat and overcoat.

"Oh!" I cried, taken aback. "Where's Olney?"

"Why?" he asked, unsmilingly.

"Because I want to see him. I had an appointment with him last night but he never turned up."

"And you did, eh? Here, eh?" He spoke with a good deal of the local accent, which made him seem very blunt indeed.

"Yes, here. We met during the afternoon out at the factory, and he asked me to come here at half-past nine."

The big man nodded. "Well, that's straightforward enough. That hat and coat yours?"

"Yes."

"I knew they weren't his. Too big for him. So it was you who jumped out of the window here last night?"

"Yes, it was."

"Silly thing to do. Why did you do it?"

"Because I don't like that sergeant of yours," I replied, "and didn't want to have to explain to him why I was here."

"Sergeant of *mine,* eh?"

"Well," I said, smiling, "if you've not some connection with the local police, something's gone wrong with my powers of observation."

"I see," he said slowly. Everything about him was ponderous and yet not dull and stupid. I liked the look of him, although I'd been sorry to see him there. "Well, your powers of observation, as you call 'em, are in good order. I'm Superintendent Hamp. Who are you?"

"My name's Humphrey Neyland."

"American?"

"No, Canadian. By the way, I've a taxi waiting outside, and if we're going to stay here I'd better pay him off."

"No, Mr. Neyland, I think we'd better ask him to take us round to my office," said the Superintendent, slowly rising. There must have been about two hundred and forty pounds of him, and it wasn't all fat either. "You can put on that hat and coat."

He didn't speak a word in the taxi, and neither did I, for I was busy wondering how much I could tell him. The department always leaves this to our discretion, though sooner or later, as I've explained before, we usually have to work with the local police. But at the beginning of a job it's better if they know nothing about us.

"It's your taxi," he said, grinning, when we arrived at the police headquarters, which were at the back of the large municipal building.

"Sure," I said, and paid the man off.

They ought to have given him a bigger office, for there didn't seem much left of it by the time he'd made himself comfortable behind his desk. I had to do my best with a little hard chair wedged between the desk and the window. There was a message on his pad and he spent a minute or so digesting it. Then he looked hard at me, out of shrewd little eyes, while he fingered his yellowy-grey moustache. And I knew then, what I had guessed up in Olney's room, that this wasn't a man you could fool with any easy yarn.

"Well now, Mr. Neyland," he began, "I'd like a few particulars from you. How long have you been in Gretley and what are you doing here?"

I told him I'd been to the Charters Electrical Company and then to the Belton-Smith factory looking for a job. I mentioned the men I'd seen at each place.

"I see," he said. "And had you known this man Olney before?"

"No, I met him for the first time yesterday afternoon, and he asked me to call on him last night, as I explained before."

"Quite so, but what made him do that?"

"We had some private business to discuss," I told him.

"Was it very important business?"

"Yes, very important. In fact, it's urgent that I should see Olney as soon as possible. That's why I called again at his lodgings this morning. I'd already rung up the factory and been told he wasn't there. They said he must be ill."

"No, he's not ill," said the Superintendent, very slowly, "he's dead. He was knocked down by a car in the blackout last night— and killed."

"I knew the other night when I landed here," I said, "that something damnable would happen in this blackout of yours. And now it has. Poor little devil! I liked the look of that man. He knew his job. I was looking forward to that talk with him. Oh damn and blast!" And I stared at the streaming window, wondering if I'd known all along deep down that something had happened to Olney and that we'd never have that talk.

"You say he knew his job," said the Superintendent, after a pause. "What was his job?"

I looked surprised. "Why, he was a foreman at the Belton-Smith factory."

"If he was only a foreman, then he was only killed accidentally in the blackout," said the Superintendent, and now I didn't have to pretend to look surprised.

"What do you mean?" I asked.

"I think you know something, and I think I know something. If you'll tell me what you know," he continued, "then I might tell you what I know. In fact, I will."

"All right then," I replied. "I know that Olney—or whatever his name really was—was a member of the Special Branch who was working here from the Belton-Smith factory. I went up there yesterday in the hope of getting into touch with him. And I did."

"Yes," he said. "As a matter of fact, what you say only confirms this message here. Now where do you come into all this, Mr. Neyland?"

I took a scribbling-pad from his desk and wrote on it two numbers, one a private London telephone number and the other—well—just a number. "If you ring up that number—and you'll get straight through—and mention that other number, you can check up on me at once."

"I'll do that now," he said, and put through the call. "Spycatching, is it?"

"Yes. But it sounds better if you call it counter-espionage. And don't tell me there can't be any espionage in Gretley, because we happen to know there is."

"I wasn't going to tell you anything of the sort," he growled. "What I was going to say is that I can't see why you chaps have to make such a mystery of it and don't work with the police."

"We do sometimes," I replied. "But after all, for all we know, there might be some busy Fifth Columnists among the police "

"What!" He bristled, and clenched a gigantic fist. "Why, let me tell you, the police of this country——"

"Are a wonderful body of men. I know. That's what I think. But I've seen one or two chief constables who didn't give a bad imitation of Fascists."

He grinned. "So have I, lad," he whispered. Then the call came through, and I occupied myself in filling and lighting a pipe.

"Well, Superintendent," I said, when that was over, "you know what I know. Now what do you know?"

"We've had two bits of luck over this business," he began slowly. "At first it looked like just another accident, and we've had plenty here since the blackout came down on us. But I happened to notice that he'd got a patch of clay on his overcoat that didn't belong anywhere near the place where we found him. Then early this morning I had a notion where his coat might have picked up that clay, went along there and had a look round with two of my men, and we found a little notebook. And it's my belief that when he was knocked down, somehow he managed to throw this notebook away just before he lost consciousness. Then he was pulled into the car that knocked him down, and dumped where he was found, about quarter to ten last night, at the top of Upper Market Street. In short, it doesn't look like just another accident."

"I'm certain it wasn't," I said confidently. "He was killed, and just in time to prevent him from telling me what he'd found out. Because he told me in the afternoon he was on to something. But you've got that notebook?"

"Yes, I have it here, though there doesn't seem much in it."

"What did you find in his pockets?"

"Here's the list," said the Superintendent, bringing it out. Usual sort of stuff. Loose change. Five pounds ten in his wallet, along with identity-card and so on. Pen. Pencil. Knife. Cigarettes. Box of matches."

"And a lighter, eh?" I asked quickly.

He looked surprised. "No, there was no lighter."

"We've got to get back to that room of his, sharp," I cried, jumping up. "While we're talking here, for all we know, some-body may be going through it now."

"He'll have to get rid of a fifteen-stone constable first," said the Superintendent, chuckling, "because there's one sitting in that room this minute. He took over when we left. No, I know you didn't notice him, but perhaps you don't notice everything. What's this lighter business?"

"Anybody who's likely to be working with any of us in the department is given a special lighter for identification purposes. There are certain things we say too, of course——"

"Signs and passwords." The Superintendent snorted. "I don't know. Sounds to me like a lot of school-kids having a game."

"And what did Olney look like? Did he look as if he was having a game?"

"Ah, you've got me there," he replied coolly. "But I'm only a police officer. I'm not used to this fancy work."

I took my pipe out and pointed it at him. "Superintendent," I began, "you forced my hand because I had to know about Olney. I don't want to work with the police—there are too many of 'em—but I'd be glad now to work with you."

"It'll be a pleasure, Mr. Neyland." And he grinned.

"Fine. But before we start there are one or two things you've got to understand. This game may look like fancy work, but believe me it isn't. Nazi agents killed my best friend and his wife. That's how I came to drift into this counter-espionage business. I believe a Nazi agent, right here in this town, under your very nose, killed Olney last night. Fancy work! Believe me, it's just this kind of fancy work that's done just as much as tanks and planes have to plant the Nazis in Norway, Holland, Belgium, and France. And the same kind of fancy work is helping the Japs to take the Far East to pieces right now."

"I believe you're right, Mr. Neyland," he said in his slow sagacious fashion, "I believe you're right. But I'm just a plain policeman—though I'm no fool——"

"I know you're not," I told him quickly.

"And I don't understand all this spying and Fifth Column business."

"You've got to remember that this is a very complicated war," I said. "And the official line on it here—the kind of stuff they hand out at Warship Weeks—isn't very intelligent. They're always trying to turn it into the last war, and it just won't fit into the pattern. You can't make it a simple affair of different flags, national anthems, patriotisms. We've had to lock up some British because we know they want Hitler to win. On the other hand, we've got some Germans here who are doing all they can to help our side. Right?"

"Right," he said, twinkling at me. "Now before you go on—and I don't want you to stop—I must tell you I generally have a cup o' tea about this time. Could you do with one?"

I said I could, and he put his head outside and bellowed for two cups.

"The way I see it is this," I went on. "Though there may be millions and millions on each side that support that side simply because their government and country support it, the real fight is between those who still have some belief in and affection for ordinary people and those who only believe in the Fascist idea. Joe Stalin may be as tough as hell, but in the long run he's plotting and planning to give the folk who believe in him the best life possible. Winston Churchill——"

"Now don't say anything against Winston," he interrupted. "I believe in him."

"I'm not going to. I say Winston Churchill may think sometimes he's living in the Eighteenth Century and have lots of wrong notions about this war, but I believe he wants to fight and work to give the ordinary people a chance, even though some of his friends don't. And nobody doubts that Roosevelt stands for the common man. The same applies to all the folk who line up behind these three men."

"I agree," said the Superintendent, getting up to take the tea from the constable at the door. "Now have a cup o' tea but don't stop. It's this other lot, this Fascist lot, that I want to know about."

The tea was very strong and very sweet, and I didn't like it much, but I pretended to enjoy it. "I've had to do a deal of thinking about this Fascist lot, because it's very much part of my job. Of course, you get Germans who work for Hitler just because they think he stands for Germany. But we're not worrying about them. It's the people who aren't Germans but who yet work for Hitler that give us the trouble and need understanding. Sometimes, of course, they're doing it just for the money they get, which as a rule isn't very much. Now and then they've been blackmailed into working for the Nazis. This is an old Gestapo trick. They find out something to your discredit, and so compel you to work for them, and once you've started you daren't stop. But the really difficult and dangerous people are the ones who sell out because they believe in the Fascist idea. Sometimes, of course—as in France—they think only the Nazis can help them to keep their power or money or both. Then again some of them have been promised big jobs if they help and the Nazis win. Oh yes, you and I have probably sat opposite men who were thinking what they'd do to us once they were *gauleiters*. With some—as I believe it was with Hitler himself and a lot of his gang—it's the idea of revenge that inspires them. They're all twisted to hell inside, and are just waiting to kick the face in of everybody who's ever laughed at them. And all of 'em just hate the democratic idea, and despise ordinary decent folk. And that's the type we have to look for. And don't forget that when we catch him, he may be singing *Rule Britannia* at the top of his voice and be smothered in Union Jacks."

"And there are some of 'em here in Gretley, eh?"

"We know that valuable information has been coming from Gretley. We know—and so do you—that there's been a certain amount of sabotage in Gretley. And we think that Gretley may be one of the provincial headquarters and clearing-houses of information and espionage. And I know that Olney was on to something. And you know that last night somebody murdered him."

Superintendent Hamp nodded, drained his teacup noisily, and got up. "I'm going to work on that," he said, looking very grim. "There'll be an inquest, of course, but it won't mean anything." He took a cheap little notebook from his pocket and held it up. "This is the notebook. Yes, I know you want it. But so do I, and I'd like to keep it for the rest of to-day. And as you said, we'd better get back to that room of his. Come on."

In the corridor we ran into that sergeant with the chin, and I'll swear it wobbled when he caught sight of the pair of us.

"Sergeant," said the Superintendent sharply.

"Yessir?"

"This is Mr. Neyland. He's a friend o' mine. And this is Sergeant Boyd."

We looked at each other and nodded. There didn't seem to be anything to say. I walked on while the Superintendent stayed behind to give some orders to the sergeant. The sleet had dwindled to a mere cold drizzle. I remembered then, as I looked at the inhospitable street, that I had to get out of the hotel and must find somewhere else to stay. The *Queen of Clubs?* I could probably get in by putting some pressure on Fencrest or Mrs. Jesmond, and there was something to be said for being on the spot up there, but

on the other hand it was outside the town and it wasn't my idea
of a sensible lodging.

"Any objection to my taking over Olney's room?" I asked the
Superintendent, as we trudged through the slush. "No? Well, you
might put in a good word for me with the landlady there, Mrs.
Wilkinson. She only wants to do what's right, poor woman, but
she's not so sure that anything to do with me is right."

"She's a decent little body," he replied, "and you'll be as well
off there as anywhere, specially as the town's very full. Also, I can
pay a call on you there without too many people knowing about
it."

"I'd thought of that too. And, if you don't mind, I'd like you to
do a bit of checking up for me—save me lots of time."

"Oh no, I don't mind," he said, with enormous irony. "I've
only got half my men away, and the town crammed with folk,
nearly twice as many as we had before the war, and special forms
marked *Urgent* and *Priority* and God knows what arriving by the
dozen by every post, all to be puzzled out and filled in, so naturally it'll be a pleasure to turn over half the force——"

"All right, all right, I get the idea," I said irritably. "Forget it.
Imagine I'm just here for my health and that this is an inland
resort. But you might remember that while the forms are
coming in, the secret information is also going out, and that in
some quarters the name of Gretley's beginning to stink. But I can
get by. I've done it before."

"Not in the best o' tempers, are you, this morning?" he said
quite amiably.

"No, I haven't been for days, for weeks and months, perhaps
for years. Forget it. All I ask you to remember is that there are
some useful questions that it might take me days to find the
answers to that you could answer in five minutes. After all, you
must know what goes on round this town."

"I know as much as the next man." He gave me a friendly bang
on the shoulder. "And anything you ask, I'll try to answer. So take
it easy."

We were back in Raglan Street. It suddenly occurred to me
that little Mrs. Wilkinson probably didn't know yet that her
lodger was dead. I asked the Superintendent, who said that she'd

been told late last night and had identified the body this morning.
An envelope in Olney's pocket had given them the address.

I didn't hear what the Superintendent said to Mrs. Wilkinson,
but I saw her myself a few minutes afterwards and came to an
agreement about the room. I felt it was a rather ghoulish business
arranging so quickly to move into the room of a man who'd only
been dead about fourteen hours, and our talk about it reminded
Mrs. Wilkinson that she was close to a tragedy—though she only
thought it was an accident—and she wept a little. Meanwhile the
Superintendent was going through the room upstairs.

I joined him, and together we made a very thorough search.
There was no lighter. I didn't expect there would be, because
even when we don't use them as lighters in the ordinary way we
take care always to have them with us.

"This doesn't surprise me," I said. "It was ten to one he'd have
it on him, and now it's probably another ten to one that somebody in this town has that lighter. You'd better take a good look
at mine. Olney's was exactly like it."

The Superintendent examined it closely, and then said he'd
recognize any companion lighter anywhere at any time. "And if
I do see one," he went on, "the fellow that owns it will have to
do some very careful talking to me. Well now, you'll be wanting
to go through that notebook later on. Suppose I call here about
nine or so to-night and bring it with me, eh? Right! Now I've got
plenty to do the rest of to-day, chiefly on this Olney case, but if
you'd like to jot down the names of a few people you're interested in, I'll try to get you what information we have."

"Good enough." And I scribbled half a dozen names on the
back of an old envelope. He gave them a glance, nodded, and
lumbered out without another word. I heard him telling Mrs.
Wilkinson below that he'd already arranged for the constable to
pack up Olney's things and then take them away. As a matter of
fact, the constable came back and started packing even before I'd
left the room.

Now that the Superintendent had gone, and I'd nobody to
exchange ideas or spar with, I didn't feel so good. The news of
Olney's death, coming as it did in the middle of a sparring match
with the Superintendent in his office, hadn't really registered

with me deep down inside. Then it was just exciting news. But now it became real. I remembered the little man, and the way he looked at me over those steel rimmed property spectacles of his, and the flashes of humour and intelligence that came out of him even during that short talk. Then I thought of what had happened to him, the way he'd been flattened out in the slush and dumped round like a sack of potatoes, and first I felt sad and then I felt angry. I didn't spend any time wondering whether anything of the sort was going to happen to me, because that's a waste of time, and, anyhow, I didn't care a damn. But I did make up my mind to give the job everything I'd got, and be as tough as I could on it. Whatever you may think, I hadn't really wasted much time so far in Gretley, for every move I'd made had brought me something, but because I was feeling sour anyhow and didn't want this particular job, perhaps up to now the edge of my wits had been a bit blunted and I'd been inclined to make all the easier moves.

I went back to the hotel, packed up, had an early lunch, paid my bill with no regrets, and then took a cab back to Raglan Street. This time I met Mr. Wilkinson, who was a railwayman and looked rather like a melancholy old spaniel. His idea was that we could win the war by dropping whole armies into Poland, and he said he was sorry he was too old to go himself. I said there were a lot of people I'd like to drop into Poland any night, but that most of them weren't very young. For two people who each thought the other a bit mad, Mr. Wilkinson and I didn't get on too badly.

The sleet and drizzle of the morning had now changed to a mere wintry mist, and I went out into it to discover where Dr. Bauernstern lived. I'd already asked Mrs. Wilkinson, but she'd never seen the woman before and had only vaguely heard of her existence. I got the address from a telephone book at the nearest post office. *Dr. Margaret Bauernstern, 87, Sherwood Avenue.* It was about a mile from Raglan Street, on the edge of one of those big housing estates that look so good on paper and so damned depressing in reality. Sherwood Avenue consisted of semi-detached villas, a few half-dead young trees, and a good deal of dirty snow. What daylight there had been was already fading by the time I stood outside Number 87. A middle-aged housekeeper, foreign and probably Austrian, answered the door, and told me severely that Dr. Bauernstern wasn't to be seen at this time except by patients.

"All right then," I said. "I'm a patient. Where's the surgery, please?"

There were no other patients about, and it looked as if the practice wasn't flourishing, at least in Sherwood Avenue. But it was a neat little surgery.

For a moment or two Dr. Bauernstern didn't recognize me, and for that matter she looked very different too. To begin with, she was wearing a white overall coat, and I could now see her hair, which was smooth and dark brown. Then, of course, she looked far more business-like and confident, the doctor in her surgery. I must say she looked pretty good. I could see that she had an excellent figure, with those rather square shoulders that nearly all women recently have been pretending to have. Her face looked worn, though, and the cold glare of the surgery light was hard on it.

As soon as she did recognize me, she looked angry. Then she pretended she'd never seen me before. "Good afternoon. What's the trouble?"

Well, I thought I might as well tell the truth while I was about it. "It's nothing much," I said, solemn as a judge. "I can't pretend to be very ill. But I feel depressed all the time, I sleep badly, and I can't enjoy my food."

"Let me see your tongue."

I did, and rather enjoyed sticking it out at her.

"I imagine," she said, "that probably you're smoking too much and not taking enough exercise. And when did you last see a dentist?"

"Not for a long, long time," I said, shaking my head. "You see, I've been so busy. But don't bother about my teeth. Just give me something that'll shake me up a bit and then settle me down—y'know——"

There was a sharp ring at the front door, which was only two yards or so from this surgery door. I heard the housekeeper open the front door and a deep voice outside. The next moment the housekeeper was knocking at the surgery door and releasing a flood of frightened German. The doctor hurried out, and as soon as she went I peeped through the little bay window. It was a policeman. But whatever he wanted, it didn't take long to get rid of him.

But this interruption completely shattered the little comedy we'd been playing. She returned looking rather as she'd done the night before, her eyes bright with anxiety and a secret terror. She closed the door behind her, but didn't come forward into the room.

"This is stupid," she said angrily. "What do you want? Why did you come here?"

"I came here to tell you something," I said, without smiling. "Your woman said you were only seeing patients, so I became a patient."

"I suppose you thought I wouldn't know there was nothing wrong with you?" She meant, I think, just because she was a woman doctor. Evidently she was that irritating type of touchy professional woman, always instantly on the defensive.

"Neither you nor any other doctor could tell me anything or really discover anything on that amount of evidence. And for all you know, Dr. Bauernstern, I may be in the grip of some terrible disease."

She nearly smiled. "You came here to tell me something?"

"Yes, and to ask you something too. Both quite important. But look here," I added, "can't we go somewhere else to talk? This is a bit grim."

"I thought you prided yourself on being a grim person."

I stared at her. Perhaps this was a deliberate line of hers, this suddenly coming out with a remark that suggested she'd known you quite a long time.

"All right," she went on, "we'll go somewhere else to talk. I have to have an early tea on Thursday, because I go along to the children's hospital before five." She led me across the hall but turned to have a word with the housekeeper about tea. I noticed that the housekeeper's expressive eyes were full of alarms and warnings. It was shocking how these two women were giving everything away.

The sitting-room was very pleasant, not very English, but no worse for that. Dr. Bauernstern had now taken off her overall coat. She was wearing a dark red dress that suited her very well, although it seemed to emphasize her prominent cheek bones and the hollows underneath them. But she was a handsome woman in spite of looking both too severe and too fragile. I knew I wasn't seeing her at her best. She didn't know how to handle me, and this kept making her stiff and angry, and of course it was an essential part of my game to keep her uneasy, worried and annoyed. And if you think this is a poor game to play on a tired woman, just remember what the German and Japanese troops have done to a lot of women far more tired than this one was.

"It's about your patient, Olney," I began, looking hard at her.

"What about him?"

"He's dead."

People are always faking surprise—lifting the eyebrows, widening their eyes, opening their mouths, and the rest of it— but if you are watching them closely they can't often take you in. Now this woman didn't try any of those tricks. On the contrary, whereas she was genuinely surprised, in fact deeply shocked, she pretended not to be. To take that line deliberately would have been a lovely bluff, but a woman would have to be an actress of genius to bring it off, and so far it had seemed to me that this Dr. Bauernstern was a very poor actress. So now I was reasonably certain that she hadn't known Olney was dead. And that was something I'd gone there to learn.

I explained to her very briefly what had happened to Olney, not mentioning, of course, that he'd probably been pulled into the car that knocked him down and then dumped elsewhere. She wasn't to know about the murder angle.

"There's another thing," I continued. "I told you I wanted to ask you a question. It's this. Had he a weak heart?"

"Yes," she replied. "I suppose you're wondering if that made the accident more dangerous? I'd say definitely it would. I'm terribly sorry. I liked him."

"Yes, no doubt you did. But I'm also wondering how many other people knew he'd a weak heart."

"He may have told lots of people. Some patients—people, I mean—often do."

"I know. They've bored me for hours with their medical anecdotes. But do you know if Olney went to any other doctor here before he came to you?"

"I haven't the least idea," she said coldly. "And I don't see what right you have to cross-question me like this."

I grinned. "None whatever, Dr. Bauernstern."

Some tea arrived. I could see that that housekeeper would much preferred to have been serving me with prussic acid. She was a terribly obvious woman, that housekeeper, and I'd have hated to share a secret with her.

Now that the tea was in the room, the doctor had to change her manner, however much she may have disliked me. "I feel an awful fraud," she said, as she poured out, "every time I hear anybody calling me Dr. Bauernstern."

"But it's your name, isn't it?"

"It's my married name," she explained. "You see, my late husband was the famous Dr. Bauernstern—you may never have heard of him, but he really was famous—as a children's specialist in Vienna. He died two years ago. And now I still can't help feeling embarrassed, because it's just as if I were trying to masquerade as somebody who knew ten times as much as I know."

"I see. But why didn't you decide to practise under your own name? Lots of married women doctors do, I believe."

Now she looked proud and defiant. "Because people would have thought I was ashamed of a name that sounded German. And of course I was proud of it. My husband was a great man."

"Was he an exile?"

"Yes, of course. When the Nazis took over Austria, he lost everything—except his great reputation. They couldn't take that away, although they tried hard enough."

All this was said with great bitterness, of course, but I'd heard other people talk just as bitterly about the Nazis and found out afterwards that they'd been taught just how to do it during their special espionage course in Berlin. And this line didn't require much acting.

I glanced round the room, but this wasn't the kind of woman who keeps personal photographs in her sitting-room. There was a ring at the front door, but neither of us bothered about it.

"You were in Vienna yourself at some time, I suppose, eh?"

We're always reading about eyes lighting up, but this woman's really did then. It was just as if somebody had suddenly switched her on. "Yes, I spent two years in Vienna, working at my husband's hospital—though he wasn't my husband then, of course—because I hoped to be a children's specialist too."

"And why aren't you?" I asked bluntly but not too rudely, as I was really interested.

"Why aren't you—well—something that I can see you're not just now?" she demanded, like lightning. And I must admit I was taken aback for a moment. Why wasn't I looking after a big clean sensible job in some wide sunlit place instead of sitting there wondering how soon I could trap one of these people? To hell with it. And I knew she saw it all written on my face, but instead of looking as if she'd scored a point, in a game in which she'd been losing so far, her eyes, in fact her whole face, seemed to soften and look more friendly. I'd have to watch myself with this woman.

And then Mr. Perigo walked in, cool as you please. "Now you did promise me a cup of tea if I ever found myself in this part of the town," he began, holding out both hands to her in his affected way. "Oh yes, Mr. Neyland and I know each other, don't we?"

"We run into each other all over the place," I said, sounding a bit sulky.

Our hostess was busy with the teapot again, and I noticed for the first time that there were several extra cups, as if visitors could be expected at this hour. As if she knew what I was thinking, she said casually to both of us: "Thursdays and Sundays at this hour are about my only chance of seeing people at a reasonable time of day."

"Yes, of course," said Mr. Perigo, who seemed to be in good form. "Everybody's so frightfully busy these days, everybody but me. So I run about, like a chattering rabbit, and *pretend* to be busy, though really, of course, I'm not doing a stroke of work. What *is* there for a man like me to do? I tried talking to the soldiers, but I could see they absolutely *loathed* it. And nobody wants me to look after a machine or hammer bits of tin or whatever they do in these absurd factories. So I run about, and of course get poorer and poorer and poorer. Now what about you, my dear fellow? Have you been given some splendid responsible post at either of our two factories yet?"

"Not a thing," I said. "But of course there hasn't been time yet for my application to go through to the Board."

"I dare say. But they ought to have *jumped* at you. Mr. Neyland comes all the way from Canada to help us—and you can see he's just the virile methodical type they need—and yet they keep even him hanging about. Disgraceful!"

He gave us both a look that suggested that the whole business was an elaborate joke. They talk about alarm and despondency, but Perigo's line, taking all the seriousness out of the war effort, was infinitely more dangerous. He was worth more to Hitler than even our week-end orators.

"And isn't the news really shocking?" he asked brightly.

"Is it?" said Dr. Bauernstern, without any interest and giving a tiny shrug.

"Now don't tell me, my dear, that you don't even *care.*"

"All right, I won't," she replied, smiling a little. "But do have something to eat, won't you?"

"No, thank you," said Mr. Perigo, showing us those porcelain teeth. "But if you don't mind, I'll smoke a cigarette. Now, I have a lighter somewhere, a nice new lighter."

As he said this, he gave me a glance out of an eye that looked a thousand wicked years old. I watched for the lighter coming out. But it didn't.

"I must have mislaid it," he said, holding out his palms. "No, please, don't trouble, Dr. Bauernstern. I'm sure Mr. Neyland has a lighter somewhere."

"I can give you a match," I said. And I saw that our hostess was looking a trifle puzzled, as if she guessed that more was meant than had been said.

There didn't seem much sense in staying, for though there were several things I could usefully have said to either of them alone, I didn't feel I had anything to say to them together. Mr. Perigo didn't offer to leave with me, although he must have known he couldn't stay long, because the doctor would have to go along to the hospital very soon; so I took it that he had something important to say to her. She came to the door with me, which I didn't expect her to do, and we lingered just behind it for a minute.

"Do you happen to know," she asked, "what Mr. Perigo really does?"

"No, I don't. He says he just runs round and chatters."

"Yes, I know. But I find that rather hard to believe. Don't you?"

"I find nearly everything about Mr. Perigo hard to believe," I said deliberately. "And some things about you, Dr. Bauernstern, aren't easy either."

"What do you mean?" She sounded more surprised than angry.

"I don't quite know—yet," I said, speaking the exact truth. "And thanks for the tea. I enjoyed it."

I hurried back to Raglan Street, told Mrs. Wilkinson I didn't expect her to supply me with any food that night but that I would be back by nine at the latest, and went out again, taking with me the two books I'd borrowed from *Prue's Gift Shop.* I'd only read one of them, but changing both would give me a good excuse for returning to the shop. When I arrived, the young assistant with the yellow smock and the cold in the head was just finishing blacking out the windows, and Miss Axton herself was serving a customer. I went straight across to the bookshelves and pretended to be examining them until I saw the customer go and then the assistant, who was told by Miss Axton to hurry off home and take herself straight to bed. But then another customer, a fussy woman, came in, and messed about for the next ten minutes or so, trying to choose one of those little bunches of artificial flowers made of leather or cloth.

Miss Axton's handling of this irritating customer was well worth watching. Her voice was completely under control and never stopped being politely helpful. But I saw her give the idiotic woman a look that was very revealing. If the woman herself had noticed it, she would have hurried straight out. It seemed to spring, this look, from some hidden depth of cold fury, and it was quite murderous. I was fascinated all over again by this tall handsome blonde, who looked at first sight as if she were some old-fashioned young beauty just taken out of cold storage. Nothing about her, except the superficial things, her green smock, her plaited hair, her obvious manner, suggested the kind of woman who'd want to run this sort of shop. What she was giving was a rough character performance, no doubt good enough for Gretley, as that kind of woman. Really it was like seeing a high-powered streamlined car crawling away from a greengrocer's back door, loaded with vegetables.

As soon as the fussy woman had gone, Miss Axton came across to me, smiling. My mind had gone clean off the books, so I grabbed the first two I could reach for.

"Do you really want these?" she asked, still smiling.

"Well, I think they'll do," I said hastily.

"Look at them," she commanded. I did, and they certainly weren't my kind of reading, if the titles were anything to judge from.

"All right," I said, "you win. I couldn't read these on a desert island. The fact is, I'd been standing here so long that when you came up, I felt I ought to have made my choice. But I'd been thinking about something else."

"So I imagine," she said, taking the two books away and then making a note of the two I'd brought back. "What were you thinking about?"

A little boldness wouldn't do any harm here, I thought. "I was thinking about you."

She looked up, raising her eyebrows. "Then you'd better tell me, hadn't you?"

"Not now," I said. "As a matter of fact, I looked in to remind you that you promised to dine with me quite soon. What about to-morrow night—at the *Queen of Clubs*? I had a really good dinner there the other night, and though I might not be able to do you quite as well as Mrs. Jesmond did us, I can do my best. By the way, I saw you there that night. The night before last it was."

"Yes, I remember. I could dine with you to-morrow there— thank you very much—but not before half-past eight. I promised to attend a public meeting at seven o'clock. It's a patriotic meeting, so I feel I ought to be there, especially as we shopkeepers arc particularly asked to attend. And things like that are good for business too," she added, and showed me a handbill announcing the meeting.

I saw that the local M.P., the mayor, and Colonel Tarlington would be speaking. "All right, suppose I go along with you, and then as soon as it's over we can go straight out to the *Queen of Clubs?*"

"Excellent!" she cried. And I remember thinking that I'd never heard a woman say "Excellent!" like that before. It's not a thing somehow you expect to hear a woman say. But I'll already made up my mind that this was no ordinary woman.

"Have you found two books you really want?" she asked, after a moment.

"No, I'm afraid I haven't. Do you want me to go?"

She laughed. "No, it's not that." She hesitated a moment, then added in a half-whisper: "But I'd like to close this damned shop. It's been such a dreary long day. You don't seem to be in a hurry——"

"I admit it. I'm not."

"All right then, this is what we'll do. I'll close the shop—before another of those awful women finds her way in—and we'll finish our talk upstairs and have a drink too. And then you can tell me what you were thinking."

"That would be grand," I said, with enthusiasm, and meant it too, because it was just what I'd wanted. I was curious to see what she'd do now. Well, all she did was to lock and bolt the shop door, show me the lighted stairs at the back, switch off all the lights in the shop and promptly join me on the stairs. And I was positive that people who own shops and really care about them don't leave them for the night as casually as that. They tidy them up, linger here and loiter there, consider the day's takings, perhaps check the cash entries, and so forth, taking an easy but fond fare-well of their shops. This brusque shutting up of shop was quite out of character with what she'd said to me when we first talked, her little speech about giving the people of Gretley a chance to appreciate her charming little things. Of course she may have had a particularly bad day in there, and so feel impatient, but it seemed to me that the real reason was that she was either uncon-sciously or quite deliberately dropping the character. There was something about me—and I don't mean my beautiful eyes—that inclined her that way, but it was important to know whether it was unconscious or deliberate.

The little sitting-room upstairs was interesting just because it hadn't any character at all. It looked like a sitting-room in an hotel. Nobody owned it. There wasn't a suggestion of any tatty Prudence of the Gift Shop, but it didn't suggest any other kind of woman. Yet this Miss Axton had a strong personality, even though as yet it wasn't easy to define. Nevertheless, she'd furnished this room and spent four months in it and it hadn't taken on any character at all. Well, that was no accident.

She murmured something about the drinks, and I heard her unlocking the corner cupboard. I turned round in time to see the best row of bottles I'd seen for some time. Miss Axton was very lucky in her wine merchant.

"Now the real miracle would be if you happened to have some Canadian rye," I said, just the big dumb boy from the Wild West.

"Well, I have," she replied coolly.

"For Pete's sake!" I yelled, almost overdoing it. "I've almost forgotten what it tastes like. Sure you can spare it?"

She poured me out about half a tumbler, and gave herself a hefty gin-and-lime. Then she switched off the top light, leaving only a shaded little standard lamp in a corner. We stood holding our glasses, smiling, near the fire. The scene had gone all intimate, almost in a flash. We raised our glasses, bringing them together so that for a moment or two our hands came into contact. Then we drank, still smiling at each other. She put her glass down and so did I, but we still remained standing, facing each other.

I knew then, though I don't know how and why, that this woman wouldn't be angry if I kissed her, and I felt that it would be a good thing if I did. So I slipped my arms round her, as easily and coolly as I knew how, and kissed her. And don't forget this was no girl, though she might look it at a distance, but a mature woman. Her response was very interesting. It was efficient, experienced, almost enthusiastic, but quite impersonal. Then, making no comment on this little interlude, we sat down.

She remembered, as I thought she would, that I was after a job with the Charters people, and now asked me what had happened. I told her that my lack of experience in this kind of work was against me, but that Heacham was putting my name before his Board.

"I ran into one of his directors that afternoon," I went on, "and I didn't feel he was going to be enthusiastic about me."

"Who was that?" she asked.

"Colonel Tarlington," I said. "Do you know him?"

"I've just said How d'you do to him," she replied. "Somebody said he had a lot of influence in the town, so I thought I'd better smile at him sweetly. But he's not my style."

I told her that Heacham had shown me all round the works, and threw in carelessly that I'd been impressed by the new heavy anti-tank guns they were beginning to make. Also, for good measure, I gave her the calibre of the guns, only it wasn't the right calibre.

"Look here," I went on, "I oughtn't to have said anything about those guns. Keep it to yourself, of course." And I couldn't help wondering how many asses were saying just the same thing over a drink at the very same time.

"Of course," she said, looking solemn, "I'm very discreet."

"I'm sure you are," I said, looking as if I thought she was wonderful.

"Another drink?" she asked, smiling.

I had a notion then that she wanted me to go, and as I was ready to oblige her, I said I wouldn't have another drink. As soon as I got up, she got up too. I reminded her that she was dining with me the next night, and she reminded me that I'd also promised to go to the meeting with her.

"You'll have to go out the back way," she said. "And as it's a bit tricky, I'll come and let you out."

She used a torch this time instead of switching on any lights, and I followed downstairs and across a little store-room at the back of the shop. After she'd unbolted the door, she hesitated a moment before opening it. The torch went out, and there we were, behind the door, close together in the dark. This time it was she who moved in and kissed me, doing it as if she just couldn't help it. She did it very well too, but I couldn't help wondering.

I didn't spend much time wondering, however, because I remembered then that the little Hippodrome theatre was only just round the corner, and after going down several wrong side-streets in the dark I managed to find the Stage Door. There I asked for Larry, and was told that he was on the stage, but would be up soon to change for the finale, and was taken along to his dressing-room. This was a stinking little hole, where three of them dressed, and it looked like the back of an old clothes shop. It was the last dressing-room but one at the end of a dimly lit corridor, and I knew that the end room was occupied by Fifine. I knew, too, that unless my timing had gone all wrong, Fifine ought to be going down soon to do her act.

I waited in the open doorway of Larry's room, hoping that I would see Fifine pass. I could just hear the show going on, but it sounded miles away. The corridor was deserted, dim and forlorn. I can remember feeling curiously empty and sad, like a ghost waiting there.

Then Fifine came out, with a gaudy but stained wrap huddled round her. She locked her door. I didn't withdraw but stared at her with a wide fatuous grin, which made her dismiss me contemptuously as she sailed past, reeking of grease-paint and a strong animal smell of warm flesh and hair. She was older than she'd appeared to be from in front, and a queer tough type.

They must have told Larry that somebody had called to see him because now he came flying round the corner, just as Fifine disappeared.

"I wondered if it was you," he said, breathlessly, looking oddly solemn behind his idiotic make-up. "The other two chaps will be up in a minute. Are you going to try and get into her dressing-room?"

"Yes, if I can open the door," I told him. "You and I had better be talking out here, near her door, when the other two fellows come along. Then you'll have to keep watch for me somehow while you're changing."

We moved farther down the corridor, near her door, until I was standing where a hand behind my back could easily reach the keyhole. I'd had to open other people's doors before, and the department had for a long time now let me have a small bunch of instruments that made short work of most locks. As I stood there, leaning against the wall, with Larry covering me by leaning against the wall too, apparently in earnest confidential talk, I began to try the lock. Larry's partner, the middle-aged pansy, and some other man now appeared, gave us a curious look but went at once into the dressing-room.

"Cover me until I get in," I muttered to Larry, "then go and change, but leave your door open, so that you can warn me." I turned and tackled the job properly, and half a minute later was inside her dressing-room.

The table in front of the mirror had the usual make-up stuff on it, and nothing else except a pack of dirty playing-cards. Underneath the table, however, I found a screwed up bit of paper that had numbers written on it in pencil, and as this had been thrown away and probably forgotten, I took it. Then I found her handbag, hanging behind a fur coat on one of the hooks. It was a biggish handbag, and it wasn't locked. It was filled with the usual stuff—a compact, mirror, a few keys, some money—but I was disappointed to find that there wasn't a single letter. Most women carry letters in their handbags for weeks after they've first received them, but this woman didn't. There was an old professional card there, though, and I saw that on the back of it had been scribbled what appeared to be half a dozen telephone numbers. I copied these out, and then returned the card to the bag and the bag to its hook. And if there was anything else worth examining at leisure, then I must have missed it. I was back in the corridor, with the door locked behind me, at least five minutes before the woman was due to return.

Larry came out, although he hadn't quite finished changing, and followed me along the corridor, away from Fifine's dressing-room. We stopped at the end, where we could see anybody coming up the stone steps.

"Okay?" he whispered.

I shook my head, and looked as if I thought I'd wasted my time. After all, although Larry had been useful, I didn't have to tell him everything.

He was disappointed. "Nothing doing at all?"

"Doubt it," I said. "Probably we've been a bit too clever."

He shook his head, and I felt sorry for the poor little devil, standing there in his dreary fool's paint. Obviously he'd been building on this Fifine story, and had probably been seeing himself as a member of the Special Branch. I put a hand on his shoulder, which was now wearing an evening dress coat that had known far better days, long before it had met him. "I'm much obliged, all the same, Larry," I told him. "And I'll try to see you again before you leave town."

"If you stayed on through the second house," he began, cheering up a little.

"Can't be done," I said. "But if anything exciting breaks, I'll let you know."

"You promise, Mr. Neyland?" He was like a kid.

"Sure!" And I gave that dress coat another little thump. "And I must get out now before too many people begin asking questions. Tell me where I can get anything to eat round here?"

As we went downstairs together, he told me there was a little café down the street that was open at night. We could hear Fifine getting a thumping round at the end of her act, and I wondered just who was in front to-night, counting those twists and turns of her fine big shoulders and legs.

The little café was open all right, and an anæmic girl there pushed in front of me an unappetizing mess of fried fish-skin and bones, watery mashed potatoes and cabbage, and a cup of warm grey mud that she said was coffee. Two soldiers yawned in a corner. At another table a little middle-aged woman, who might have been the sister of my landlady, Mrs. Wilkinson, was shrinkingly feeding herself as if eating in public was an act of wild indecency. From the radio there came bits of some play about jewel thieves, who all seemed to talk like old-fashioned bad actors. There are some places that strike you as being absolute dead ends, and that café was one of them.

On the other hand, that upstairs back room at 15, Raglan Street, began to look almost like home when I went back there, just before nine, to meet the Superintendent. Mrs. Wilkinson had turned it out and changed it round a bit, and had then left me a nice fire. I had time to smoke a pipe and to do some thinking before the Superintendent arrived. He made himself easy and comfortable at once, I was glad to see.

"I'm sorry I can't offer you a drink," I said, "but I haven't got any, as you can easily understand."

"Quite so, Mr. Neyland," he said, lighting his pipe, which

looked several sizes too small for him. "A cup o' tea suits me, if you should be having any."

I asked Mrs. Wilkinson to bring us some tea, then settled down opposite him, feeling better than I'd done any time since I arrived in Gretley, partly because I liked this big policeman and also because it was a relief to be able to talk fairly frankly about the job instead of going round putting on an act. Don't forget that although I'd now done nearly two years of this sleuthing for the department, and knew most of the dodges in the game, I still thought of myself as a civil engineer who'd only taken this on as his war work. Anyhow, whatever the reasons might be, I was feeling better.

"I promised you that notebook," said the Superintendent, producing it, "and here it is. You'll probably want to tackle it when I'm gone."

"Thanks, I'd rather do it that way," I told him. "And here's something for you." I gave him the telephone numbers I'd copied out in Fifine's dressing-room. "There isn't a telephone directory here, and one of your chaps can easily find out whose numbers those are."

He took a quick look at them. "I can tell you one of 'em here and now," he said, pointing. "This second one's the telephone number of the *Queen of Clubs*—y'know."

I told him I did know.

"You can have the rest in the morning," he went on. "But it's funny you should ask me about that particular number, because the *Queen of Clubs* seems to keep popping up in this case. Does that surprise you?"

"No, it doesn't. But go on."

"Well, first, about Olney's movements last night. When he left the factory, he got a lift in a car to Colonel Tarlington's house. That's all straightforward. He didn't go there on your sort o' business but for the factory. It seems that Colonel Tarlington, who rather likes to hear himself talk in public, had agreed to go to the factory next week in connection with their Warships Week, to make a speech to 'em in the canteen, and Olney had to see him about it."

"Seems queer to me that Olney should go," I said.

"Nothing queer about it. Olney was on the Canteen Committee of the factory, and one of 'em had to see Colonel Tarlington. I may say I've seen the colonel myself, and checked up on all this. And he told me where Olney'd gone next, because Olney had told him. Olney was calling in at the *Queen of Clubs* for a drink and a sandwich."

"There again, that seems a queer move to me," I said. "A place like the *Queen of Clubs* isn't the kind of place a little works foreman would go for a drink and a sandwich. And Olney struck me as a man who'd never step out of the character he'd assumed. However. Where did he go after that?"

"On his own two legs he didn't go anywhere after that," said the Superintendent. "Because, if you ask me, he was knocked down and killed not three hundred yards from the front door of the *Queen of Clubs*. As you know, his body was found a couple of miles away. But he never took it there himself."

Mrs. Wilkinson brought in the tea, and we said nothing more until she'd gone and we had our cups in front of us. The Superintendent then produced a little time-table of Olney's movements. It looked all right to me.

"Does anybody at the *Queen of Clubs* remember seeing him there?" I asked.

"One of the waitresses does," said the Superintendent. "And she said that Olney spoke to Joe—that's the barman in the cocktail bar—he's thought to be a bit of a character——"

"I know him," I said. "Some of the customers seem to think they're very lucky if Joe condescends to shake a cocktail for them, but I don't get like that about barmen myself."

"It's because they've more money than sense. Anyhow, I had a word with this Joe, and he doesn't remember Olney. Says he talks to dozens of people every night, and of course remembers all the regulars and the more important customers, but can't be expected to remember everybody. And it was the girl who served Olney with his glass o' beer and sandwich. Well, there you are, Mr. Neyland. It's a fairly clear picture. Olney sees Colonel Tarlington on factory business. No mystery about that. He calls in the *Queen of Clubs* to have a drink and a bite. He's then on his way here, to keep his appointment with you. He went along to the bus stop at the corner, then decided to walk down the road to the next. Between the two bus stops, where we found his note-book, he was knocked down. They've been taking up one side of the road just there—you remember I told you about the clay there—and it's just the place if you want to run a man down, for if anybody should be looking it'll seem an accident. Ten to one somebody left the *Queen of Clubs* at the same time he did, jumped into a car, then followed him and let him have it."

"Or knew he was going there," I said slowly, "and waited outside in a car."

"That's right," said the Superintendent. "Now about the time. He was still in the *Queen of Clubs,* the girl says, at about half-past eight, but she doesn't remember seeing him there after that. There's a bus down at twenty to nine at that corner, and we can assume that he missed that. The next one passes the place where he was killed just after nine, and the driver of that bus didn't notice anything happening round there. It was all clear when he passed. So we can assume, I think, that he was probably killed between about quarter to nine and, say, nine o'clock. So, we want to know what people were doing at that time last night."

"Colonel Tarlington, for instance," I said. "He knew where Olney was going."

"And he's also a magistrate, chairman of this, that and the other, and not the sort you ask to explain his movements."

"I dare say not, but I'd like to know them all the same," I said sharply.

"Don't worry. The colonel told me of his own accord what he'd been doing after he'd seen Olney. He'd been hoping to get down to his club—the Constitutional—but he'd had to wait for an important personal telephone call from London, and it didn't come through until quarter to nine. Just to make sure," the Superintendent added, dropping his voice as if he were half ashamed of himself, "I checked that, and found that he had taken a long personal call from the Ministry of Supply that started at quarter to nine and lasted till nine o'clock." He grinned. "I did this for your sake, my friend. It was a waste of time as far as our case is concerned, because nobody could suspect Colonel Tar-lington."

"Quite so," I said smoothly. "Now did you do anything about that list I gave you this morning, Superintendent?"

His big hand dived inside his coat. "I haven't got much for you, Mr. Neyland, but I've done what I could. I know as much as the next man about what's going on in this town, but we're not the Gestapo, y'know. Well, first, this Mrs. Jesmond. She lives out at the *Queen of Clubs,* though she's not always there, for she travels about a bit. Came from the South of France just before France packed up. Plenty of money. And one of my chaps tells me that she's overfond of young officers."

"I know all that," I said. "And a bit more. I know she owns the *Queen of Clubs.*"

The Superintendent whistled. "I thought this chap, Settle—"

"He's only the manager," I said. "And his name's not really Settle but Fencrest. I've run into him before, and he's no good."

"What's the idea?"

"I don't know yet," I said truthfully. "The whole lot of 'em up there'll stand watching. Mrs. Jesmond's in the Black Market, and not only to get more food and drink for her roadhouse. I'd say she's operating herself, or at least putting money up. There's a fellow who calls himself Timon—from Manchester—who's certainly in it with her. You might put an enquiry through about him." And I described the swarthy fat man with the Manchester accent, and the Superintendent made a few notes.

"But I'm not sure how far she goes yet," I went on. "She's obviously a bad citizen, the type that'll do anything for money and luxury, the type that sells out to the Nazis. She may take these Air Force boys up to her room for her own private fun, but then again there may be a lot more than that in it."

"What do you want me to do about her?"

"Nothing just yet," I told him. "Let me handle it. Now what about Mrs. Castleside?"

"Not much there," said the Superintendent. "Young wife of Major Lionel Castleside, who's rather a swell and been stationed here, in charge of anti-aircraft batteries, for about six months. She's not been married very long, I gather, but I'm told she was married before, to some chap in India, and then left a widow—"

"Yes, I remember," I said. "That's her story. And it isn't true,

And she knows I know it isn't true. I've seen her before, and
now she fancies that she's seen me before, and not at her first
husband's funeral in India either. This girl looks a fool, but she's
been clever enough to fake up this yarn and catch Castleside.
Now she's terrified of being found out. These are the people
the Gestapo boys like. They have a hold over 'em, and they use
it to put the pressure on. It's their favourite trick. That's why I
put Sheila Castleside down on that list. Her husband's an officer.
She's knocking about, chiefly in bars, with other officers all the
time. She looks a fool and isn't, which means that if she keeps her
ears open she can learn plenty. And if they've put the screw on
her, she may have to pass on everything she learns."

"I see," said the Superintendent, his little eyes twinkling away.
"And I think that young woman spends a lot of her time—and
other people's money—up at the *Queen of Clubs,* doesn't she?"

"She does," I said. "I may risk a show-down with her very
shortly. Which reminds me." I made a note to ring up London in
the morning, for there were several enquiries I wanted them to
make there, and one of them was about Sheila Castleside.

"Next on the list," said the Superintendent, who'd been looking at his notes, "is this Perigo. I had a word with him myself,
quite friendly, a few weeks since. As a matter of fact, Colonel Tarlington, who's a bit hot, said something about him to our Chief
Constable, who put me on to him. Colonel Tarlington met this
Perigo somewhere and didn't like the look of him nor the sound
of him at all, so we had to check up on him. Nasty bit o' work, I'd
say, whatever he might be up to. I got the idea when I saw him,"
he added mournfully, "that he'd been trying to paint his face."

"You got the right idea too," I said, grinning. "Now Perigo says
he used to have a little art dealing business in London, and that
it went broke, but that having a bit of money left and nothing to
do, he came down here because a friend lent him a cottage just
outside the town. That's his story."

"I know it is." And the Superintendent sounded quite angry.
"That's his story, and the devil of it is—it's quite right. Yes, we
checked it. Art business, cottage, everything, all quite right.
What do you think of that?"

"Not much," I said. "It's what I expected. Perigo's too clever a man to dangle a story in your face that he knows wouldn't stand examination. He told me all this the very first time I met him, fairly pushed it at me. I knew then that his story was absolutely watertight. He also told me that he was down here trying to amuse himself. Well, if he is, so am I, and Gretley's a famous health resort. In short, he's phony as hell. And *very* clever. One of the things he knows, for instance, is that Mam'zelle Fifine, whose acrobatic act you can see at your Hippodrome this week, isn't quite what she seems. Have you seen Fifine?"

"I'm taking the wife to-morrow night, with luck," said the Superintendent solemnly. "I'd rather see a film myself, but the wife likes these turns. But what's this Fifine?"

"She's a hefty young woman—probably just about your style, Superintendent—who does a lot of wonderful twisting and turning on the trapeze and invites you to count the number of times she does any particular twist. She has the whole audience counting, and it's very popular. It's also very useful to her and the people who employ her, because it means that there in the spot-lights, with everybody looking on, she can hand out a message in numerical code."

"Now, now, now!" cried the Superintendent, "that's too fancy for me."

I knocked out my pipe against the grate. "Have another cup of tea? Good! What I'm really doing now—and doing it very successfully, you'll notice—is keeping my temper. I'm not going to tell you all over again where the Nazis and the Japs have got to, using methods that you say are too fancy. Just look at the map some time, and ask yourself if perhaps we're not living in a very fancy world."

The Superintendent looked at me over his cup. "You're right there. Many a morning I've had to ask myself if I was dreaming. All right, lad." And he reached over and patted my knee. "Forget it. And go on."

"I took that short list of telephone numbers I gave you—or at least I copied it—from Fifine's dressing-room to-night," I told him. "And here's a list of numbers I also picked up from the floor of that room. It's one she used earlier in the week. I'm not a cypher expert myself and I don't intend to waste my time trying to work it out, but I'll send it to our experts. You see, all you have to do is to sit there, counting with the rest of the audience, and then you have your message. This show goes from one industrial district to another, and it's easy for all the people concerned to come in and see the show. It's not one of their neatest or subtlest ideas, but it's not bad. And I can assure you that one of the people round here who knows what all that counting's about is our friend Mr. Perigo. I sat next but one to him at the Hippodrome the other night and saw at once that he was on to it."

"Then let's pull this woman in," cried the Superintendent.

"If we do, we break one link, that's all, and twenty others more important slip out of our hands. No, that's all right. I didn't mean to worry you with Fifine. Leave her to me. But I wanted to show you that I know a few things about Perigo. Who's next?"

"Well, there's this Miss Axton at the shop," he began doubt-fully, "but I can't imagine why you put her down."

"I wondered if you had any information, that's all," I replied, grinning. "I've just had a very pleasant drink with her to-night. She has a surprising lot of good liquor left in that sitting-room of hers above the shop. She interested me for two reasons. First, because when I first talked to her, she went out of her way to tell me a lie. Secondly, because she's obviously acting a part. But, mind you, an awful lot of women tell lies and act parts. Who is she, do you know?"

"Niece of Vice-Admiral Sir Johnson Frind-Tapley," the Super-intendent recited from his script, "and very well-connected gen-erally. She lived abroad for several years before the war. Then she was in America when the war broke out, and stayed there until last summer, then came back and opened this shop here. Plenty of money. A sort of hobby, I suppose, this shop is. The wife's been in for little presents and knick-knacks once or twice, she tells me, though she doesn't fancy this Miss Axton, she says. Too stuck-up and not really a nice woman, the wife says. You know how women go on."

I lit my pipe. "I can quite see what your wife means, y'know. But Miss Axton's dining with me to-morrow night, and I might learn a bit more about her then, if there's anything worth learn-ing. But she sounds quite okay."

"Of course she is. Wasting your time there, Mr. Neyland. That is," and he grinned, "if you were really on the job and not merely amusing yourself." Then he looked serious and tapped his notes impressively. "This last name you've got on here——"

"Well? Dr. Bauernstern, isn't it?"

"It is. And I'm sorry to see it here. I'll have to put my cards on the table here, Mr. Neyland. Of course if you want me to talk to you simply as a police officer, I will, and let it go at that. Because you *could* get me into trouble." And there he hesitated.

"Listen, Hamp," I began, deliberately using his name without his official rank, "one of the worst features of this job I have to do—and I don't like doing it and I'd *much* rather be working in my old profession, as a civil engineer, is that I'm hardly ever talking straight to anybody. I'm fishing for information. I'm trying to catch them out. I'm playing a part and trying to discover if they're playing a part too. Now I'm not doing that when I'm here talking to you. I may not be telling you all I know——"

"Don't worry, Neyland," he said, grinning. "I'm not so thick as I look. I knew that much."

"But if I don't tell you all I know, it isn't because I don't trust you, but simply because there are some kinds of vague suspicions, hints, hunches, that are best not talked about. If I told them to you, the way you took 'em might easily spoil 'em for me. You see what I mean? Right! But short of that, I trust you absolutely and want you to trust me. It's a relief and a pleasure to me, Hamp, to talk straight out and to stop acting. So for God's sake, never mind the police officer business, but tell me all you know, and all you think and feel."

"All right," said the Superintendent, looking relieved. "About this Dr. Bauernstern. Now I'm sorry—though not surprised—to see her name down on this list you gave me. I'm sorry because I like her, and I think she's been badly treated. She's a good doctor and, I believe, a fine woman, and I know she's done wonders with those poor kids down at the hospital."

"But she married an Austrian," I said, not wanting to be told what I knew already. "And she thinks he was a great man, and she's not going to change her name or anything like that, and she's been having a tough time."

"Ah, I see you know a bit about it already. I must say it doesn't take you long to get about and pick up information. Well, as Dr. Bauernstern—I mean, the husband now—had to register with us and report and all that, I knew something about him. He told me once what he thought of the Nazis, and I've never seen a man so sad and so bitter. And talk about doctoring! That chap could work miracles. There was a little niece o' mine he cured when my sister had tried everybody—big specialists in London and all that—and they'd all given her up. Anyhow, he died. He wasn't young. He must have been old enough to be his wife's father. I fancy she married him because she'd such a great respect for him as a doctor and a man."

"That's the impression I had from what she told me," I said. "I may say, I met her first last night. She was waiting in this room—for Olney, she said, because he'd been her patient. I called to see her this afternoon and got myself invited to tea. She told me a bit about herself and her husband. Then Perigo came in."

"Perigo?" The Superintendent didn't like this.

"Yes, Perigo. Pops up all over the place, doesn't he? I don't think they were old friends, but he knew her all right. Well, what's the rest of her story?"

It was obvious he wasn't enjoying this. He looked very worried. "She hasn't had a very good time since he died. Of course it's a very German sort o' name, and lots of people started saying things long before they bothered to find out a few facts. She's a woman with a good deal o' pride, and I don't blame her for it—so you can imagine how she took it. Another thing was that she'd made a few enemies by being outspoken about local conditions—housing and all that—and of course that didn't make it any better. Then, on top of everything, there came this business of her husband's brother."

"What was that?" This was really new.

"Her husband had a brother, younger than him, who also had to run from the Nazis. This chap, Otto Bauernstern, was a metal-lurgical chemist, and quite an expert in his own line. After a lot o' trouble he gets a job at the Charters Electrical works. This was last summer. Then an agitation starts to get rid of him. Among the people who want to get him out is the man we've mentioned already, Colonel Tarlington——"

"Yes, he pops up quite a lot too, doesn't he?" I said, all bright and breezy.

"Well, as I suggested before, the colonel's all right—has a great deal of influence round here—but between you and me he's apt to run his patriotism a bit hard. Anyhow, he said he wasn't consulted, as a member of the Board, when this Otto Bauernstern got his job in the works, and that he objected to a German or Austrian being inside the works every day and half the night. And other people took the same line. Including," and here the Superintendent dropped his voice to a confidential whisper, "our Chief Constable, who's a great pal o' Colonel Tarlington's. About a month ago, it all blew up, and Otto Bauernstern was told to leave the works and the district—sharp. Well, he left the works all right, but then he clean disappeared. He packed up and left his lodgings, saying he was going to London, but he's never registered himself in London or anywhere else, because we asked that it should be reported to us when he registered himself anywhere, and it hasn't been."

"He didn't live at his sister-in-law's house—the doctor's—did he?" I asked.

"Oh no, though of course he often saw her. She's very bitter about the way he's been treated, because she says all he wanted was to help us beat the Nazis and instead of letting him do his work in peace we go and persecute him all over again. There's no doubt she's very bitter."

"Which leaves two possibilities," I said. "First, that she might feel so bitter that some smooth Nazi agent has persuaded her that she might as well help the great German race, to which her husband belonged, to defeat the stupid British. Secondly, that the whole story's a fake, and that these Bauernsterns never were genuine exiles at all. There's been a certain amount of planting agents as exiles—yes, and some of 'em could show you the scars they still had from beatings in concentration camps—it's always done very thoroughly."

"There's still another possibility, Neyland," said the Superintendent, looking at me severely, "and that is that this woman's neither more nor less than what she makes herself out to be, that she's a decent fine woman who's just had a lot o' bad luck. And that's what I happen to believe, and more than once I haven't been able to look her in the eye without being ashamed of some o' my townsfolk. She's worth a hundred of most of 'em."

This declaration of his, which he gave out with tremendous emphasis, ought to have made me feel rather contemptuous, but for some odd reason, which I couldn't discover, it made me feel vaguely uncomfortable, as if I were ashamed of myself. Yet I'd nothing to be ashamed of. Immediately then, I felt irritated. But this Bauernstern woman always seemed to have an irritating effect upon me. She was producing it now even without being there, through her champion, the Superintendent.

"All right," I grunted, "she's wonderful. But she doesn't behave like a woman who's got nothing to hide. She was frightened when I saw her here last night. She was very much on her guard when I saw her this afternoon. Now why?"

"Because of the way she's been treated," he replied promptly.

I shook my head. "No, there's more than that in it. And by the way, do you really want to lay your hand on this fellow, Otto Bauernstern?"

He leaned forward, and whispered: "No, I don't. That is, not if he's what I think he is. Why do you ask?"

"Because I've a pretty good hunch where he is right now," I replied. "He's tucked away in an upstairs room in the house of your friend, his sister-in-law, Dr. Bauernstern."

"Are you sure?"

"No, but I'm willing to bet a box of cigars to a peanut that he's there. It was written all over those two women this afternoon—especially that housekeeper woman, whose face is death to any secret—that they're hiding somebody there, and now it's obvious who that somebody is."

The Superintendent brought both his hands down on his knees with a loud slap, then got up. There was a look of utter disgust on his face. "Well, I wish to God you hadn't told me."

"Wait a minute," I said. "Don't imagine you're going there to pull him in."

"Now I know where he is, what else can I do? He's got to be charged for failing to register."

"I have authority from the department—and I can show it to

you, if you like, though I'll have to take it out of the lining of my bag—to demand full co-operation from the police in any district where I'm operating, except the Metropolitan area. Do you want to see that letter?"

He grinned. "Perhaps I'd better while we're at it. You see, I haven't worked with one o' your sort before."

I slit the stitches in the lining of my bag, then showed him the letter. He was quite satisfied. In fact, he couldn't help being impressed. "That's all right," he said, uneasy again now. "Does this mean you want me to get a warrant now and take in Otto Bauernstern?"

"No, it doesn't. It means that I insist upon your leaving him alone, and that I take full responsibility."

His face immediately lost that look of distaste. "That's different. Mind you, I think you're wrong about those people. I'd stake my pension on that woman, Dr. Bauernstern, being straight, and I'm not a bad judge o' character."

"I've no doubt you're a very good judge of character, Superintendent," I said, "but we happen to live in very strange times, when people's minds are working in very strange ways. It's a very complicated war this, and we keep making the mistake of trying to simplify it. Money, politics, ambition, personal prejudices, spites, hidden desires, are all mixed up in it. I've had so many surprises that now I refuse to allow myself to be surprised any more. And I'm not staking anything on anybody being straight until I know for certain they are."

He looked hard at me. "I fancy you were a happier man, Neyland, before you took on this job," he said, to my astonishment.

"I haven't been a happy man for some time," I found myself replying. "I had my little share, and then I lost it, and I don't expect any more. Well, I may call on you in the morning to do my telephoning, if you don't mind. Thanks for coming along to-night. Now I'll have a look at poor Olney's notebook."

I settled down with it as soon as the Superintendent had gone. It was a queer sad business looking at those scribbles, all that was left of a man. The people in the Special Branch, as Olney was, don't work in the same way as we in the department do. They spend far longer in one place, doing an ordinary job, and this means that their whole approach and technique are different. Olney's notebook might at first sight have appeared to belong to any foreman in an aircraft factory. It was filled with notes about his work there. But I knew of course that he wouldn't have made a last effort to prevent it falling into the hands of the people who ran him down if it hadn't contained some indication of how his mind was working. The last two or three pages here were really his final message to me, and would have to take the place of the talk we were going to have. So it was up to me.

The *Queen of Clubs* was there, marked by a big query. There was also a rough diagram, showing a mysterious *X* in the circle of the town and then lines from it, with a note that ran: *One P.O. in the town and another outside?* Another note said: *What about a window?* Another merely announced *Probably America.* Another referred back to a note made a couple of months ago, which I discovered, after some difficulty, to be this: *Both men certain he had trace of deep scar on left cheek.* On the very last page there were three words that it was impossible to decipher at first because a fat triumphant tick had been scrawled across them, but finally I came to the conclusion that these words were: *Look for scar.* In addition there were several separate words on the last three pages, and one or two of them had been heavily underlined, notably *Flowers* and *Sweet*.

Well, there it was. I made my own notes from these of Olney's, and then compared them with such scraps and wisps of information I'd already acquired myself. It didn't look too promising, as you can imagine. And one grim fact stuck out a mile, and that was that these people we were after had discovered who Olney was and had guessed that he knew too much and so had struck before he could make any further move. (There was too that very disturbing business about his lighter.) It might be my turn next. Before turning in, I wanted to let some air into the room and clear it of smoke, so I turned off the light and opened the window. And for a moment or two, I stared, not very hopefully, at that damned blackout.

6

THE Superintendent was out next morning when I went round to his office, but he'd left instructions that I could use the telephone. I had several queries for the department, about Fifine, about the Bauernsterns, and another that involved the Canadian Pacific Railway. I knew they would work fast, so I hung on for the replies and so was there most of the morning. The Superintendent came in just as I'd finished. I gave him Olney's notebook, and then asked him if he'd had any luck about the list of telephone numbers that I'd copied in Fifine's dressing-room.

"I've got 'em," he said, "but I think you're going to be disappointed. Here's the list." We looked at it together. "Now, you see, one's the *Queen of Clubs,* as I told you last night. The first one's the stage door telephone of the theatre itself, which doesn't mean very much, does it?"

"Not a thing," I said. "But what about these other four?"

"Well, this next is a bit of a surprise, I'll grant you," he said, pointing. "I ought to have remembered it at once. It's the Charters Electrical Company. Why a female acrobat should want to ring up the Charters Electrical Company, I can't imagine."

"They employ about six thousand people," I said, showing no interest, "and she could easily say that one of 'em's a friend of hers. Next, please!"

"This chap's a chemist, well known, quite respectable, and he tells me that he keeps grease-paint and all that for the professionals and also supplies 'em with aspirin or any medicines they want. It's a little side-line of his, dealing with the professionals. All quite straight and above board. So's the next. I've gone into that. There's no telephone where this woman's lodging, and this is next-door but one, where they have an arrangement to take messages. It's quite usual."

"I never saw such a lot of blanks," I said, disgusted. "What's the last one? Newsagent, fancy goods?"

"That's it. I know the shop. Silby's the name. Sells papers, cigarettes, and odds and ends, and used to take betting slips in the
old days. Also, an accommodation address. It's no use me going
round there because they know me—I've had some bother with
them before about betting slips—so I thought you might like to
go round yourself. Here's the address—Mewley Street. Do I see
you again to-day?"

"Probably not," I said gloomily. That list of telephone numbers had looked so promising at first, and now—what was left of
it? Though at that I attached more importance to the fact that the
Charters Electrical Company's number was amongst them than
I let the Superintendent think. He told me how to find Silby's
shop in Mewley Street, which was between the market square
and the Charters works.

It was a miserable street, thick in black slush, and Silby's
shop didn't look out of place in it. There must be hundreds and
hundreds of shops just like it all over England, and God knows
who first thought of them. It sold papers, racing specials, sexy
paper-backed novels, post-cards showing women with fat legs
and behinds, sixpennyworths of astrology, dream books, and
a lot of other cheap trash. In peace-time it probably did a good
trade in cigarettes and chocolates. It belonged to a kind of sub-
world of "cigs, chocs and film mags." It was a furtive-looking
little establishment, long overdue for the ash-can. There was a
middle-aged couple pottering about in it. Mr. and Mrs. Silby, no
doubt. They had a half-blind, bloodless look, like creatures who
crawled in and out of the rotten woodwork. Both of them held
their mouths open all the time and made a wet snuffling noise
through their noses.

"Yes?" said Mr. Silby.

I'd intended to tell them some smooth little tale about wanting to use the telephone occasionally, but now I couldn't be bothered. I decided to be tough, and have done with it.

"You Mr. Silby? All right. Well, I've just seen your telephone
number here among several others, in the possession of a certain
person——" I halted there, and saw in his pale eyes a flicker of
fear. The woman came closer, and I had an idea she was frightened.

"Look here, who are you?" he asked, but in an uneasy, quavering tone.

"Never mind who I am," I said fiercely. And that's where, if he'd been an honest man, he could have told me to get to hell out of it. But of course he didn't. "I want to know how your telephone number came——"

But the woman interrupted me, being eager to explain, as I thought one of them would be. "You see, sir, what 'appens is that with us being on the telephone, like, an' so many people not 'aving one, we 'ave an arrangement with some customers who gives our number to their friends an' then we take the message for 'em and charge sixpence. It's reelly like what we do with letters. Just for a convenience, you might say."

"Got a list of these telephone people?" I asked sharply.

"Oh yes, sir, an' you can see it if you want. Show the gentleman the list, Arnold."

Arnold showed me the list, and of course it didn't mean a thing. If you weren't Smith on that list, then you made it Brown or Robinson. Just as I'd handed the list back over the counter, I noticed among the bits of rubbish on the unswept floor, near my foot, a cigarette end that was rather longer, slightly fatter and much cleaner than you'd expect a cigarette end to be in there. I picked it up, then halted a few yards down the street to examine it. As I'd suspected, it was an American cigarette, and I could just read *ield* printed in fine script on it. A *Chesterfield*. Silby had a customer, who'd called there quite recently, who smoked Chesterfield cigarettes. And I was willing to bet all the money in my pocket that no ordinary customer in that back-street smoked Chesterfields, which you couldn't buy anywhere in Gretley. It seemed to me about fifty to one that whoever it was who threw down this cigarette-end had gone there to enquire about a telephone call. Having arrived at these odds, I happened to look round, and there standing in his door-way, like a quivering giant termite, was Mr. Silby, keeping a jellied eye on me.

Mrs. Wilkinson had kept some of their lunch for me, and I ate it up in my room, while black rain fell on the back garden. I had a fairly long report to forward to the department, and as this had to be done in code, it took me most of the afternoon. After posting it at the corner, I hurriedly returned through the rain, had a cup of tea, and then sprawled on the sofa and dozed. I kept slipping in and out of bright little dreams. One minute I'd be back with Maraquita and the boy, Paul and Mitzi Rosental, on some diamond morning in Chile, and then the next minute I'd be lying on that sofa in Raglan Street, Gretley, at the dark end of a January afternoon, feeling stale, oldish, and not quite real, like a ghost. I didn't like it. Dreams oughtn't be as clear as that and come and go so quickly. Another queer thing, which annoyed me, was that I kept thinking about that woman doctor, Bauernstern, and though I couldn't remember her face properly, and didn't want to, I seemed to see her eyes, greeny-brown, brilliant and sad. This annoyed me simply because the woman didn't mean a thing to me personally, and as I'd knocked off the job for an hour or two, I didn't want to be bothering about suspects. But there it was.

At ten to seven, more by luck than by clever navigation, I managed to arrive through the pitch darkness at that back door, behind which I'd kissed Miss Axton the night before. The meeting was to be held in the public hall in the square, not three minutes away, so we had time for a quick drink upstairs, where Miss Axton was once more very lavish with her Canadian Club rye. As a matter of fact, though I've a good head, I downed my rye, which I took straight, so quickly that I felt the effect of it right away. Miss Axton—it was queer I didn't know her first name— was looking very grand, and more than ever the green-and-gold, fire-and-ice queen. There was nothing about her manner to say that we'd done some kissing the night before, and on the other hand nothing to suggest that she was really denying the fact. Most women would have been definitely warmer or cooler towards me, whereas she seemed to be exactly as she was when we first began talking the night before. But that may have puzzled me simply because I kept forgetting that she was a mature woman and not at all the mere girl she seemed when you first took a peep at her.

When we were ready to leave, I suddenly remembered I'd never rung up the *Queen of Clubs* to order our dinner, so now I got through to Fencrest, calling him very carefully "Mr. Settle", but in such a way as to remind him that he was still Fencrest to me, and told him bluntly that I expected to be very well looked after up there, and he promised eagerly that he would do his best. I thought Miss Axton eyed me curiously as I rang off, but she didn't make any comment and I merely put on a bit of a swagger, doing an act as the tough unscrupulous male making his arrangements to spoil the female.

But as we went out, she did say one thing. "I thought as you ordered dinner, it didn't sound as if there was much of a war on."

That was my cue. "When a man's taking a beautiful woman out to dinner, even yet, there isn't a war on."

And she put a hand on my arm, giving it a tiny squeeze, as a reward for that half-witted announcement. I remember wondering how long this game could last, seeing that now nearly every word we spoke and every move we made was hardly less than an insult to the other's intelligence.

But talk about insulting anybody's intelligence! I hadn't seen anything yet. That meeting! Goebbels could have put it straight on the air. If the war effort could survive meetings like that all over the country, it ought to be able to defeat Hitler.

The hall looked like a cheap coffin on a very large scale. It showed a lot of flags, proving definitely that it was on our side. It was comfortably filled with members of the employing, shop-keeping, suburban classes, the working folk having their meetings in the factory canteens. The Mayor of Gretley was in the chair and read out his opening remarks so slowly that even words like "which" and "where" began to take on a strange and rather sinister significance, as if there was black magic about. After telling us that the local member of Parliament needed no intro-duction, he introduced us to the local member of Parliament. This was an excitable and self-important little man, who looked like an angry wedding guest. His trick was to shout platitudes at us in a furious voice, as if we'd all been arguing for hours and his patience was exhausted. Apparently he held some very minor government appointment, but he tried to give us the idea that he and Churchill split the war work between them. He wasn't very consistent. He blamed us because, he said, we didn't realize this was our war, but at the same time he gave us to understand that the war really belonged to him and a few friends of his in

Westminster. He was angry because there was far too much crit-
icism, too many of us were "sitting about and criticizing", but he
was also annoyed because we were all far too complacent, and he
said that complacency was really the great danger. I got the idea
from him that hardly anybody was playing the game, though he
didn't tell us what game. In the end it turned out that he and the
Empire were fighting for freedom, that they'd always stood for it,
and that now they refused to let it die. For which we all gave him
a good round.

The next speaker was a tall gloomy man, Sir Something
Somebody. He took a very simple line. Our trouble was, he said,
that we employed a lot of Germans to talk over the air to Germany, promising the German people this and that, whereas what
we ought to do was to sack all these German broadcasters, and
all their friends the Left pink intellectuals, and tell the German
people we proposed to kill as many of them as we could, thus
showing them that we didn't propose "to stand any nonsense."
This would inevitably lead, though by what steps he didn't tell
us, to an early and complete victory. At the end of this extraordinary little speech, which might have been written for him by
Goebbels, I asked myself why I spent my time trying to nose out
Nazi agents, when somebody like this Sir Something was worth a
dozen agents to Hitler.

Now came the man I really wanted to hear, Colonel Tarlington. I hadn't seen him since we met outside the offices of the
Charters Electrical Company, but somehow I seemed to have
heard a good deal about him, in one way and another. He looked
as he had done before, like a last-war general in mufti, stiff, well-
brushed, ruddy. He spoke very well in his own clipped style, and
obviously knew his job on the platform. He roused the audience
as the other three speakers had obviously failed to do. So far I'd
been listening idly, with more than half my mind elsewhere, but
now I listened hard and took care to miss nothing.

Taking the bluff hearty line—"I'm a plain man with no frills"
Colonel Tarlington announced that he was in favour of a real
war effort, with no sloppy sentiment about it. Men who went
on strike or tried to argue about their precious rights ought
to be sent into the army or, if they gave any further trouble,

be promptly shot. He hinted that Labour leaders had taken
advantage of their position to blackmail the country. He said
that a lot of fantastic nonsense was being talked about post-war
reconstruction. We hadn't won the war yet, and even when we
did win it, we should be poorer than we'd been before, and it
was up to all sensible men to make certain in the meantime that
the position of employers, private enterprise, and the necessary
control of Labour by Capital, were not weakened. He asked us to
remember that the Communists were still busy in our midst, and
taking full advantage of some of the sentimental nonsense that
was now being talked about Russia. Finally, what this country
needed was far more of the tough old British spirit, the spirit that
had carried the flag into every corner of the world.

There was, of course, a great deal more of it than that, but that
was the general line. I noticed several reporters taking full notes,
and knew that some of the more provocative phrases would certainly be quoted outside the local press. There were one or two
shouts of protest from the back, but they were quickly drowned
by the applause of the Colonel's admirers in front. But not even
all this audience was entirely pleased, for I noticed some thought-
ful and bewildered faces near me. Colonel Tarlington had done
a very good job.

"What did you think of that?" Miss Axton asked, while the
Mayor was winding himself up to propose votes of thanks.

I replied very deliberately. "I think Colonel Tarlington's an
extremely clever man."

She shot me a bright blue glance, but there wasn't time for
any more talk. As we began to leave the hall, I caught sight of a
worried little face that I thought I recognized, and then I saw that
its owner recognized me. It was Heacham, of the Charters Electrical Company, and he quickly pushed his way through, excused
himself to Miss Axton, and took me on one side.

"I wrote to you to-night, Mr. Neyland," he began. "We had
a Board meeting this afternoon, and your name came up, as I
promised. I told them about your lack of experience in our kind
of work quite frankly, at the same time giving your various qualifications and experience in handling labour. As I expected, there
was some opposition from the Board, on the ground of your

lack of experience, but then, rather to my surprise, one director, who carries great weight, suddenly said he thought we should give you a trial, just because we are so short of good men. So I've written to say that if you hang on here and come and see me about the middle of next week, I should have a proposition to put to you."

"Thanks very much," I said, hiding my surprise. And I couldn't help thinking grimly that if I'd really wanted this job it would never have fallen into my lap like this. "By the way, do you mind telling me who was the director who put in a good word for me?"

Heacham smiled. "Don't say I told you. But you've just been listening to him. It was Colonel Tarlington."

I was feeling distinctly pleased when I rejoined Miss Axton. Things were moving at last. I thought she looked curiously at me again, but she didn't ask me who it was who'd taken me on one side. We were now in the press of folk at the outer doors. I heard somebody say it was still raining hard.

"Here, I'm sorry," I cried, speaking the truth too. "I clean forgot that the *Queen of Clubs* is about two miles away, and I don't suppose there's a chance of a taxi now."

"There's a bus goes quite near to it," she said, "and there ought to be one in now. Let's run for it."

We did, and just caught it. We had to stand and there were too many wet clothes about, but Miss Axton didn't seem to mind. Now I'd have said about her that she was the type who would have minded very much, who would have demanded that a thing must be done properly or not at all, who was naturally fastidious and rather intolerant. But she had a trick of behaving unexpectedly, and by this time I was giving it some careful attention.

As soon as she came out of the cloakroom at the *Queen of Clubs,* I hurried her into the cocktail bar, where the smooth broad-faced Joe was presiding. Most people were eating now in the dining-room, so that there were only a few people in the cocktail bar, and nobody I knew among them. I ordered two double martinis from Joe.

"You don't like them sweet, do you?" said Miss Axton.

"No, they mustn't be sweet, Joe," I said.

"I'll do my best," said Joe, showing a gold tooth, "but these days, when we're so short of everything, it's hard to stop 'em being sweet."

This repetition of the word "sweet" reminded me of something but I couldn't think what it was, and during the next two minutes I kept on wondering. Then I remembered. One of the odd words that Olney had put down on the last pages of his notebook had been "Sweet." While I was mulling this over, I noticed that Joe was offering Miss Axton a cigarette.

"I seem to remember you like Chesterfields," Joe was saying, "and I still have a few left."

"Pretty hard to get, aren't they?" I said, after refusing one for myself.

Joe winked. "When I was at Borani's, I knew one or two of the young fellas at the American Embassy, and before they all got short, they let me have a few to be going on with."

"Smoke 'em yourself as well as give 'em away, eh?" I said carelessly.

"Sure! And, believe me, I don't give too many away."

So it looked to me as if either Joe or somebody he knew had visited Silby's shop not so very long before I'd gone in there. It wasn't likely that anybody else had a stock of Chesterfields in a place like Gretley. Again, it was about five to one that nobody who'd been casually given a Chesterfield by Joe up here would have taken it away and then lit it somewhere very near Mewley Street and Silby's shop. But of course Joe or one of his pals might visit Silby's for reasons that didn't interest me.

We were just finishing the martinis, which were very strong, when Miss Axton said: "Who was the man who spoke to you in the hall? I've seen him before somewhere."

"That was Heacham of the Charters works," I said. This seemed the moment to spill it. "As a matter of fact, he was telling me that his Board look like offering me a job."

She smiled at me. "That's fine, isn't it?"

"Grand! But the curious thing is—between ourselves—that the Board were going to turn me down, for lack of experience in electrical engineering and so on, when one of them spoke out for me. And do you know who that was?"

"I can guess," she said calmly. And for once took me completely by surprise, because I was certain she was going to play it the other way and pretend she knew nothing about it. "Colonel Tarlington."

"Now how on earth did you know that?" I asked, blank as a whitewashed wall.

She jumped straight in with both feet. "Because, last night, after you'd gone, I remembered what you'd said about the job, and so I rang up Colonel Tarlington and told him about you."

"Well, that was swell of you," I said, looking as if I wanted to start kissing her again. "But I didn't know he was a friend of yours." And I thought she'd better have the rest of it. "Don't you remember, you told me you'd just said *How do you do?* to him and that he wasn't your style."

"And that's true," she said, without a flicker. "I don't know him very well, and he isn't my style. But I have met him, and I thought I was entitled to tell him that you seemed to me the kind of man they ought to employ. And he didn't mind my ringing up. He said he was grateful. And you ought to be grateful too."

"But of course I am," I said, pumping out some enthusiasm. "I hope I'll be able to make you realize that."

It seemed to be a big night at the *Queen of Clubs.* The dining-room was full, the only vacant table being the one that Fencrest had kept for me. I saw Mrs. Jesmond, who was with two or three officers and some women, and at another table, with a military party, I noticed Sheila Castleside. But this time Mr. Perigo was not to be seen. The dinner was quite good, and they found for me a bottle of excellent *Meursault,* of which Miss Axton, who certainly wasn't afraid of a drink, had her fair share. We talked mostly about America during dinner. I knew she'd been there, for the Superintendent had it in his report on her, and she told me how she'd stayed with friends in California until she felt she ought to come back and do some war work. Then she'd tried one or two jobs, but couldn't get on with them, so had finally opened the Gift Shop. And, of course, the whole yarn simply didn't make sense, but it wasn't time yet to tell her so. Moreover, she was really enjoying herself, no doubt about that, and I've often wondered since why she was enjoying herself so much that night. The band was plugging away most of the time, and once during dinner we danced. Then just after the waiter had brought me, after some pressure, a little more of that brandy which Mrs. Jesmond gave us two nights before, an Air Force fellow came over and was introduced to me, refused a drink, but begged Miss Axton for a dance.

No sooner were they on the floor than Sheila Castleside dashed across. She was all excited as usual, and might have been a bit tight, but she was looking very attractive, with that long impudent nose of hers and those amusing eyes, one a shade darker than the other.

"Where have you been?" she demanded.

I said that I'd been knocking about, fairly busy most of the time.

"Why have you brought that awful woman with you?" she said, pulling a face. "You know I loathe her. I told you."

"I know you did, Sheila," I said, grinning, "but after all I'm not your husband, so you mustn't ask me questions like that."

"If you knew as much as I do," she began, then suddenly shut up.

"Well?"

"No. Sorry I spoke. After all, if she's a friend of yours." And she shrugged her shoulders.

I caught her eye. "Sheila, you and I have been meaning to have a talk, a serious talk, haven't we?"

She looked rather frightened, but nodded in agreement. "I'm ready when you are."

Ever since she came over I'd made up my mind that this was the best next step. And the enquiry I'd put through the department to the Canadian Pacific that morning had given me all I needed. "All right, only we can't talk in public. If you can pull yourself out of your party and I can leave Miss Axton with one of these airmen for half an hour or so, is there anywhere here where we can go and talk? And when I say go and talk, I mean go and talk."

"I know you do, blast you!" she said. "There might be some spare sitting-room upstairs. You try to find out, and so will I."

"Then what?"

"The first one to find out can pass the other a note," she said. "Has the Axton piece touched this brandy?"

"No, she hasn't. Want it?"

"Cheers!" She swallowed the precious stuff in one gulp. "Don't buy her another one. She isn't worth it. See you later."

I watched her rejoin her party, then after a minute or so she bounced across to Mrs. Jesmond, who had to turn away from the table to hear what she said. That looked as if she were enquiring about that sitting-room. I thought of another way of doing it, and as Miss Axton was still dancing and didn't look like stopping for a few more minutes, I hurried out and went in search of Fencrest. But he wasn't in his office, and he wasn't in the lounge or the cocktail bar, so I gave it up and went back to the dining-room, just in time to order drinks for Miss Axton and her dancing partner.

I told Miss Axton apologetically that I had one or two people there I wanted to have a word with and also a long-distance telephone call to put through, and asked her if she'd mind staying on to dance while I did all this. She looked hard at me for a second, as if wondering what I was up to, but then smiled and said, of course, she wouldn't, for she and the Air Force felt they were perfect dancing partners. I said they looked pretty good too.

Sheila was no longer talking to Mrs. Jesmond, and as Mrs. Jesmond had looked my way several times and smiled, I thought it was about time I went across. I hadn't long to wait, for the band began playing a waltz, which Miss Axton liked best of all, and off they went.

Some of Mrs. Jesmond's crowd were dancing, and she made me sit down beside her. She looked even more downy, peach-like and corrupting than before. I had a great desire to take hold of that long neck and do something with it, but whether it was to stroke it or wring it, I'm not sure. I asked her if she'd seen Mr. Perigo.

"Not since he came, quite uninvited, up to my sitting-room, the other night," she replied.

I took a long shot here. "You know what happened that night," I said. "I came up to find you. As a matter of fact, I got lost. Then I saw Perigo standing outside a room, not waiting to go in but obviously trying to hear what was being said inside. I hesitated a moment, then walked straight up, and at that moment your friend, the man from Manchester, opened the door."

"Is that exactly what happened, Mr. Neyland?"

"That's exactly what happened, Mrs. Jesmond," I replied firmly. "And what's this chap Perigo's game, anyhow?"

"I'm not sure," she said, opening her eyes wide but speaking softly. "I've wondered if it might be blackmail. What do *you* think?"

"He says he's a retired art-dealer who's down here because a friend lent him a cottage."

"That," said Mrs. Jesmond, "is too silly."

"It amused me," I said easily, "and in order to have a little more amusement I asked a friend who knows about things to find out about Mr. Perigo. The result was very entertaining. It seems that Perigo *is* a retired art-dealer who was lent a cottage here."

She opened her cigarette-case. "I'm surprised," she said slowly, tapping her cigarette, "though he does know about pictures. Incidentally, he was lying the other night when he said he'd spent hours looking at my pictures. He'd only seen them once before. Of course he lies all the time, and not stupidly either. He's not a fool, y'know. You heard the way he talked about the war the other night? That was quite deliberate, of course."

"I had that impression," I said carefully, "but he always does that to me. Seems to be—well—fishing. Mind you, he knows my own views aren't the usual short-sighted nonsense."

She looked at me speculatively, and I noticed then that she needed a light for her cigarette. But as I began fumbling for my matches, she shook her head.

"Don't trouble, thank you. I have a nice new lighter here and I insist upon playing with it." And out of her bag she produced the little crimson-and-black lighter that was exactly like the one in my pocket, and also exactly like the one that Olney showed me the afternoon before he was killed, the one that was afterwards taken from his body. These lighters can't be bought anywhere, and are quite unlike any others that can be bought. Either this woman was one of us or this was Olney's lighter. And now I had to think fast. If I showed her my lighter and she wasn't one of us, yet knew what the lighter meant, then I told her what I was and probably ruined everything I'd done so far. The risk was too great. I compromised by saying: "I've one rather like it—a present from an old friend."

It was quite plain this didn't mean anything to her and that therefore she had no connection with the department, the Special Branch or M.I.5. So now I had to know how she came to be in possession of that lighter.

"This friend of mine," I continued, as she stared at me placidly, "makes these lighters, and there aren't many of 'em about. I'll bet you didn't buy that one in any shop in Gretley."

"No, I didn't," she said, with a slight smile. "It was given to me—as a nice surprise present—last night."

I tried not to sound too eager. "And who gave it to you?"

She didn't seem to mind the question. In fact it pleased her. "Derek Muir gave it to me—you know him, don't you? That tall boy—he's a squadron-leader—dancing with the little fat girl in green."

I looked across at the chap, whom I remembered as one of the young men I'd seen with her. I had no doubt whatever she was telling the truth. And a very awkward bit of truth it was too. This had been Olney's lighter, I was convinced. How had this Air Force lad got hold of it? He would have to be questioned, and it would have to be done so tactfully that he couldn't possibly guess what was behind this lighter business. I was wondering when and how to approach him, without making Mrs. Jesmond suspicious, when a waitress came up, asked me my name, and then slipped a note into my hand. Mrs. Jesmond saw all this, of course, and when I asked her to excuse me while I read the note, I saw on her face that faint curl of derision with which most women seem to greet any evidence of an intrigue that concerns another woman. But I may have been wrong. She may have been thinking I was nothing but a plain donkey.

The note said: *Room 37 soon as you can! S.C.* And if this didn't mean that Sheila Castleside wanted me to meet her at once upstairs in Room Thirty-Seven, then it didn't mean anything at all. I took a quick look round the room but couldn't see Sheila, so I thought she must have already gone upstairs. Miss Axton was still waltzing away in a queenly Nordic fashion. I turned to Mrs. Jesmond and said rather lamely that I must put through a long-distance call.

"Of course," she said, smiling. "But take care you don't get into trouble."

"Trouble?" I said, as I got up. "Why should I?"

"I don't know," she said, "but sometimes these long-distance telephone calls *do* land one into trouble. So take care."

It was very quiet upstairs and I didn't see anybody. The lighting was dim and it was several minutes before I found Number Thirty-Seven, which was at the end of a corridor and in its dim remoteness seemed miles from anywhere. I knocked, then walked in. It was not a sitting-room but a bedroom, and Sheila wasn't there. The room wasn't being used, but there was a light on and an electric fire that must have been switched on at least quarter of an hour before I came in, for it was quite bright and the room was fairly warm. The double bed was covered with a deep pink eiderdown, and there seemed to be lot of pink about, so that the total effect was very feminine in the wrong sort of way. There was a short sofa on one side of the electric fire and an easy-chair on the other. You could sit and talk in the place, but it did announce pretty plainly, in its blushing satiny style, that it expected something a bit different. Having taken all this in, I still stood just inside the door, wondering if I'd made the mistake or if Sheila had.

Then she came charging in, with such haste that the door slammed to behind her, and no sooner had she glanced at the room we were in than she turned on me furiously. "My God, you've a nerve, haven't you? Bringing me here!"

At that moment I heard a tiny click. Somebody had locked us in. Sheila had heard it too, and now angrily tried to open the door.

"Just a minute," I said quietly, as she was about to shout at me again, "before you start making a scene. Look at this." And I showed her the note I'd received.

"But I had a note from *you*," she gasped. "Where is it? Oh—I tore it up. And you ought to have known—that's not my writing at all."

I didn't bother asking her how she expected me to know that that wasn't her handwriting. It was necessary to calm her down, because for all I knew the person who'd arranged all this might be expecting her to make a scene, bang and kick on the door, and so advertise the fact that we were in there together.

"Now listen, Sheila," I began, "somebody has passed these phony notes to us and then locked us in. I don't know why. It may be just damned silliness or it may be something worse. But our best plan is to take it easy. We came here to have a talk, so let's have a talk. And don't worry about it's being anything more than a talk. Anyhow," I added, with a grin, "nothing's more likely to keep me in order than this kind of bedroom. They ought to show 'em to young men who are thinking of entering monasteries. Now sit down, and take it easy."

This had the effect I wanted. She sat on the sofa, watched me settle into the easy-chair, and then began to giggle. "We only want some new luggage and some confetti on the floor, and it would look like the beginning of a honeymoon."

"Well, it isn't," I said, I was wondering how to start, because I didn't want to give too much away. We were quiet for a few moments.

Then, to my surprise, she said "Kiss me."

I stared at her. "Well, for Pete's sake! A minute ago you were ready to scream your head off, and now——"

"It's quite different," she said impatiently. "And I know that in a minute you're going to talk quite seriously and probably be quite horrid to me—and in spite of that, I like you—so I'll feel better and more confident if you kiss me. Just in a nice friendly way."

So I kissed her in a nice friendly way, because, of course, I wanted her to feel better and more confident. But I took good care to march straight back to that easy-chair. I also lit a pipe. If the smell of my Navy Cut ruined this pink boudoir, that was just too bad.

"Well, Sheila," I said, "you've got to understand, to begin with, that everything we say in here is strictly between ourselves. Right? Good! And the other thing to understand, right away, is that I'm not a bit interested in your private life and don't want to interfere just for the pleasure of interfering."

"Do you like me?" she asked, in her sudden childish way.

"Yes, I do, Sheila," I told her.

"I thought you did. You like me but disapprove of me, don't you?"

"That's about it," I said, grinning at her. "Well, as soon as I saw you in the bar of the *Lamb and Pole,* the other night, I knew I'd seen you before. Then I remembered, but to make sure I made a few very discreet enquiries— no, you needn't worry about that— and now I know most of it."

"Wasn't it on that C.P.R. boat—the *Duchess of Cornwall*—you saw me?" she asked, suddenly looking like the ghost of herself.

"Yes. A fellow I saw something of in that ship fell for you, I remember. You were in the women's hairdressing shop and you also did manicuring. Your name then was Sheila Wiggitt. Afterwards you let yourself rip with a passenger, there was a row, and you were sacked."

"And not for the first time, believe me," she said, half miserably, half defiantly. "Other girls could get away with anything, but the minute our Sheila put a foot wrong, out came the scandal, and out she went. My God, but I'd some stinking luck. And believe it or not, half the jobs I lost just went because I wouldn't say *Yes.* I always seemed to land in that kind of job. It started when I was sixteen and went to work at a confectioner's, and the man who owned that place seemed to think we were part of his confectionery. What's your name? Humphrey, isn't it? Well, Humphrey, I tell you—I'm not making excuses, but I never had a chance from the start. My father disappeared when I was a kid. I'd no brothers or sisters, and Mother was sweet but a complete fool."

"All right, Sheila," I said, "but you're not on trial, you know. What about the Indian widow business?"

"I'd got tired of being myself, so I thought I'd turn into somebody else—sweet and sad and pure, and, of course, better class. So I bought myself some nice black and put up, on my last ten quid, in an hotel in Salchester, where a lot of officers were billeted. I told some of the women my sad story—going out to India the girl bride and then losing my husband so suddenly— and by this time I'd almost persuaded myself it was true, and just couldn't help crying when I told my story. Then I got myself engaged, within a fortnight, to Lionel, who never doubted a single word I said. By this time I hadn't a bean, so I told him a fairy-tale about an old aunt who was dying and went off to Scotland, where I put in a couple of months as a waitress. Then I told him my aunt was dead and had lost all the money she promised me. But we got married, and all I had to do after that was to see nobody caught me out about my past. You'd be surprised what a lot you have to invent when you're pretending to be quite a different person, but I used to enjoy doing it. Often, when I was talking about myself, I *felt* quite different. But then at other times, specially these last few months, I'd get fed up with all this silly lying. I've often felt like throwing it in their faces that I never went to a finishing school in Paris or was presented at Court or went out to India, but that I'm a cheap little bastard from a back street who's washed dishes, scrubbed counters, served farm labourers with their half-pints——"

"And what's wrong with serving farm labourers with half-pints?" I demanded.

"Nothing—in theory, though anybody can do it, for me," she retorted. "But you don't realize what silly snobs these people are. These women I have to mix with now—I don't mean here, but going round with Lionel—they're unbelievable. But of course I have to keep it up, and believe me I've had some narrow escapes."

"Tell me frankly, Sheila, why have you to keep it up?" This is where we got down to it.

She hesitated a moment, then said slowly: "You can say if you like—because I don't want to be shown up and find myself back again on the treadmill. I wouldn't deny it. But there's another reason. When I first married Lionel, I wasn't in love with him. But I am now. And though he doesn't mind me knocking about and enjoying myself, he still sees me as he first saw me—as the poor sweet kid in black who'd had such a tragic life and cried so easily. He never forgets all that. He has a kind of thing about it all. And if he found out that I'd told him—and his family—a lot of fairy-tales, and all the rest of it, I know he'd never forgive me, probably never speak to me again."

She stopped, and I saw her eyes glisten with tears. Then she began quietly sobbing. After a minute I went across and put a hand on her shoulder, and she pressed her wet cheek against this hand.

"Take it easy, Sheila. And thanks for telling me it all."

"Telling it all! My God, I could go on for hours. And you

needn't thank me, because honestly it's a relief to be able to talk about it to somebody and stop pretending." She was all right again now, and accepted a cigarette. "But what's the idea? Who are you, anyhow?"

"I'm just a chap who knocks around," I said. "But you can trust me. Now tell me this—and it's very important. Is there anybody who knows or guesses that the yarns you've told about myself aren't true?"

She tried to bluff now. "Why should there be anybody?" she asked defiantly.

I looked hard at her. "I said this was important. Don't let's waste time. We may have the practical jokers who locked the door coming back soon. Tell me—who knows—or guesses?"

Her mouth trembled a little. "I don't see you've any right to ask that. I mean, what does it matter to you? That's my funeral."

"I'll put my cards on the table," I said impressively, for I couldn't afford to waste much more time. "I'm here to prevent people committing certain crimes against the country. Now one of the ways in which these rats can force others to work for them is by blackmail—that is, by threatening to expose them, by making good use of a hold they have over other people. Is that clear?"

She nodded. "I knew there was something queer about you."

"Never mind about me. The point is this—I soon saw that you were pretending and also that you were frightened, and that it would be easy for the kind of people I'm after to make use of you. Now come on, Sheila. We haven't much more time."

"One person definitely knows. And I think two others have guessed something. These two are Mrs. Jesmond—and Mr. Perigo. Both of them have a way of looking at me and dropping sly remarks that make me think they've guessed something."

"All right. I'm not surprised. But who knows definitely?"

"Joe—you know, the barman here. That's why I always pretend to think he's so wonderful. You heard me go on about him the other night. I do that because I'm frightened of him, I hate him really."

"Has he asked you to do anything for him, in return for his keeping quiet about you?"

"No, he hasn't, not yet, but he's made it plain that he is going to, quite soon," she said. "He told me so, a few days ago. He didn't say what he'd want, and I couldn't make out whether he was going to ask for some money—or—well, you can imagine. But he warned me that he didn't propose to keep quiet much longer without being paid in some way for it. And he showed me that he knew a lot about me."

"I see." And now I hesitated. Should I ask her to make him show his hand? Before I could decide, she spoke again.

"There's another one who knows or guesses something about me," she continued. "I forgot her because I don't see her as much as I do the others. But I think you ought to know. It's your big blonde lady friend below, Miss Axton. Every time that woman looks at me, she's telling me she has me taped. And how *she* could know anything beats me. But I'll swear she does. That's why I told you I couldn't bear her."

"Does she often come here?" I asked. "She talks as if she hardly knew the place, but I noticed to-night that Joe said something to her that suggested she was a regular customer in that bar."

"I've not often seen her here," said Sheila, then added shrewdly: "If she's thick with Joe—and I'll bet you're wondering if he told her about me—then it must be outside this place, and that doesn't seem very likely to me. Anyhow, as I told you, she's a howling snob. Here, what time is it?"

It was after ten, I told her. "We've got to get out of this," she said, jumping up, "or somebody'll be telling tales to Lionel when he comes back. What on earth are we going to do? And, anyhow, who was it who played that trick with the notes?"

"Did you say anything to Mrs. Jesmond, after you left me and went across to her, about wanting a sitting room?"

"Yes, I did. After all, she lives here and I thought she might know something about it."

"She not only lives here," I said, "but she owns the place. And I think she's responsible for this trick with the bedroom. She's done it partly out of devilment——"

"Didn't I tell you the other night she was a dangerous woman?"

"And also perhaps on the chance of compromising us both

and so obtaining some little hold over us, which might be useful to her. It's the same method, you see."

"All right, Sherlock Holmes, but what do we do now? I don't want to have to scream the place down."

I went to the door. "It all depends on whether they've left the key in the lock," I said, bending down. "It seems they have. And as there's plenty of space under the door, it's easy. I suppose those drawers are lined with paper, aren't they? Just hand me a piece, will you, Sheila? Thank you. Now I'll perform the old trick of escaping from the locked room."

"What a man!" she cried, in good spirits again now. And if the trick was old, the audience was new and tremendously admiring. Almost holding her breath, she watched me slide half the sheet of stiffish paper under the door, poke the key out with the little gadget I use for my pipes, so that the key fell on to the paper, and then slide the paper and key under the door towards us. I gave her the key and put the paper back in the drawer. When I came back, she had the key in the lock but hadn't yet turned it.

"I don't know yet who you are and what you're up to, and you've been terrifying me for days," she said, almost into my ear, "and you haven't really been very nice to me, and my Lionel's ten times as good-looking—but I think you're heaven."

And she twined her arms about my neck and gave me a most luxurious kiss, then quickly unlocked the door and fled. I didn't follow her, because it was obviously much better for us to go down separately. I spent the next five minutes behind that door wondering how many more women I'd be kissing on this Gretley job. For that wasn't my style at all, and particularly just now, when I was feeling so sour and not at all young and hopeful. I've had it explained to me since, by somebody who ought to know, why I, who never pretended to be a charmer and was never a chaser, found myself in the way of these kisses just then; but that explanation, which is, anyhow, a bit fancy, doesn't come into this part of the story, so we can skip it.

I was still leaning against that bedroom wall, smoking and thinking, when the door was quietly opened, and there, looking not nearly as surprised as I felt, was Miss Axton. "What are you doing up here?" she asked.

"I'm smoking and thinking," I said.

"But why here? And what a ghastly bedroom!"

"It isn't mine. I just borrowed it for an hour to smoke and think in. Kindly provided by the management."

"It was Mrs. Jesmond who said she thought you were up here."

"Mrs. Jesmond is the management," I told her. "Did you know that? Most people don't. But I see you did know."

"Well, I did, as a matter of fact," she said coolly, and stared again at the room for a moment. Then she looked at me, not smiling.

"You looked so happy waltzing down there that I didn't like to disturb you," I said apologetically. "I had an idea you preferred dancing to talking, and I was doing my best to give you the sort of evening you wanted. Let's go downstairs, shall we?"

She put a hand on my arm as we walked down the dim corridor. "I was looking for you to tell you that several of those Air Force boys, with some girls, are moving on to Wing-Commander Sullivan's house, where apparently there's some kind of party going on—dancing to the gramophone—and drinks and things. I've been asked to go on, and so have you, for that matter——"

"Not me, thanks," I said. "I like the Air Force but not at this time of night, and I wouldn't be paid to dance to the gramophone. But you go, of course—though I hoped we'd have some talk."

"So did I. And if you're not sleepy, why shouldn't we? I'll go on there for an hour—these boys amuse me and I adore dancing—while you go back to my place, give yourself a drink, and wait quietly for me. I'll be back by half-past eleven. One of the boys will drive me back, and I'll take care not to ask him in. Look—here's the key of the back door. You know the way. The only thing is—be as quiet as you can going in."

She gave me a lingering, meaning look, and I tried my best, without appearing too fatuous, to return it. "That's grand," I said. "Now there's just one thing——" And I hesitated. "I feel a fool not knowing your name, for I can't keep on calling you Miss Axton, can I?"

She said I couldn't, and told me her name was Diana.

"Just the name I'd have wanted for you," I cried, and was

rewarded by a bit more pressure on my arm. "Now tell me, Diana, do you know an Air Force lad called Derek Muir? Is he still here?"

"Yes. He's going on to the party too. Why?"

"I just want a quick word with him, that's all. Do you mind introducing us?"

The party, which I noticed didn't include Sheila, was getting ready to move on, but Diana Axton pulled young Muir out of it and introduced us. I took him into a corner.

"It's about the lighter you gave Mrs. Jesmond," I said.

I saw he didn't like this, though my guess was that he felt rather ashamed of being so thick with Mrs. Jesmond, who was old enough to be his mother.

"Any business of yours?" he asked, raising his eyebrows.

"Yes," I said, "or I wouldn't be asking you. But I'm not interested in the fact that you gave it to Mrs. Jesmond. What I'd like to know is where you got it from."

"Well, there's no particular mystery about that," he said, obviously feeling a bit better. "It belonged to Joe here, and I gave him fifteen bob for it. There he is, if you want to ask him. Hoy, Joe!"

Joe was crossing the entrance hall, and was wearing a dark overcoat and looking as if he was in a hurry to leave the place. But he turned and stopped, and we went across to him.

"It's about that lighter you sold me, Joe," said young Muir. "And better settle it between you, chaps, because obviously I'm wanted." His playmates, who'd been deciding who was to ride with whom, were now crying out for him. I exchanged a quick knowing look with the tall smiling Diana, who was probably ten years older than the rest of the girls in that gang, but at that made them look like ten cents.

Joe hadn't looked too pleased about being held up, but now he was his usual cheerful obliging self. "Have to cut it short, if you don't mind," he said to me, "because I've done quite a night's work, believe me, and I've somebody to see. And if you want another lighter like that one, sorry I can't oblige you."

"Mrs. Jesmond showed it to me," I said confidentially, "and the point is—I lost one exactly like it."

"I see," said Joe, dropping his voice too. "Well, I found that

lighter. Not in here, of course, otherwise I'd have turned it in to
the management. I found it down the road, one morning. I've
got a quick eye, and I often spot things that other people seem to
miss."

"Then it's probably the one I lost," I told him.

He shook his head, smiling. "No, it isn't."

I thought I had him now. "How d'you know, Joe?"

"That's easy, Mr. Neyland. When did you arrive in this town?
Tuesday? Wednesday?"

"Last Monday," I said, not so pleased with myself now.

"I found that lighter the Wednesday or Thursday before," he
said, "and I kept it for a week, in case somebody said they'd lost
it—for it's a nice little job, as you know—and then when nobody
said anything about it, I flashed it at one or two of the boys in the
bar the other night, and Mr. Muir offered me fifteen bob for it,
and I let him have it—to oblige him. Anyhow, I'd a good notion
what he'd do with it." And he winked. "Sorry, Mr. Neyland, but
that's how it is—see? Anything else?"

"Not a thing, Joe," I said, looking more cheerful than I felt. He
nodded, grinned, then hurried off. The wing-commander's party
had gone. There was no sign of Sheila or Mrs. Jesmond, and no
reason now why I should hang about any longer. Besides, the
last bus would be going in a few minutes. It arrived at the corner
very soon after I did, to my relief. The rain had stopped, leaving
behind it a cold black sponginess through which the bus seemed
to have to push its way. And we all sat humped in our seats as if
life had done with us. But it hadn't.

7

OTHER things being equal, as they say, I like to do what I'm told,
so when at last I arrived at Diana Axton's back door, I did what
she'd told me to do, I let myself in as quietly as I could. And when
I noticed the sliver of light, coming from under the sitting-room
door upstairs, I was quieter still, and took at least a couple of
minutes softly negotiating those stairs. But, anyhow, the man
and the woman behind that door were very busy talking, and not

in English. When I reached the little landing, I rushed them, and was inside that sitting-room, staring at them, almost before they knew they weren't alone. It was a cosy little party, well supplied with drinks and cigarettes. The woman was Fifine.

I'd never seen the man before. He was a tall, straight, clean-shaven man, possibly about fifty, with stiff grey hair, and he was wearing dark clothes. For a moment, while he stood there, glaring at me, he was one kind of man, and then as soon as I spoke he turned himself into another kind of man. It was as if one character had been sponged out, to be replaced by this other one, smaller, humbler, far less dangerous. It was superbly done, but just not quick enough.

"Sorry to startle you," I said, smooth as cream, "but Miss Axton specially asked me to be as quiet as I could. She's been dining with me at the *Queen of Clubs,* and as we've something to talk over, she suggested I should come back here and wait for her while she put in another hour's dancing at somebody's house."

I began taking off my overcoat, and the man at once helped me, as if he'd been doing nothing else for years. I knew any explanation would come from him, because Fifine had had a very nasty shock, looked badly rattled, and didn't know yet what her cue was. But I thought I might help them out a bit.

"Haven't I seen you at the Hippodrome here this week?" I said, grinning at her.

"Yes," she said slowly, in her thick clotted English, "I am appearing there. It was good, eh?"

"Very good," I said. "Everybody was talking about the act. Well, as Miss Axton particularly mentioned my helping myself to a drink, I think I'll join you." I made a motion towards a bottle of brandy on the little table. They'd had about a half of it, I noticed, and still had some in their glasses.

"Allow me, sir," said the man, with a deference which was obviously part of the character he had at once assumed. And he poured out for me a generous helping of the brandy, and care-fully handed me the glass. I sat down, but he remained standing. Fifine, who had been sprawling in an easy-chair when I first burst in on them, was still sitting, but was now upright and far nearer the edge of her chair. I took a sip of the brandy, and looked cheer-

fully and expectantly from one to the other, waiting for the story.
I knew, though, that it would come from the man.

It did. "I must explain, sir," he began, speaking with great
precision, "that I am in service in this neighbourhood. But when
I was younger and before I had an accident that left me slightly
lame, I was a performer in the circus and at vaudeville shows.
And not only did I know this lady and all her family very well—
they were all performers like myself—but I was married to her
older sister."

"Which makes him your brother-in-law," I said to Fifine, who
cheered up a bit after this fatuous remark. Before, she'd been
very uneasy. Now she smiled.

"Naturally," the man continued, "we'd a great deal to talk
about. But I'm busily employed during the day, and she's at
the theatre until late in the evening. I can't ask her out to my
employer's house, and she can't ask me, as late as this, into her
lodgings."

"No, no, no, quite impossible," cried Fifine, and would have
said more only the man gave her a sharp look.

"I occasionally visit the shop here for my master," said the
man, "and it happened that I mentioned our predicament to Miss
Axton the other day——"

"And she suggested you should come up here one evening
when she thought she'd be out late," I said, and then, as if
astounded by my insight and wizardry: "And probably, to-night,
she forgot."

"Undoubtedly. I hope you don't feel we have made ourselves
too comfortable," he went on, indicating the drinks and cigarettes, "but Miss Axton, who's very kind, did say that we could
help ourselves."

"Of course! And why not?" I had another sip of the brandy. I
saw him give Fifine another quick look, and now they both finished their brandy.

"Shall I clear away these things?" he asked.

"No, don't bother," I told him heartily, and made it plain that
they couldn't go too quickly for me. Fifine was fastening her fur
coat, and the man was putting on his overcoat. I had a good look
at him during this last minute or two. His face didn't match with

his talk at all. It looked tough, resolute, unscrupulous. And as he bent forward slightly, adjusting his overcoat, his left cheek, heavily top-lit, suddenly showed a trace of a scar that wasn't visible before.

Just as she was on the point of going, Fifine gave me a surprise. "I saw you behind at the theatre last night," she said. She managed her voice pretty well, but she couldn't keep the suspicion out of her eyes.

"Yes, I know you did," I told her. "I was visiting young Larry, one of your company. I've known him some time."

"He is not a good comic actor," she said.

"He's terrible," I said. "But then, he shouldn't have gone on the stage."

"I am sorry I had to leave it," said the man, who now that he was wearing his big overcoat and a white silk scarf and was about to put on a black soft hat, did suggest the theatre rather than the pantry. "Ah, that was the life! You will explain to Miss Axton, sir? Thank you! Good night."

As soon as the door below had closed, I took their glasses and washed and dried them in the little kitchen and put them away, and then emptied the ash-tray that was filled with the cigarette-ends they had left, re-arranged the easy-chairs, turned off the top light, and settled down to look as if I'd been doing some serious drinking while I waited for Diana Axton's return. The bottle of brandy they'd punished was prominent on the little table, and so was my glass. I decided not to take another drink until she came, for actually I was in no mood for drinking, but that as soon as I heard her below I would take a quick big gulp, which would give just the impression I wanted it to give. Then I lit a pipe and did some thinking, chiefly about the man who'd just left, for it seemed more than likely that this was the man Olney had been wanting to find, the man who had the "trace of deep scar on left cheek" mentioned in Olney's notes. Of course he might be hanging about just outside the door below waiting to catch Diana and to tell her what had happened, but I didn't propose to go down and see, even if it would be possible to see. What I did do, however, was to switch off the standard lamp for a few minutes and to open the window to clear the room of some of its cigarette smoke. And when I had closed the window and drawn the curtains and switched on the standard lamp, I saw that it was nearly half-past eleven. She had said she would be back about half-past and I had a notion that she was a woman of her word in these matters.

There are times on jobs of this sort when, without having set any machinery in motion yourself, without possessing any kind of direct evidence, you just know that things are about to happen. This was one of those times. I could feel that the whole job was about to go tearing along the runway.

I thought she'd have had another key to that back door (though I suppose if I hadn't been there she could have gone round to the shop entrance and unlocked that), but she hadn't. I took that big quick gulp of brandy before I hurried down to let her in, so that when I gave her a hasty sort of kiss just behind the door, she got the impression at once that I'd been doing some very steady drinking. And of course she noticed the state of the bottle—trust any woman to do that—as soon as she arrived in the sitting-room. Also, my hair was a bit rumpled, and I'd held my breath going downstairs so that my face was red, and I put on a fuzzy, half-sleepy, half-excited manner.

"Well!" she cried, taking it all in. "I don't think you've been too miserable, my dear." She used that easy bantering tone which suggests intimacy at once. And I saw that something had happened which had left her delighted and triumphant. She was the fire-and-ice queen all right.

When she came out of her bedroom, she gave me a long glittering look, and said: "I believe you're tight, Humphrey."

"You bet your life I'm not, Diana," I said, with too much emphasis. "It's just seemed a long time, that's all."

She came very close. "I'm sorry," she said softly. "And I've bad news for you. Somebody else is looking in soon, and I'm afraid you'll have to go when he goes."

"Oh hell!" I sounded absolutely flattened out. "Now listen, Diana——"

"It can't be helped," she said, in the same soft, intimate tone. "Besides, there'll be other nights. That is, if we're going to be friends."

"Friends!" And I hope I looked as reproachful as I sounded. Then I put in a bit of passion, thick voice and all. "My God, you don't know what you're doing to me, Diana."

"Don't I? But perhaps I do."

Well, perhaps she did, and perhaps she didn't.

I took her in my arms and kissed her hard, and she responded exactly as she'd done the night before, in that oddly efficient almost enthusiastic but impersonal style. It was like having a lesson from a first-rate instructress.

"I'm going to be frank with you," she said, after we'd broken away and I'd had some brandy and she'd taken some herself. "And when I say frank, I mean it. I've not had much kissing lately, and I could do with plenty. I like it, with the right person——"

"I'm the right person," I announced, grinning.

"In some ways I think you are—or might be." She looked hard at me. I noticed all over again how clear and pale a blue her eyes were, and what a cold unflinching look they had. There wasn't a glimmer of tenderness in them, and there never would or could be, and, if you ask me, without tenderness, and the fun and affection that go with it, the whole business between the sexes is just a messy battle. "But I'm in a difficult position, my dear. The few men I know whom I can trust aren't the kind of men I'd want to make love to me. The other kind—who might be possible as lovers—aren't men I know I can trust. And I'm not going to have a lover unless I can trust him. No, I don't mean the ordinary feminine trusting—I'm not talking about that at all——"

"I didn't think you were, Diana," I said. "You're not an ordinary woman. But what do you mean? Because whatever it is, I'm for it a hundred per cent."

"I want a man who, war or no war, will tell me all he knows," she said coolly. "If I ask him questions, I expect him to answer them. And of course not to answer anybody else's questions, but to be very discreet. And I had an idea you were that kind of man, Humphrey."

"So I am. You try me," I said eagerly.

"That's what I mean by trusting him," she went on, as if I hadn't spoken. "I'll do anything for him once I'm convinced he'll do anything for me."

I grabbed hold of her again, to help the scene. She didn't resist, but she didn't co-operate, as I knew she wouldn't. "For God's sake, don't keep on telling me, but just try me, that's all. This is enough to drive a fellow off his nut. If it's something about this war business that's worrying you, well, you know what I think about this war—and that's not much. Here, kiss me, and tell me what you want to know."

She kissed me all right, but then we heard a buzz from the door below. "There he is," she said, breaking away. "And I'm sorry he's butting in, but it's very necessary he should, and if I'm positive I can trust you, then—well, there'll be lots of other nights, won't there?" And off she went.

I'd made a bet with myself, when she first mentioned this other chap who was coming, as to who it would be, and now I knew I'd lost it badly. For I certainly didn't expect to meet Mr. Perigo. But here he was, one huge, false, porcelain smile, looking like a little pink-and-white alligator.

"My dear lady," he cried, as soon as he saw me, "I'm surprised but delighted, but quite delighted. Really, this is most unexpected. Though I don't know why it should be, for I've heard you say some very refreshing and sensible things about this nonsensical war that we're trying to fight for the Russians and the Americans. How are you, my dear fellow? Is it true that you're about to do something very grand and responsible at the Charters Electrical Company?"

"I'm meeting the Board next week," I replied, "but of course I don't know how we'll hit it off."

"They'll take you," said Diana confidently. "But you mustn't ask for more than eight-fifty a year, with a possible rise at the end of the first six months."

"You see," said Mr. Perigo, sparkling away like a malicious catherine-wheel at the pair of us. "Here's a charming and handsome woman who isn't content to be merely decorative, who knows how to be useful in this ridiculous world, *and* who realizes that a salary of eight hundred and fifty pounds a year can probably be nicely augmented in one way and another."

"In one way *and* another," she repeated. She then gave me a direct glance of invitation, and said calmly: "Mr. Perigo was wondering if they've started making the Amberson anti-Stuka device up at the Charters place."

"Certainly they have," I said promptly. "They've made about ten, but production's held up because they think they've been using the wrong type of carrier for it. Also, the men who were demonstrating it complained about the fumes."

"Wonderful!" cried Mr. Perigo. "But surely they didn't *tell* you all this, humph?"

"No, they didn't. But I was shown all over the works, and I've a habit of keeping my eyes and ears open." I was fairly loud and boastful, but didn't overdo it. And I saw Diana give him a look that asked him to confirm that what she'd hinted to him about me was nothing less than the truth.

"Quite so," he said. Then, as if answering that look she'd given him, he went on: "But I've no need to tell you, my dear, that in fact we don't want anybody else working for us at the Charters factory."

"Of course not," she said calmly. "But he won't stay long at the Charters factory——"

"If you're thinking of the Belton-Smith show, Diana," I said, "don't forget I tried there, and they wouldn't look at me."

"That's because you tried from outside," she said, "but once you've been with the Charters people a few weeks, there's going to be an opening at the Belton-Smith factory, and we can get you in easily enough."

"You see," cried Mr. Perigo. This was to me. Then he turned to her. "And you were perfectly right, of course. What it is to have a clever woman's intuitive power! Well, now then——"

But she stopped him, and with a gesture and tone of sharp command. "No. No more to-night. We've all said quite enough, as things are at present. There must be a definite test before anything else is said." All this, of course, was to Mr. Perigo and not to me, but then she turned to me, pulled out a smile, and said: "I'll be in the shop all day to-morrow, but Saturday afternoon's nearly always our busy time, so perhaps you could look in during the morning." Then she seemed to draw herself up in a grand queenly style, and she addressed us both. "How stupid these people are!" she cried, with more colour and warmth in both her face and her voice than I'd ever noticed before. "How can they expect to keep their power and yet be so stupid! The world isn't going to allow itself to be ruled by idiots. We have the leadership, the devotion, the audacity, and the brains. What have these poor fools got?"

It was a theatrical sort of speech, but she meant it, for like so many people of her way of thinking, as I'd often noticed, it was just when she showed you what she was really thinking and feeling that she became theatrical and artificial. They are all alike, these dupes of the Führer, somewhere at the back of their minds there's always a performance of grand opera going on, with Adolf and themselves in the leading roles. As Diana Axton stood there, queening it over us, she could hear the augmented orchestra fiddling and booming away.

Mr. Perigo looked at me, and I looked hard at him, while Diana stood listening to her orchestra, and at once we read the truth in each other's faces. I produced a cigarette and my special lighter. "Won't work," I said, shaking the lighter. "You got a light?"

He had his lighter, identical with mine, out in a flash. "I'd give you this one," he said, as he held it to my cigarette, "only it's a present from an old friend."

"Don't think of it," I said. "I'll take care my lighter works to-morrow."

So that was that. Now we looked at Diana, who was just coming out of her happy reverie of Nazi brains over the world, and we said good night to her. She was still half-lost in grandeur, and I was very glad that I wasn't staying. She returned to this earth just in time to give my hand a very tender squeeze when we reached the bottom of the stairs, and that was all. Then Perigo and I slipped out into the darkness.

We didn't speak for a minute or two, not because we hadn't plenty to say, but because both of us knew that there might be somebody hanging about there, waiting for us to leave Diana's place. So we didn't say a word until we'd slowly edged our way through the dark into the square. It was now just after midnight, and to say that Gretley seemed to be asleep doesn't begin to do justice to the time and place. Gretley seemed to have vanished. We might have been crawling about in some enormous cave, with only a few faint patches of phosphorescence to light our way. When a truck came groaning through the square, it seemed to have descended from some other world. Once again I felt I was groping round in hell.

"Where are we going, Neyland?" asked Perigo, who was little more than a voice in the dark.

"We can go round to my lodgings if you like," I said, "but if it's all the same to you I'd like to look into police headquarters. The Superintendent there knows all about me—we've been working together to some extent—and if by any chance he's still there, I've one or two things to say to him, and even if he isn't, I'd like to use their telephone line."

"They don't know about me there," he said, "but I don't think it matters if they do know now."

"No, I don't think it does, Perigo," I said. Then I explained how Olney's murder had brought me into touch with Superintendent Hamp. Perigo didn't know anything about Olney. By the time I'd finished telling him, we'd worked our way round to the back of the municipal building and I was looking for the door that would be open all night. When we got inside, I was lucky enough to find that the constable on duty was the one who'd seen me with the Superintendent once or twice before. He said the Super would be coming in soon—and I got the idea that something had happened to keep him up—and in the meantime Perigo and I could wait in a bare little room next to the Superintendent's office.

So there we were, Perigo and I, staring and yawning at each other in the hard light of two naked bulbs. The room had a mixed smell of disinfectant and stale cigarette smoke. The fire had gone out. We sat on two chairs that must have been much too small for any policeman. Perigo looked a hundred years old, and I felt about seventy-five. He admitted that he was very tired.

"I have to do so much running about and bright chattering on this damned job," he said, "that by the end of the day I'm all in. Next time I'm going to be an elderly invalid, a bad heart case, and people will have to come and see me. Only, of course, they won't. But it's murderous having to sustain a character who must never stop amusing the company all the time. If that's the life of a social parasite, then he earns his keep. But I did learn how to be pleasant to all kinds of insufferable people in my business. I had a business, y'know, Neyland."

"I know you had," I said grinning. "I checked up on you at once."

"What happened was that I genuinely retired—I was hoping to do some writing—and then I felt there must be something I could do in the war, and a nephew of mine, who's in M.I.5, suggested this counter-espionage business, which I must say, in spite of many drawbacks, I still find rather fascinating. How did you come to be in it?"

I told him briefly. Then I asked him how he'd managed to convince Diana Axton so suddenly that he was working for the Nazis.

"You don't know the sign they're using now?" he asked.

"No, I don't. I knew several of the old ones, of course," I told him, "but I understood it had just been changed. This was a handicap, though of course the way I was playing it, I wasn't going to pretend I was in the know, but only a disgruntled Canadian, who really didn't care about the war, and so could be bought—or—" and I grinned—"seduced."

"I was working that too, as you saw, though without any possible seduction," he said, "though even there, as you may have noticed, I baited the trap a little, with a bait the Nazis understand only too well. For, believe it or not, Neyland, it wasn't previously my habit to use rouge or over-emphasize my sibilants and, in short, behave like an old pansy. But I learned this morning, when I was up in London, what the new sign and password are. I'll show you." And he put the first and second fingers of his right hand stiffly across my wrist, making a "V." "Then you say, 'That's V for Victory and I don't mean a small V, but a capital one.' That's what you say. Got it? Then the other great mind places the forefinger of his or her other hand across your two fingers, turning the V into A, and at the same time says brightly, 'That's good. I'll remember that.' Wonderful, isn't it? God, what an idiotic world we're living in! To think that millions of lives may depend on such antics! But there it is. Just try it, Neyland, for you may need it soon."

I did, to his satisfaction. Then he went on: "I thought I'd try it on the Axton woman, because I'd suspected her for some time and she seemed pretty stupid, so I tried to get hold of her for to-night, but discovering that she was engaged to dine with you, I arranged with a wing-commander who knows all about me to throw a late party to which she'd be invited. I tried it on her there. She fell at once, and insisted that I should take a look at you as a possible new recruit. I wasn't sure about you, of course, just as you weren't about me. But how had you spotted her so soon?"

"Chiefly because, as you say, she's so stupid, so eaten up with conceit and Nordic greatness inside, that she doesn't watch what she's doing. To begin with, she obviously wasn't the type of woman who'd keep that sort of shop. She told me she'd got it as a bargain and it didn't take me five minutes to find out she was lying. Then she didn't take the trouble to sustain the character of the woman who would keep such a shop. Her own sitting-room hadn't any character at all, which meant that she daren't let it express her real self. Then again, with her social background, she could obviously have got herself into some bossy parading job in one of the women's services—a high-up Wren or something of that sort—which would have suited her temperament. She didn't, because she wasn't on our side. She'd played about in Nazi Germany, gone to Nuremberg at some time or other and been told by Goebbels that she looked like a Wagner heroine, and had been sworn in and taught a trick or two, and then quietly told to ship herself across to America, to do what mischief she could to us in the early days of the war. Then she'd been told to return here, and set up shop where she could be most useful."

"But why the shop, when, as I agree with you, she wasn't the type?" Perigo asked. "Assuming she had the money to do it, and we can suppose she had, why didn't they tell her to instal herself in a country house, just outside the town, and entertain the young officers. Like our friend, Mrs. Jesmond," he added, with a grin. "You know, of course, there's nothing there for us."

"Yes, she's just playing about with the Black Market, just a handsome, luxurious, lecherous rat," I said. "She doesn't matter to us, but I'd like to see her spending the rest of the war washing up in a canteen."

"Oh come now, Neyland," he protested. "She's a charming decorative woman——"

"We've paid too high a price for such charming decorative

women," I said, "and I've seen too many other women, each worth a hundred Mrs. Jesmonds, kicked along the gutter by everything she represents. From now on, let the Mrs. Jesmonds work or starve."

"You're too bitter, Neyland," he said gently, and looked at me in a friendly speculative way. "I've seen it in you from the first. There's something——" But he merely ended with a gesture.

"Never mind me," I told him, more harshly than I felt. "We were talking about Diana Axton. That shop, I'm certain, is more than a mere front. They're not so stupid, even if they aren't the world brains she obviously thinks they are—the poor mutt! My own guess—and a reference to flowers I found in Olney's notes makes it a pretty good guess—is that Prue's Gift Shop is a neat little Nazi post office. These little bunches of artificial flowers in the window could spell out a message to anybody who stopped a moment or two outside there——"

"Like Mam'zelle Fifine's admirable arms and legs," he said, grinning. "You noticed them, I think?"

"I did. And I also noticed you noticing them. I saw her to-night." And I told him about meeting Fifine and the man with the scar on his left cheek. Perigo didn't know anything about this man, and I had a notion then that he didn't see the local picture quite as I did. But then I hadn't said a word yet about my two chief suspects, and I decided I wouldn't, not because I didn't trust Perigo, but because it was better if each of us still followed his own trail. I hinted as much.

"What about Joe?" he asked.

I told him about the lighter, which Joe claimed to have found ten days ago, but which I knew to be the one taken from Olney. I also told him about finding the half smoked Chesterfield at Silby's shop, whose telephone number Fifine had on her list. I pointed out that Diana Axton knew Joe far better than she pretended to do. And I asked him if he knew what Joe had been doing in the interval between Borani's being bombed and his arrival up here. "You see, I was told he came up here partly because he'd lost his nerve," I went on, "but he didn't come up here until after the regular heavy bombing had stopped. Besides, there's nothing wrong with that guy's nerves."

"What a pleasure it is at last to have such an intelligent colleague!" said Perigo, who though he now looked about a hundred and fifty years old, was waking up a bit. "I realized from the first, of course, when you were listening to our chatter in the bar of the *Lamb and Pole*, that you were a shrewd and observant man, but I'm really surprised, perhaps almost a little envious, at the progress you've made in a few days. Remember, I've been here for months."

"That's different," I told him. "You had to build up a part, whereas I walked straight into one. Furthermore, the people we're after are now getting over-confident and careless. Diana Axton may be the silliest of them, but look at the way she's been leading with her chin. And then the way they knocked off and lugged round poor Olney—why, this Superintendent knew at once it was murder."

"But, in spite of his having the lighter, that couldn't have been Joe," said Perigo slowly, "for at the time Olney was run down Joe was serving drinks in his bar."

"No, that wasn't Joe. But I think Joe met the man who did it later that night or next morning, and was given the lighter."

"I agree with you that Joe's in this somewhere," said Perigo. "In fact I've been keeping an eye on him for some time. I asked them in London to tell me something about his movements after Borani's was bombed. It seems that Joe, who has a Mexican passport, went to America towards the end of 1940. What strings he pulled to obtain permission to return, I don't know, but it can't have been easy. Unless, of course, his own Embassy quite innocently got him through."

"You know, Perigo, I have a notion that the set-up here might have been first planned in America," I said. "Diana was there, and Joe was there, and perhaps we may find out that one or two others were there too. Where does Joe live?"

"He has a room at 27, Palmerston Place," replied Perigo promptly.

That's as far as he got, because at that moment in walked that sergeant with the long chin, Boyd. He didn't look as if he liked me now any more than he liked me when we first met, but he couldn't escape the fact that his Super and I were working together at something. And obviously he wondered what the blazes little Perigo was doing there, but I let him go on wondering.

"I've been talking to the Superintendent," he began, looking about two feet above my head, "and he says perhaps you'd better go down there."

"Down where?" I asked.

"Canal. We've just pulled a car out, with a woman inside it. And the Superintendent thinks you'll be interested."

Perigo and I looked at each other. Sergeant Boyd didn't like that. "He didn't say anything about anybody else going down," he said pointedly.

"I'm wondering how to get home—three miles away—not how to get down to the canal to see a drowned woman," said Perigo hastily. "Perhaps I'd better stay here, though."

"Can your people take an inquiry at this hour? What is it—nearly one?"

"They can take the inquiry, but usually they can't do anything about it. I wouldn't call it a twenty-four hour service they give us. Why? Is it Jeeves with the scar you're wondering about?"

"Yes," I replied.

"Why don't you ask us?" said the sergeant. "We live here, y'know. And if by Jeeves you mean a valet-butler kind o' chap, plus a scar, I think I know who you mean." He waited then, of course. He was that type.

"Well, do us a favour—we're only trying to rid this country of some of its most dangerous enemies," I said nastily, "and tell us who this chap is. In order not to waste your time, I may add that he looks about fifty, has stiffish grey hair, very careful precise English——"

"Yes, I know," said the sergeant. "Name's Morris. He's Colonel Tarlington's valet-butler. Queer chap. I've had a few words with him now and then. But he's all right, y'know. He was in the last war with Colonel Tarlington—his batman. Everything in order."

"I see." One foot had been doubled under that little chair, and now I stamped it hard. "Well, Perigo, better not bother about that inquiry, but wait here if you like."

"I'd rather wait here than walk three miles," said Perigo, stand-ing up rather uncertainly. "Is this the best I can do, Sergeant?"

"You'd do better next door, where at least there's a fire and you might get a cup o' tea. Now we'll have to be getting along," he said to me.

They had a car outside, and in five minutes we were nosing our way somewhere near the canal. We stopped finally at a hell of a place. There were two more cars and a truck there, and their dimmed headlights shone mournfully on the green slime of the canal bank and the thick greasy water. There were piles of old junk and rubbish about. It seemed just the end of everything down there. We weren't far from being a lot of old junk and rub-bish ourselves. There didn't seem any particular reason why the black weight of the night shouldn't press still harder and flatten us all out. Then, outside some sort of shed place, for which we were making, I saw a woman standing, and when the sergeant flashed his torch, I saw her face. It seemed to be hollowed out by fatigue and sadness to a thin ivory mask, yet it also seemed then the most beautiful face I'd ever seen, and my heart turned over.

It was Dr. Margaret Ann Bauernstern. She didn't see us prop-erly, and probably didn't want to see us. She merely stood aside, moving in that slow mechanical fashion of people who are tired through and through. Pushing back some tarpaulin they'd hung up at the entrance of the shed, we went inside. Several hurri-cane lamps were burning there. I saw the big bulk of the Super-intendent and a couple of policemen. They were staring down at something, and looked like men lost in an evil dream. I felt lost with them. There, laid out among more old junk and rubbish, still reeking of the foul water, was the body of Sheila Castleside.

Probably it wasn't more than half a minute before the Superintendent spoke to me, but it seemed like hours. I'd time to think about that talk Sheila and I had had in that bedroom at the *Queen of Clubs*—it seemed days ago, though it was only three hours or so—and to remember that last, nice, silly girl's speech she'd made to me before she twined her arms about my neck and kissed me. Ever since I was eighteen, and thrown into the last war, I'd seen men die, for even apart from the war and a few sensational chapters since, I'd never been far or long away from death, for big engineering jobs in rough country, like the ones I took on in South America, produce a fair crop of casualties. But this was different, and much worse. When Maraquita and the boy were killed, I'd known nothing for days, except, of course, that last blinding quarter-second when I knew we were for it and still had time to damn for ever my murderous recklessness. Then I went out like a light, and was pulled back afterwards to a world that wasn't the one, and never could be the one, I'd gone tearing around in, bright and idiotic at seventy miles an hour. I didn't expect much in this second world, where the murdering fool lives on while the woman and the child are smashed to pulp, but somehow even here I hadn't thought of this dirty little stroke, though now I began to wonder, even before the Superintendent spoke, whether I ought to have thought of it, whether this wasn't, in fact, my fault.

"She went in about half-past eleven," said the Superintendent. "A fellow across the way, going home, saw and heard it, and got on to us. She was driving her own car, one of these little affairs, and hadn't a chance to get out."

"Any sign that she wanted to?" I asked him.

"No. Thinking it might be suicide?"

"No, I'm certain it wasn't suicide. Nobody would choose this way of doing it. Besides, she wasn't thinking of suicide. I had a long talk with her to-night at the *Queen of Clubs*. What's Dr. Bauernstern doing out there?"

"She'd been late at the hospital, and I happened to catch her," he said. "Couldn't do anything, of course. Our police-surgeon's in bed with a temperature of a hundred and three. Has Dr. Bauernstern gone home?"

"No, she's standing outside, looking like death herself."

"Thank you," said a voice, and for a moment I didn't recognize it as hers, "but I'm here, and quite prepared to answer any questions—that is, if Superintendent Hamp gives you proper authority to ask them."

He could tell—for who couldn't?—that she thought I was poison, and he knew she'd had a weary long day and was almost all in, and he didn't want to enter into any fancy explanations about me there and then, so I didn't blame him when he hesitated. She came nearer and sat down on an upturned box. It was all in slow motion. It was like a meeting of old ghosts.

The Superintendent must have felt all this and have made up his mind not to give way. "Sergeant," he roared, "take these men and go through that car now. You've all got torches, haven't you? But don't splash the light about. Take some sacking for the windows. Sharp now!"

That got rid of them. I took a pull on myself and leaned over and looked hard at the body.

"Had she been drinking up at the *Queen of Clubs?*" asked the Superintendent.

"She may have had a few," I said, "but she was sober enough when she left me, which was just after ten."

"Did she say where she was going then?"

"No. And when I left—say, about half-past ten—I looked round for her, but couldn't see her. She hadn't gone there with me, by the way, but I'd had a rather long talk with her, and wanted a final word with her."

"She may have dashed off and had a few quick strong ones somewhere else," said the Superintendent gloomily. "I believe she was a young woman who liked to be gadding about."

"Yes, she was. But not down here by the canal," I told him. "That's got to be explained."

"Not if she was drunk, it hasn't."

"I don't think she was drunk. And I don't think she committed suicide. And I don't think she missed her way in the dark," I said sharply. Just as the Superintendent had had to do a bit of bellowing to break the spell, so I had to talk sharply and seem rather tough. "Do you mind, Dr. Bauernstern?" And I turned to her. "I wouldn't ask you if I didn't think you'd do it better than I could."

"What do you want?" she asked, without any warmth or interest. She'd quietly worked up a hate against me that stuck out now like a two-foot knife.

"Will you feel very carefully at the back of her head? It's important, or I wouldn't trouble you. And we mustn't lose time."

She must have looked enquiringly at the Superintendent, for he told her quietly to go ahead.

All this part seemed to be in dragging slow motion too. She

asked us to bring a couple of lamps nearer. Tired as she was, and I think profoundly unwilling to do anything I wanted her to do, she went to work with a beautiful easy skill that gave me a kind of sad pleasure to watch. When her probing fingers finally halted, and she looked up, I could tell by her face that my guess had been right.

"There a *hæmatoma* here," she said slowly. "I can feel it. The blood's collected under the scalp. This means that either she hurt herself badly as the car went over, striking the back of her head against some part of the car, or——"

"That somebody knocked her out, probably with a rubber cosh," I said. "And that's my guess. They were down here somewhere, talking in the car. She was difficult, so she was knocked out, and the car was started and sent into the canal. You'll notice," I turned to the Superintendent, "it's the same method as before. Murder looking like an accident."

"Does that square with what you've discovered, doctor?" he asked.

"I don't know much about this kind of injury," she said, with an obvious effort, "but somehow I can't imagine how she could have given herself such a blow, merely striking her head somewhere as the car went over. It seems much more like a deliberate blow. I think," she added reluctantly, "that Mr. Neyland must be right."

To hear her mention my name like that, though of course I'd heard her say it before, gave me an extraordinary pleasure. Somehow I must have had the notion that she'd completely, perhaps deliberately, forgotten my name, and now that I knew she hadn't, I was ridiculously pleased.

"This girl, Sheila Castleside," I said, "expected to be black-mailed quite soon. She didn't know what form it would take, but I did. That's why I had this talk with her to-night. There wasn't any real harm in her, poor kid, but she'd a rather sticky past she wanted to hide and in order to give herself a leg-up in our wonderful social scale, she'd told a lot of fancy stories about herself, pretending she'd been a young widow in India and so on. She'd kept up this pretence even with her husband and his family. She married him in the first place to promote herself from being a waitress and a manicure girl to a nice young lady, but then she fell in love with her husband, and it was chiefly because of that she didn't want the truth to come out."

"She told you all this, eh?" said the Superintendent.

"Yes, but I'd guessed she was in a spot," I went on, "and I also knew that certain people might put the screw on her, for reasons that she didn't understand. Well, it's my guess that one of them got hold of her to-night, to tell her what was expected of her——"

"Which was—well, something in your line, eh?" said the Superintendent, who'd almost forgotten that Dr. Bauernstern was still listening to us.

"Yes. She hadn't expected that. She thought they'd be wanting money—or—well, let's say a little personal attention from her. But when she discovered what it was they did want—and I hinted to her to-night what I thought that would be—she wasn't having any, refused to fall for the blackmail, and threatened to tell me or you or her husband what the game was and who was playing it. That settled it. She had to be killed—and at once. That's how I see it." I looked down at the wretched thing they had fished out of the stinking canal. I remembered the impudent nose, the ripe smiling mouth, the oddly-coloured bright eyes. "And if my guess is right, she's as much a war casualty as any lad torn apart by machine-gun fire. And she's also just another casualty in another and worse battle, ordinary human nature *versus* a social system that's diseased in every part of it. They grow up, bright and smiling, thinking heaven's round the corner, and then we proceed to kick 'em to hell."

"I didn't know you felt like that," said Dr. Bauernstern, softly and wonderingly.

"You don't know what I feel," I said harshly. "It's late, and I'm talking too much."

"You needn't tell me it's late," the Superintendent grunted. "But I'll have to ask you to look in at my office for a minute, doctor. Perhaps you'd drive us there."

He stumped out to give the sergeant some further instructions. Margaret Ann Bauernstern looked at me for a moment or two in a detached but essentially feminine way, then bent over the body, as if the dead girl was only sleeping and had to be left easy and comfortable.

"I saw her once or twice," she murmured. "Once—I remember—I envied her. She seemed so pretty and gay—enjoying life—even if it was all rather silly. Every woman wants to be like that sometimes. It must have been her husband—a tall, good-looking young man—I saw her with. I thought they obviously adored each other. Yes, I was envious for a minute."

"There was nothing for you to be envious about," I said, and I tried to make it sound dry and unfriendly. "And I'll tell you something now. When I caught sight of you standing out there——"

"Looking like death," she whispered.

"Yes, looking like death. Exhausted, worn-out, apparently finished. With just a hollow shell of a face. And I thought to myself, 'That's the most beautiful face I've even seen'. And it seemed to hurt me."

She stood very still, looking at me, quite close, yet remote, mysterious. "Why are you telling me this?"

"Not to make anything of it, don't worry." I was dry and unfriendly now, all right. "Why I mentioned it has really nothing to do with you. But when anybody—and I'm not thinking particularly about women now, for it's more likely to happen with men—does something or has something that suddenly knocks me sideways, I feel I ought to mention it. I once went six hundred miles just to tell old Messiter that his Carnova Dam was a masterpiece and nearly brought tears to my eyes. I feel better then. It's like paying a debt."

"And now that you've told me, you feel better," she said, with more mockery in her voice than in her face.

"Yes, and it's all clear. We can go straight on disliking and mistrusting each other. That's all right to me. Come on, Dr. Bauernstern, let's go."

She drove us to the municipal building. Perigo wasn't there, but he'd left a note for me saying that he was getting a lift in a lorry going near his cottage, and that he'd look me up some time the next day, when he'd be feeling less old and tired. It didn't take the Superintendent long to go through some necessary bit of routine with Dr. Bauernstern, and as I'd now more to say to her than I had to the Superintendent, I suggested she should drop me at my lodgings. I didn't tell where I was staying until we were in the car.

"It's 15 Raglan Street," I said then.

"But isn't that——"

"Yes, where poor Olney was staying. We met there, you may remember."

"Yes, I remember. The night he was killed."

"The night he was murdered," I said emphatically. "Yes, Olney was murdered, just as I'm certain this girl was murdered to-night. You're not doing badly in Gretley, are you?"

She didn't reply to that, but steered her car, which was a beastly little brute, in silence through the darkness. Somehow she gave me the impression that she wasn't ever going to speak to me again. It was that kind of silence. So there we were, two people crawling through the blackout with nothing to say. It wouldn't do.

"All quiet in Gretley," I went on, "and not a mouse stirring. Except murder. Except treachery. Except the good old plans to sell out the poor devils of people."

"If you can't say anything real, please be quiet."

"That's real enough, lady. It's all happening."

"It may be. But you're not being real while you're saying it. You're striking attitudes and showing off. At this time of night too!"

"All right, I'll stop striking attitudes and showing off," I said grimly. At least I hope it sounded grim and not merely peeved. "And you might as well pull up, because I think we're nearly there."

She did. "Well? And please try not to be bad-tempered about it. I've had a very long day, and I react badly to exhibitions of bad temper."

"I'll be as smooth as silk. I want to have a talk with your brother-in-law, Otto Bauernstern."

Tired as she was, that made her jump, then instantly whirl round on me. "I don't understand. Why should you want to talk to Otto? Besides, he's disappeared."

"So I was told. But my guess is—he's in your house. That Austrian woman you employ gave it away."

"She *told* you!"

"No, of course not," I said. "But it was obvious from her manner that she was nervous about visitors, that there was something or somebody in the house that was making her nervous, and then it wasn't hard to link it up with your brother-in-law."

"Do you enjoy going about spying on people?" she asked bitterly.

"You can cut that out," I said. "What I enjoy or don't enjoy doesn't come into the picture. But I want to have a talk with Otto Bauernstern."

"Well," she said defiantly, "you're some kind of policeman, aren't you? A new British version of the Gestapo——"

"Sure! I'm always taking old men and boys down into cellars and beating the daylight out of 'em. Go on."

"Then," she said, "you've only to tell the local police, who've been told by patriots like Colonel Tarlington to hound down poor Otto, that he's in my house, then they can put him into the nearest cell, and you'll be able to talk to him for hours—and he won't be able even to escape from it."

I kept my temper, though it wasn't easy. This woman had a power of irritating me—and had had it right from the first—that I hadn't met in anybody for years. "I told the local police," I said quietly. "At least I told Superintendent Hamp, who by the way, you can count among your friends. He was annoyed when I told him, because he thought it would mean he'd have to take action, but I pointed out that this was my affair and that I preferred to have Otto Bauernstern where he was."

"Why did you say that?" she asked, dropping the bitter mocking tone.

"Because—to go back to the beginning again—I wanted to have a talk to him in your house. And I'll be glad if you can fix it up as soon as possible. Let's say—to-morrow afternoon."

She thought for a moment. "I want to be there myself," she announced finally. "Otto's—well, in a highly nervous condition. He's a rather unstable type, and all this persecution and hiding haven't improved him. Four o'clock?"

"Four o'clock," I repeated. "Just a nice friendly cup of tea on a Saturday afternoon. I think to-morrow looks like being a busy day. I've got to work fast now," I said, talking to myself rather than to her, "otherwise, somebody else we know will soon meet with a nasty accident. They go in threes, and we've already had two. Well, thanks for the lift, Dr. Bauernstern. Margaret Ann," I added.

She surprised me then. "It's Margaret usually," she said, though without any particular expression. I hadn't moved, though I was about to go, and now I knew, though there wasn't much to see, that she was looking at me speculatively. "Before all this—you were—some sort of engineer?"

"Yes. First in Canada, then in South America. Big useful jobs—though I wasn't the top man, of course—in big useful places, with lots of light and air. Yes, very different from creeping about in blacked-out alleyways baiting traps."

"Yes. And, I was thinking, you must have been different then," she said slowly.

"You've said it, Margaret. Very different. As you were—working and studying and planning for the future—there in Vienna."

"How did you know that?"

"You told me a bit the other afternoon. And I watched your face light up. You don't often see faces light up like that now."

I waited for her to reply, but she didn't. Then I heard a tiny sound, and knew she was crying. I had to take a grip on myself. "Hurry up and get some sleep," I said. "You're all in. Good night, Margaret—and don't forget—four o'clock to-morrow."

8

BEFORE I try to tell all that happened that last day, Saturday, when, because of some mounting impatience I'd never felt before while working for the department, I bustled the whole job into the bag, I ought to give you a sketch of the background, so that you can keep it in mind all the time. A cold wet Saturday in late January, 1942, with the Japs swarming nearer and nearer Singapore, and pushing down towards Australia, temporary stalemate in Libya, no bombing of Germany because of the weather, and a general feeling of uneasiness and disillusion. A cold wet Saturday in Gretley, with a half-hearted sort of market in the square, dripping queues here and there outside the shops and, later, the picture theatres, and everywhere the steam and reek of wet clothes. Never quite full daylight, and with the black-out waiting just round the corner. If you thought of the war as a kind of tunnelling from one sunlit valley to another, then this was about the middle of the tunnel, where you smoked your last cigarette but one in the damp raw gloom and wondered if you ever had sat about laughing with your friends. And through the scene, this background to the action, moved the patient people, taking what was given them and asking for no more, except in their hearts, remembering absent faces, waiting for letters that never came, willing if necessary to die for a Gretley that had hardly ever come to life for them. Their slow patience, their lack of fire and fury, puzzled and half angered me, perhaps because I could never make up my mind whether they were half-dead or simply better people than any I'd known before. I wanted them to blast Hitler and all his kind off the face of the earth, and then tear down Gretley and everything like it, throwing the last of its dirty bricks at the retreating backs of the gang that had kept them imprisoned there. I mention all this because I think something of this impatience and bitter bewilderment, fed too by my hatred of the cold wet dingy town, found its way, that Saturday, into my handling of the job.

The middle of the morning found me in the Superintendent's office, where Perigo, whom I'd explained to the Superintendent, joined us. I'd already put through a call to London, been given some information by the department, and been told, probably because I sounded so impatient, to go ahead, using all the powers given me, and to get immediate results as best I could. The Superintendent, who was nothing but a large-scale map of worry but didn't know how to begin speeding up his usual police methods, had started trying to check up on Sheila's movements after she left the *Queen of Clubs* the night before. And he told me I was doing nothing but guessing, and that guesses were no use to them. They needed cast-iron evidence before thinking about arrests.

"I know all that," I told him, "and I don't blame you. But I'm not going to work that way. I don't propose to play the game. In fact, I'd suggest there's no more playing the game until the last of all these rats has gone, and we're all friends and want nice fair play."

"There," said Perigo, showing us all his porcelain, "I agree with our friend. I hadn't time to do more than glance at the paper this morning, but what I saw did suggest that our attitude as superior amateur sportsmen is becoming a trifle dangerous."

"I'm not a superior amateur sportsman," said the Superintendent heavily, "but an inferior professional policeman. And I've had about a couple of hours sleep since I saw you last, Neyland, and I'm working as hard as I can to get some real evidence. It seems to me you haven't enough to last you three minutes in court."

"I know I haven't. But I also know that valuable information has been streaming out of Gretley, and I know who's been collecting and distributing it. I also know there have been two murders that looked like accidents, and that very soon there may be another. And I think I know who did the murdering. But we might sit here from now until Christmas trying to get the sort of evidence you want. What we've got to do is to bluff and bustle 'em until they're convicting themselves. You found nothing in that car of Sheila's, I suppose?"

"Nothing that meant anything," he replied. "I didn't expect we would. And so far there's nothing to prove that anybody was with her——"

"Except that little matter of the clout on her head," I said sharply. "Which makes it certain to me she was murdered. But the man who murdered her doesn't know we've found that bruise on the back of her head. Now are you both willing to try it my way?"

Perigo was, as I knew he'd be, and after hesitating a moment or two, the Superintendent said that he was too.

"Then let's get busy," I said. "It's what? About quarter to eleven. Perigo, Diana Axton trusts you, as she calls it, and isn't quite ready to trust me yet. So hurry round there, in a state of great excitement, and tell her that you've an urgent message for Joe that she must give him at once. The point is, of course, he'll

take it from her. Tell her that there was some attempted sabotage
last night out at the Belton-Smith works. A man who looked like
Joe was seen by somebody, hurrying away. And the police believe
they can prove he was there. They have some evidence that points
to him. The time? About half-past eleven. You've got that?"

He repeated it at once. Perigo was very quick. I didn't bother
to find out what the Superintendent thought about the move.
"Then there's another thing," I went on. "Let slip afterwards
that Sheila Castleside drove into the canal late last night, and
her drowned body was taken out early this morning, and that
it looks as if she was tight. She'll tell Joe that too. But be very
urgent about it. She must tell him at once. *Achtung, achtung!*"

As soon as Perigo had gone, I remembered that I had to make
an appointment with Colonel Tarlington. I rang him up at his
house and then at the Charters works, where I found him. I told
him that I was very anxious to see him as soon as possible, about
my possible job with the Charters Company and one or two
other things, and he was very polite, said that he was engaged all
day, and had to have an early dinner out, but would be back home
about ten that night, if I didn't mind going out as late as that. I
said that I'd be delighted. Then I added: "I've just heard that Scorson of the Ministry of Supply put in a good word for me when
he spoke to you on Wednesday night. And I've been wondering
if that made any difference. It did? Oh—fine! Ten o'clock then."

"I don't wish to seem inquisitive," said the Superintendent,
who enjoyed a bit of heavy irony, "but what was that last little
story about?"

"Well, you'll remember that between quarter-to-nine and
nine on Wednesday night, just when Olney was being knocked
down and carted around, Colonel Tarlington, as you told me,
was taking a personal call from London. It was that call I was
referring to."

"So I gathered," he said. "But did this Mr. What's-it put in a
good word for you?"

"Colonel Tarlington just agreed he did," I said, keeping a
poker face. "By the way, where could I find a little thick black
grease—the kind you might find in an old engine, you know?"

"How much do you want? And what's the idea?"

"As much as will go comfortably into an ordinary envelope," I told him, and then waited until he'd told the constable on duty to find some. "As for the idea, the less you know about some of my present methods the better, Superintendent. But I think you'd make more effective use of this than I should." And I handed him the half-smoked Chesterfield that I found in Silby's shop. "That was found last night, understand, out at the Belton-Smith factory, and was left by the man who attempted to break in and do some sabotaging. And, mind you, though I did find that cigarette-stub somewhere else, I'm willing to bet that it's Joe's."

He didn't look pleased, but he was careful enough in putting the cigarette-stub away in an envelope to suggest that he wasn't pulling against me. "Anything else?" he asked.

"That sergeant of yours, Boyd, told me last night that Colonel Tarlington's butler-valet or whatever he is—you know the man?—his name's Morris—served in the last war with Colonel Tarlington as his batman. Well, I'd like somebody to get through to the proper regimental records, find out all he can about this man Morris, where he went to after he was discharged, and so on and so forth. And I'd like all the necessary information as soon as possible, even if it means burning up the wires. And this is important for you people as well as for me," I added meaningly.

"You think there's been hanky-panky there, eh?" he said, pulling his great weight out of the chair.

"I'm not quite sure what 'hanky-panky' is, but if it's what I think it is, then the answer's Yes." And I waited, smoking furiously and without much pleasure, while the Superintendent, who might be cautious but wasn't really slow, began to demand some quick action. Then I looked at my watch. I didn't want Joe to leave his lodgings for the *Queen of Clubs* before we interviewed him, because it was essential that we should play the scene with him in his own room. But just then a call came for me on the telephone. It was Perigo, speaking from Diana's place. "She's gone," he said softly, "but I'm staying on here just to look round and see that everything's in order. There might be something she wouldn't like stupid people she couldn't trust to discover here." And I could hear him chuckling. This meant that he'd be busy and useful for the next ten minutes.

We drove round in a police car to Palmerston Place, where Joe had his room, and kept away from Number Twenty-seven until we'd seen Diana Axton hurrying out of it. Then we marched in to see Joe, who was obviously the king of the place, occupying a fairly large and very untidy bed-sitting-room on the first floor. He was wearing a fancy dressing-gown that was due for a cleaning, and he didn't look anything like so spruce and trim as he did behind the bar. But he didn't look worried. There was a smile on his broad brown face. Even the sight of me, which surprised him, didn't take the smile off his face. There were a lot of books about. Somehow I hadn't thought of Joe as a reader.

Whatever the Superintendent may have thought of this way of doing police business, he gave a terrific performance from the moment we entered that room. "Mr. Joe Bolat, isn't it?" he said, in an easy but very impressive style. "Well, Mr. Bolat, I'm Superintendent Hamp—and I believe you've met Mr. Neyland." And then he sat down, put his hat on the floor beside his chair, and looked solemnly and rather sadly at Joe.

"Well, what's it all about?" asked Joe, who didn't enjoy being stared at in this fashion. The Superintendent was a new type to him. "I've got to go and work soon, and I'm not even dressed yet."

"An attempt was made last night to break into the Belton-Smith Aircraft premises," the Superintendent began, in a slow and impressive fashion. "Some wire was cut. But the alarm was given, though not in time to secure the man. One or two people caught a glimpse of him as he ran, however, and we have a rough description of him."

"And what's that to do with me?" demanded Joe.

"That's what we want to know. You see, one of the witnesses said the man looked like you, was almost ready to swear it was you. Then again, we found this." And he produced the envelope, from which he extracted the Chesterfield stub and held it up. "A Chesterfield cigarette. Very uncommon round here. Impossible to buy 'em. But we happen to know that you smoke Chesterfields. In fact, I notice there's a packet of 'em on that table. Now there might just possibly be one or two other people round here who smoke Chesterfields, but it's not likely they look just like you. On the other hand, there might be a few men who could be mistaken for you in a bad light, but I don't fancy it's likely that they smoke Chesterfields too. So I think we're entitled to ask a few questions. For instance—where were you last night, Mr. Bolat?"

"I was working up at the *Queen of Clubs,* as usual."

"And you left there just after half-past ten," said the Superintendent, looking as if he knew everything and had never heard of bluffing. "It's after that we're interested in. Come on, now."

"I came back here," said Joe, still looking pretty confident.

"Quite so." And the Superintendent suddenly pointed an enormous forefinger. "But I gather you didn't get back here until about quarter to twelve." And the bluff worked. Joe, who obviously thought we'd already talked to the people downstairs, had to admit that it was round about that time when he returned.

The Superintendent now settled down massively, as if willing to spend years in that chair. "It's the time in between that interests us, you see. Now be careful, Mr. Bolat. You'd be surprised at the number o' people who begin to trip themselves up—sometimes innocent people too—just at this point. All we want's the plain truth. Then if you've done no wrong, then it'll do you no harm." And he waited.

Joe couldn't take it. If he'd been under suspicion of committing some ordinary crime, he'd have told us to get on with the job of proving he had anything to do with it, but I'd taken care to choose the very thing he was most anxious not to be suspected of having any part in, and now he took a chance and jumped for his alibi.

"I didn't want to get a lady into trouble," he muttered.

"Don't blame you, Mr. Bolat," said the Superintendent. "That's something none of us like to do. But we won't give away any of your little secrets. Now who was the lady and where did you go?"

"One of the regular customers in my bar is a Mrs. Castleside, wife of Major Castleside," he began, "We often have a joke together. She's quite a sport. Well, she was leaving when I was, and she had her car there, and she said she'd give me a lift. She said too she'd something she wanted to ask me. Well, if you must know, she was quite a bit lit. I don't like to say that—specially as she must have had most of it in my bar—but that's a fact. She was lit, all right. And she talked a lot of nonsense, asking me if I heard any gossip about her among the boys in the bar and one thing and another. Well, I didn't like it. And another thing was—she was driving all over the place—couldn't see properly, I guess. She'd gone the wrong way too, though I didn't notice that at first, what with it being so dark and listening to all she had to say. So in the end—and this would be about quarter past eleven—and we were still up by the park by then—I asked her to stop the car, said I was tired and I'd had enough of it, and I got out and walked home."

"And what did she do?" asked the Superintendent.

"She was wild, I guess, and I saw the car go past me, down the hill, not looking as if she knew or cared where she was going. Aw—she was lit." And Joe produced a smile of sorts.

"Did anybody see you get out of the car?"

"If they did, I didn't see them. It was dark and late—you know how it is round here that time."

The Superintendent looked as if he'd only just begun. "And exactly where was it you got out?"

Before Joe could reply, I said: "Back in a minute," and went downstairs. In the kitchen, which hadn't had a good turn out for a long time, I found Joe's landlady, who was a youngish woman and gave me the impression that she'd found life disappointing. Perhaps Joe had disappointed her.

"Joe's dressing," I told her, "and he wants the shoes he wore last night."

"I've only just cleaned them now," she said, and handed me a pair of black shoes that had been cleaned after a fashion. I tucked them under my arm, then closed the kitchen door carefully behind me. Several overcoats were hanging, bunched together, in the hall. I tried one of them, a black one and the smartest. Joe was getting careless. In one pocket was a pair of gloves, and in the other a short but heavy length of rubber, which went straight into my own pocket. Then I went to the mat behind the front door, turning my back to the kitchen, so that the landlady couldn't see what I was doing if she decided to have a peep, and smeared some of that black grease the Superintendent gave me over various parts of both shoes. After that I'd only to wipe the shoes lightly on the mat, clean the grease off my fingers, return the envelope to my pocket, and travel upstairs. But I didn't let the other two see the shoes.

It was clear they'd reached a deadlock, as I thought they would. Joe was sticking to his story that he'd left Sheila's car at about quarter-past eleven near the park. He looked fairly confident. The Superintendent did too, but I could see that he was beginning to be worried and had had about enough.

"I've just told him," said the Superintendent, "that Mrs. Castleside's car, with her in it, went into the canal, just this side of the Charters works. And he says he doesn't know anything about that."

"Well, how could I, when I left her about a couple of miles away?" Joe protested. "I surely am sorry to hear she's drowned, but she was lit all right, as I told you, and almost anything could have happened to her. In fact, I begged her to let me drive." He was beginning to feel fine now, ready to invent anything.

Well, the Superintendent had done his stuff, and now it was my turn to do mine, and to change the key. He'd had it smooth and come out smiling. Now he could have it rough.

"Stop lying, you rat," I shouted, standing over him, but still keeping the shoes behind my back. "I'll tell you when you got out of the car—and where. You got out of the car just before half-past eleven, and I can show you the place where you got out, not twenty-five yards from the canal."

This wiped the grin off his face and began to rattle him, as I intended it should. "You're too careless, Joe," I went on, like somebody in a gangster picture, "and now you're all washed up. You didn't notice all that black grease near where you stopped— couldn't see it in the dark, I guess—but you might have noticed that some of it was sticking to your shoes. Yes, these shoes. Look!" And I jabbed them in his face, where all his confidence now withered and died. I had him on the run.

"You didn't leave the car when it was anywhere near the park, did you?" I flung at him. "You left it near the place where it pitched into the canal. Didn't you? Don't tell any more lies. I can prove you were there. It's sticking out a mile."

He ran his tongue over his lips. He didn't know where he was now, and I didn't intend him to find out. "All right," he muttered, "it was all just like I said, only instead of me leaving her near the park it was near the canal."

"Oh, so you were down there, eh?" said the Superintendent. "You admit it? Anything else?"

"No, there isn't anything else," said Joe, talking fast. "I've told you all I know. She was lit. I had to get out. She couldn't drive right. I said to her——"

I hurled his shoes on the floor and put my hand over his face and pushed him back into his chair. "I'll tell you what you said to her, you rat. You told her that if she didn't get you the information you wanted, you'd tell all you knew about her." I could see that shot going home. "And she said she wouldn't, and not only that, but she'd go straight from there and tell the police what you wanted her to do. And you knew she meant it. So there was only one thing to do, you thought, and you did it. You knocked her unconscious, started up the car, steered it from the running-board, then jumped and let it go over into the canal. And this is what you knocked her out with—look—this!" And I pushed that length of rubber in his face.

That's where Joe fell apart. I'd kept him on the run so fast that he'd never had time to consider what sort of evidence we could bring against him. Now he didn't know where he was or what he was doing. He made some hoarse screaming noises that might possibly have had words inside them, and then, apparently forgetting that he wasn't even dressed, he shot out of his chair for the door. But the Superintendent was there first and put a gigantic hand on Joe's shoulder and shook him gently.

"You get some clothes on," said the Superintendent, "and then you can come along with me and make a statement. It'll put you out o' your misery."

I told the Superintendent that I'd take the police car as far as headquarters and then send it back for him and Joe. I wanted to see Perigo as soon as I could, and as we hadn't arranged to meet anywhere and there was no sense in hanging about the wet streets, I knew he'd return to the municipal building. He arrived there only five minutes after I did. I could see he'd got something, but I hurried him out to the lounge of the *Lamb and Pole,* where we could talk in comfort and if necessary use the telephone. After I'd told him about Joe, I asked him if he'd found anything while Diana was out.

"There was a small blue case I couldn't open," he said, grinning, "but I found this stuff in the bottom of a drawer. It's the usual code stuff—some of it from America—enquiring about auntie's rheumatism and uncle's horses and cattle—you know. Our cipher boys will tear through it as if they were reading the Book of the Month."

We looked it over for a minute or two, two quiet chaps doing a bit of business—something in the shop renting line, no doubt—in the lounge of the *Lamb and Pole.*

"You don't like Diana, do you?" he said, as he began putting the letters in order. "I mean, we know she's a bad citizen, and not at all on our side, but you might like her in a way. I had an idea that there might have been amorous passages between you—or were about to be. Humph?"

"No, I don't like her," I replied. "And where she made the mistake—due to conceit, of course—was in not stopping to consider that the amorous passages as you call 'em might have been just as much business on my side as they were on hers. At a guess I'd say that such heart as she has is in the possession of some monocled top-booted specimen of the *Reichswehr,* who's filled her up with hock, told her she's Brunhilde, and then treated her good and rough. And, if you ask me, the pair of 'em are alike in this—that they're clever up to a point, and then, past that point, just stupid to hell. And the trouble is—conceit. They think they're giants striding about among pigmies. They've no savvy. That kid assistant of Diana's, the one with the perpetual cold, has probably got ten times more real sense than Diana has."

"I took an instant dislike to Diana myself," said Perigo reflectively. "But then I never have liked or trusted those large, handsome, well-preserved, cold-eyed women. They keep all their feminine silliness bottled up inside until it turns to sheer insanity. Whereas the women who let out their nonsense, even overdoing it just for fun and cosiness, are often wiser than Solomon when you come really to know 'em. But now what do we do with

Diana, who's still full of pride and confidence, though a trifle worried about Joe, who's merely a useful colleague, of course, not a friend? I should like, if it's all the same to you, to handle Diana myself."

"Just what I was going to suggest," I told him. "My own idea is this—that as soon as she realizes that their little organization here is finished—instead of staying on and bluffing it out, which she easily could do, she's stupid enough to clear out at once and report for further instructions."

"I couldn't agree with you more," he said, grinning. "And I really must ask for a transfer to your department, you seem so sensible and flexible in your methods. Suppose then that in a few minutes I rush back there, more agitated than ever, and tell her that Joe's been arrested and is beginning to talk—not perhaps involving her yet——"

"That's it. Tell her the game's up here and you're clearing out yourself later to-day."

"Meanwhile I offer my help, as a companion great brain among the stupids," he cried, enjoying himself. "I take her to the station, offer to get her her railway ticket, to save time and to avoid suspicion. And then——"

"A wire to the other end, which my guess will be London, and we have her tailed," I said.

"Tailed!" he cried, beaming with pleasure. "How I wish I had the self-confidence to use these tough, professional, Trans-Atlantic terms! Yes, yes, yes, let's have Diana tailed. Now about the woman acrobat, in whom, I must confess, I take a certain aesthetic interest——"

"I leave Fifine to you," I said. "She's yours. By the way, there's a lad in that company called Larry, who has a shrewd notion what's happening and was rather useful to me."

"Larry? Let me think. Oh yes, I remember. I thought him the worst comic I've ever seen on the professional stage. But if we decide to let Fifine carry on for a few more weeks—and I gather that may be the policy—you think Larry might be useful, eh?"

"Yes, it's worth trying. But you'll have to decide. I'll be busy elsewhere to-night. I want to bustle the whole lot of 'em, the whole Gretley job, into the bag before the day's out."

Now he suddenly stopped grinning and posturing and turned himself into a serious elderly man, looking at me with friendly concern. "You're going to be careful, aren't you, Neyland?"

"Not very," I said, hoping I didn't sound too boastful. "I feel like taking rather long chances to-day, Perigo. I never wanted this particular job. Somehow this damned place depresses and irritates me. I want to be done with it. Then I'd like to ask the department to let me go. No more prowling and spy-catching. I feel I've done my share. I have my own work and I'm not bad at it. Why," I said, warming up a bit, "there must be jobs for men like me now out in the Far East. Roads, bridges, railways, to be built. Specially in China. Perigo, I want to be out in the air again, helping to make something. I don't want to dodge the war. I'll go and work in the thick of it. But I must have some air and sunlight and a straight sensible job to do. Otherwise, I'll soon be so sour and stale that I'll hate to live with myself."

"And you've nobody else to live with, eh?" And I saw that he wasn't merely being funny.

"No. I'm alone." I told him a little about Maraquita and the boy, just enough to make him understand I wasn't talking for effect.

"I see." It seemed as if he was about to add something but checked himself. "Well, about getting back to your other work, if the military can help—and I imagine that now it would have to be done under the auspices of the military—I have a friend or two in the War House and might be able to pull a string. And now I'll run away and proceed to put the fear of God into Diana. And that, when you come to think of it," he added, as he stood up, "is what's the matter with her and all her kind. They lack the fear of God."

I put through a call to the police, without asking for the Superintendent, who would still be busy with Joe, and found they had a message from London that I needed badly and got them to repeat it, and then I hurried through the rain back to 15, Raglan Street, where I began my report. Mr. Wilkinson, that great strategist among Gretley railwaymen, now had a scheme for capturing Holland that would have been very promising, if only we happened to have about five hundred large ships that we didn't particularly want elsewhere. Mrs. Wilkinson, who was now quite a pal of mine and had an odd wistful desire to hear tall stories about South America, hadn't any schemes for ending the war quickly, and indeed regarded the war not as a man-made thing at all, but as a huge natural calamity, from which the "poor Germans", as she didn't hesitate to call them, suffered just as we did. Her own war was on the shopping and catering front, and she fought it with a timid persistence and gallantry, never wanting more than her share, but quietly determined to have that share, not for her own sake but in order that her husband and I should be decently fed. There were times, and this was one of them, when I had a suspicion that Mrs. Wilkinson was really about a million years older than the rest of us, let us say the members of the War Cabinet and her husband and Humphrey Neyland, and that somewhere deep down she knew it.

At four o'clock I was in Sherwood Avenue, being shown into the sitting-room by that Austrian housekeeper as if I was a six-foot dose of poison. Margaret Ann Bauernstern was in there, waiting for me, but there wasn't any sign of Otto. This time she was dressed in dark green, with some touches of deep red at the collar and cuffs, and I thought she looked grand. I had the impression, too, that she'd taken some trouble about it, but perhaps to prove that she hadn't, and also perhaps because she'd done some crying just before she left me the night before, her manner was very cool, as if the whole tea-party was a terrible mistake, but that she was too polite to say so.

I could play this game too, in my own way, and started right away to play it. "Where's your brother-in-law, doctor?" I asked, as if I'd come for some overdue rent.

"He'll be down in a minute. We thought it better to wait until you came," she said, with a sweet, sad patience that made me want to throw things at her. "In case, you know, somebody came in unexpectedly and saw him."

I nodded. "And by the way, we've got last night's murderer."

She was astonished and didn't try to pretend she wasn't. "But that's frightfully quick. How did you collect all the evidence?"

"We didn't. But then I guessed last night who it was, and the rest was mostly bounce and bluff. But it worked."

"May I ask who it was?"

"Yes. It was Joe."

"Joe?" And clearly for once I was talking to a woman in Gretley who didn't spend half her time at the *Queen of Clubs*. I explained to her who Joe was, and felt oddly pleased that I had to do it. But I didn't mention the espionage angle, and she didn't ask any questions that would have brought out that angle, though she looked at me curiously once or twice.

The tea arrived before Otto did, so Margaret and I continued our talk, half-intimate, half-antagonistic, over the cups and scones. "What do you do really?" she asked, not looking as if she cared very much or was ready to enjoy the answer.

"I'll tell you exactly before I leave town, if you like," I replied. "But not now."

"You find me irritating, don't you?" she said.

"Yes," I said.

This was the answer she must have expected, yet when it came she was annoyed. I could see the sudden flare of anger in her eyes. "I don't often feel like hitting people," she said, "but there are times when I'd like to hit you."

"Those are the times," I told her, "when I'd be glad if you'd try."

We seemed then to have reached a dead end. Perhaps it was as well that Otto Bauernstern came in. He was about my age, but nervous, short-sighted, studious-looking, and obviously in poor shape. I didn't like him, but that may have been because his sister-in-law looked at him with concern and affection, not at all as she looked at me. He accepted a cup of tea, but didn't seem to know what to do with it. I now caught a look of appeal from Margaret, and it said plainly: "Do be careful with him." But I didn't give her even the smallest nod of reassurance, but merely stared blankly.

"You wanted to talk to me," he began carefully. He had a thick accent, but I don't propose to monkey about with the spelling to give an impression of it.

"I did. Why did you stay on here?"

He closed his eyes and wriggled his shoulders. "What else could I do? Where else could I go?"

"That's a stupid question," said Margaret, addressing me, of course. "It was safer for him to stay here, where we could look after him——"

"No, it wasn't. And you know it wasn't. I want the real answer, Mr. Bauernstern," I said severely, "and if it's any help, I'll tell you my guess at it. You stayed on here, taking the risk of being discovered and being charged with having failed to register, because there was somebody here, in this town, you wanted to keep an eye on."

This hit the target with him all right. But I noticed that it didn't with Margaret, who still looked indignant. "No, that's not true," she began, and then stopped because she saw that it was.

"But Otto, you never told me," she cried.

"Margaret, I could not tell you, could not tell anybody," said Otto, in distress. "But there was a face I saw—quickly, in a flash. Once, at night, in the Charters works. Once again, also at night, in the town."

"So that's why you would insist upon going prowling about at night? I knew there must be something, Otto."

"You see," he said to us both, "I thought I recognized this face. But I could not be sure. And it was very important that I should be sure."

"You had to be certain, for instance, that it had a scarred left cheek, eh?" I asked, and saw the blood leave his face.

"Otto!" she cried in alarm.

He smiled and shook his head. "I am all right really, Margaret, thank you." He took a grip on himself then looked at me. "It is true. But how did you know that it was that man?"

"Well, for that matter," I said slowly, staring hard at him, "how do I know that you used to be a member of the Nazi Party?"

"You beastly liar!" This was from Margaret, of course, and came like the crack of a whip.

I turned on her savagely. "Drop that. I came here to tell the truth and to find out the truth. If you think it beastly, that's just too bad. But there's a lot to be cleared up to-day, and if you can't help me, don't try to hinder me. From now on—please be quiet."

Otto was shaking. I realized now that the situation was complicated by the fact that he was in love with her, and probably had been for some time. Suddenly I felt sorry for him. I think I knew then that there just wasn't any place for him anywhere, that he was as good as dead now.

"I'll be frank with you, Bauernstern," I said quietly, giving him a chance to recover himself. "You thought you saw somebody, a German, a Nazi in fact, you'd once known. That man knew you were here, of course, and decided it was time to report that you'd once been a Nazi. He didn't go to the authorities himself, of course. He couldn't. But he passed on the information. And that's why you suddenly found yourself treated like an enemy alien. It was confirmed to me from London this morning. You left the Party, but you had been a member of it for several years and you'd tried to hide the fact. Unluckily for you, there are two people in London who remembered you as a former Nazi."

Because she was a woman, because she was fond of Otto and now saw him humiliated and crushed, and because this disclosure threatened her memories of her husband and Vienna and all that was precious, she didn't reproach Otto, but turned on me. "I think you're absolutely hateful. And I wish to God I'd never allowed you to come here."

"This interview wouldn't have gone any better in a police station," I said. "And you're not making it any better for him by abusing me. If you find it all so unpleasant, why don't you leave us to it?"

"Because I don't trust you," she blazed.

"No, no, please, Margaret," said Otto. "It is all my fault. It is true I joined the Nazi Party—I was deceived like so many others then—and I had instructions that it should be secret. I kept it from Alfred, then from you. But as soon as they marched into Vienna, and I saw what they really meant to do and what they were, I left the Party. And this wasn't easy to do. But after that I asked for nothing but to work against them, to help to defeat them, to die if necessary in helping to defeat them. Please believe me, Margaret." And he took off his spectacles to wipe his eyes, and immediately had that helpless babyish look which most short-sighted people have without their spectacles. It disarmed her, for she gave him a forgiving, tender smile and put a hand on his for a moment.

"Well, I believe you too," I said, wanting now to leave them to it. "And if you want to help, you can. In fact, what you've been wanting to do is what I want to do. I want to identify the man whose left cheek still has the mark of a deep scar. Now when you caught a glimpse of his face, you remembered somebody. Who was it?"

"I cannot tell you that until I know what authority you have to ask these questions," he replied, with some dignity. "Dr. Bauernstern has said she does not trust you. Why should I trust you? Nobody knows better than I do that Nazi agents are everywhere, even here in England."

I looked at Margaret, who now seemed embarrassed. "Nice work, Dr. Bauernstern. He doesn't trust me now. Two people who knew too much have been killed in this town by Nazi agents during the last few days. Let's wait for a third to be killed—and say *Heil Hitler!*—shall we?" Don't tell me that this was childish stuff, because I know it was. But I was feeling sore.

She didn't reply to me directly, but turned to him. "I told you, Otto, that last night Mr. Neyland was working with Superintendent Hamp, and even seemed to be almost in charge of things. I think——" and she hesitated.

Otto nodded, then looked at me. "This face I saw," he said, "reminded me of a Nazi I had seen several times, Captain Felix Rodel."

"Thanks," I said, business-like now. "Well, I know where he is, and to-night I propose to have a talk to him."

"You wish me to go with you, to identify him?" he asked eagerly. "Where do we go?"

"It's a house I haven't been to yet," I replied. "But I know roughly where it is—about a mile farther out than the Belton-Smith factory. It's called Oakenfield Manor, and it belongs to Colonel Tarlington. And I'll meet you there tonight—just inside the main gate—at nine o'clock."

He repeated these instructions in a rather wondering tone, and then asked: "You have a revolver?"

"Not here with me," I replied. "We're not encouraged to carry guns, and I can get along without 'em. Why?"

"If it is Rodel, then he is a very dangerous man."

"We'll have to take a chance on that," I said, standing up. "I'll expect you up there at nine." I turned to Margaret, who wasn't looking too happy. I didn't expect ever to see her again, and there were things I could have said, but not now. "Thanks for the tea. And—good-bye." And I hurried out. I had an idea that she said something and then followed me out into the hall, but I didn't stop to make certain, but grabbed my hat and overcoat from the stand and charged out into the cold, wet dusk. It was nearly time for the blackout again.

9

I WENT back to Raglan Street to see if there were any messages, and I found a note from the Superintendent, saying that Joe, after stiffening for a time, had finally broken down, signed a confession, and then asked to see a priest. But he'd only confessed to knocking out Sheila and then sending the car into the canal, and hadn't admitted to any espionage or given any information about it. Which meant that there would have to be more bouncing, bluffing and bustling, as I thought there'd have to be. The Superintendent added a message from Perigo, who said that he was dining that night at the *Queen of Clubs* and hoped I'd be able to join him there.

I did, at about half-past seven. We met in the cocktail bar, which was crowded, but not quite its usual self, for a worried-looking girl was trying, without success, to take the place of Joe. But I felt like drinking, and said so to Perigo.

"Why not?" he asked, with his usual cynical grin. "You've had a good day."

"It's not ended yet," I reminded him. "In fact, the big stuff is now to come. And as far as I can see, it can only be played one way, chiefly by bluff. We haven't enough evidence. And they mustn't be given enough time to see that."

"Then you ought to keep bright and sober," he said.

"I don't know about bright, but sober—yes. Even so, I feel like drinking." And I stared gloomily at the crowd, mostly youngsters in uniform with some girl friends, clustered thick round the bar. "I guess I feel old and stale and sour to night. I'm not happy about the damned war, I'm not happy about this country, and I'm not happy about myself."

"When I've brought you the same again," said Perigo, "only perhaps a little stronger, I'll talk to you." And he nipped off to the bar, and within a shorter time than anybody else there could have made it, for he'd a way with him, he was back again with two of the same, only stronger. "Now then," he began cheerfully, "let me talk to you like a wise old uncle. We shall win the war—that is, we shall definitely defeat the Axis, if that's what you mean—because a combination of the United States, Russia, China and ourselves can't, in my opinion, be beaten. Next, this country has the choice, during the next two years, of coming fully to life and beginning all over again or of rapidly decaying and dying on the same old feet. It can only accomplish the first by taking a firm grip on about fifty thousand important, influential, gentlemanly persons and telling them firmly to shut up and do nothing if they don't want to be put to doing some most unpleasant work. In my off moments—and this isn't one of them—I myself could justly be included among those persons. As for you, you're neither young enough to be wisely foolish nor old enough to be foolishly wise. And you need a change. And perhaps some woman you can respect and admire, to tell you that you're wonderful. Now let's seize that table I ordered. We'll have one more good dinner, war or no war, before this place closes down or serves nothing but watery beer."

We were in the middle of dinner when Perigo said: "Our friend Mrs. Jesmond is leaving her boys to pay us a visit. What do we say to her, d'you think, Neyland?"

"Anything that comes into our heads," I grunted. "She's due for a few surprises."

But it was she who gave us the biggest surprise. We'd been talking some time, however, before this happened. She began by telling us that she was worried about Joe, for it was the first time he hadn't turned up to work.

"You can stop worrying about Joe," I said. "He's under arrest. You'd better forget about Joe, Mrs. Jesmond."

"Curiously enough," said Perigo, "I was never deceived by Joe's manner."

"Neither was I, for that matter," said Mrs. Jesmond calmly. "A most unpleasant man, I always thought him, probably most vicious in his habits. But good at his work. And this place won't seem the same without him."

"I'm afraid this place won't be the same, anyhow," said Perigo, grinning at her.

"What do you mean, Mr. Perigo?"

"I don't think you'll be allowed to keep it going, y'know," he told her. "After all, we are in the middle of a war. Don't think I'm ungrateful. I've had some very pleasant dinners here—and found the place very useful. I think Neyland here has too. But you'll just have to go out of management, I'm afraid."

"And out of the Black Market too," I said, loading my fork with more chicken. "No, no, that's not my line of business—looking for Black Marketeers—but if I heard you were still carrying on, I'd have to report you."

"Well, I don't propose to thank you," said Mrs. Jesmond, who looked as sleek and handsome as ever. "I think you're a swine."

"Well now," I said, "I think you're an exquisite, downy sort of creature, but just not worth your very expensive keep. You're one of the luxuries we can't afford."

"He doesn't mind," said Perigo, "but I regret it, my dear Mrs. Jesmond. I've always liked you better than you liked me. I'm not as young as I might be, of course, and there I admire your taste. But I'm appreciative."

She regarded him coldly, then turned to me. "There's a rumour going round that Sheila Castleside's dead. Is it true?"

"Yes. She was pulled out of the canal last night—drowned."

"You sound pretty cool about it, considering that you spent about an hour last night with her in one of our bedrooms here."

"I'm not very cool about it. And I spent that hour talking very seriously to her." I looked her in the eye. "Anything else you'd like to know?"

"Yes. Have you seen Diana Axton to-day?"

"No, I haven't, but Perigo has. Why?"

"She rang me up this morning, just before lunch, but I was out, and she wouldn't leave a message."

"I could probably give you the message, my dear lady," said

Perigo. "At least I can imagine what it would be. She probably wanted to tell you that she was leaving Gretley this afternoon—for good."

Just a flicker, you couldn't call it more than that, passed across Mrs. Jesmond's smooth face and perhaps troubled the depths of her velvety eyes. Then she looked from one to the other of us, searchingly. "You two know something. I mean, about Diana. You'd better tell me. You can trust me to keep it to myself. I've a good reason for saying that."

Perigo and I exchanged quick glances. It was a unanimous resolution not to spill anything. Mrs. Jesmond, always sensitive to such things if not to many other more important things, knew at once what we'd resolved.

"Diana's a fool, as you may have noticed," she said, with only the slightest hint of nervousness. "She was fascinated by the Nazis at one time. Then she went to America—I hoped to learn a little sense. I think there was a man involved. When she came back, she told me she wanted to open that idiotic shop here. I thought then that she looked like making a fool of herself, but it wasn't any business of mine."

"I wonder if that's your trouble," Perigo murmured. "That nothing seems to be any business of yours. So long, of course, as you're nicely sheltered, fed, clothed and amused. This is much more Neyland's point of view than mine, really. I'm merely interpreting the look on his face."

She rose, quite calmly, and now looked at me. "I wondered last night—when I saw you with her—because I knew she wasn't your type. What's she been up to?"

"She couldn't forget Nuremberg and the master race," I replied. "And she was selling us out. Some do it for money, some out of fear or ambition, but I think she was doing it because of a mixture of romantic drivel and sheer conceit."

"Quite right," said Mrs. Jesmond, preparing to leave us. "Diana was always like that. I used to warn her. You see, she's my sister. A year or two younger than I am, of course, and much sillier. Well, one of the Air Force boys has just been telling me about quite a nice little hotel, close to one of their stations, up in Scotland. I might try that. A marvellous woman who came to Cannes—everybody went to her—told me about three and a half years ago that I'd only five more years to live. That leaves me about a year and a half, doesn't it? Quite long enough. I'm getting frightfully bored. Good night."

We stared after her, as she floated like a swan back to her table and her young men. "I'm old enough to know better," said Perigo, rather mournfully, "but that woman fascinates me. I must find out if she does go to Scotland—and where—and then the first holiday I get, I shall go up there to see what's happening to her. If the Air Force happens to be on duty, we could sit over the fire and she could tell me a few things about herself, just a chapter or two of her exquisite and appalling autobiography. But before she goes, I ought to introduce her to Superintendent Hamp, who is just as extraordinary in his own way."

"Talking of the Superintendent," I said, "I wonder if you'd tell him from me that if he doesn't hear from me before about half-past ten to-night, I wish he'd come out to Colonel Tarlington's house."

"If he does," said Perigo, "I shall come with him. Unless you'd like me to come along with you, Neyland."

"No, thanks, Perigo. I can only see one way of doing this—and it's all very chancy and might easily fail—and it's no use both of us showing our hands. If we don't meet later tonight, look me up at 15, Raglan Street, in the morning, if you've nothing better to do. And thanks for the dinner, which might easily be the last good one either of us'll have for some time."

"Still feeling sober?" he asked, as we left the dining-room.

"Sober, and depressed as hell," I replied.

I caught a bus at the corner, and luckily the fellow sitting next to me knew where Oakenfield Manor was, and told me when to get out. It was as black as ever, and squally with icy rain. The turning into the manor drive, he'd told me, was about a quarter of a mile to the left down this side road. Possibly it was only a quarter of a mile, but it seemed much farther than that to me, as I plodded and peered and felt myself getting wetter every moment. When I found the entrance it was just after nine, for I managed to catch a glimpse of my watch in the shelter of the gateway. This was where Otto should have met me. After waiting

about ten minutes, I decided he must have thought I meant somewhere nearer the house, so I went up the drive, staring about in
the gloom until my eyes ached, and finally searching either side
of the front door. No Otto. Perhaps his loving sister-in-law had
persuaded him that he was too precious a being to risk himself
on such jaunts.

I wasn't quite sure what my next move ought to be now, when
there was no Otto to do any identifying, but I went quietly prowling round the side of the house, which didn't appear to be very
large, until at last I found myself somewhere at the back, among
the outhouses. From one of these, presumably from under a
door, was coming a thin shaft of light, tiny enough, but as clear
in that blackness as a beacon signal. I went along as quietly as I
could to that door, which wasn't locked. What I did then wasn't
very clever, but the cold wet night, all my waiting about and
prowling round, and the absence of Otto Bauernstern, had con-
spired together to make me feel impatient and probably careless.
Anyhow, I went inside.

It was a longish place, which had once been a big stable, and
now seemed to be used merely for storing old furniture and
lumber, and at the other end, away from the door, as a workshop.
There was a bench underneath the shuttered window at that
end, and a man was at work there. At first I couldn't recognize
him. The light, coming from one high, dusty bulb between us,
was poor, though he had another light shaded to illuminate the
bench itself. But when he jumped up, I saw that it was the man
I'd met at Diana Axton's the night before, the man with the scar.

"What is it?" he called sharply. I saw now that he was wearing
a houseman's short coat.

I took a step or two forward. "I want to talk to you," I said,
removing my hat and shaking the rain off it.

He recognized me, and I knew in a flash that somebody,
probably Diana Axton, had told him something to make him
suspicious of me. His attitude was very different from what it
had been when he parted the night before. That ought to have
warned me, but somehow I didn't care. I had to jump in with
both feet.

"I am Morris, Colonel Tarlington's man-servant," he said.

"No, you're not," I said recklessly. "You're Captain Felix Rodel   "

He must have had the revolver, a small one as I afterwards discovered, in his hand ever since he faced me, for no sooner had I spoken his name than he fired. I felt a blow on my left shoulder that almost spun me right round, and I knew he'd hit me there. I dropped down on my hands and knees, with a hot ebbing feeling in my shoulder, and waited for the next and final shot. I never saw Otto arrive, for I wasn't facing the door, but I heard him come blundering in and shout "Rodel!" Then the revolver cracked again, and I twisted round just in time to see Otto fall. I turned again, and now Rodel was moving slowly forward to finish us off. There was a roar from the space just behind me, deafening under that low roof, and I saw Rodel slowly toppling. He gave a huge jerk, twitched once or twice, and then was quite still. He was dead. Otto, firing from the ground, and with what sounded like a large-calibre gun, must have blasted the inside out of him. But what about Otto?

Feeling dizzy and sickish, I pulled myself across to where he was lying. He'd been hit in the chest and obviously hadn't long to live. He didn't recognize me. Already he was somewhere else, muttering explanations in a German I couldn't follow. Suddenly he smiled, as if they were all friends again wherever he was and had begun playing Mozart, and a minute later he was dead.

I knew I was bleeding, and my shoulder was throbbing away, but for a moment or two I didn't feel like attending to myself. I stared from one to the other of these dead Germans, so far from anything they really understood, already stiffening and growing cold in this old stable somewhere in the English blackout. One of them, the soldier-spy, had been lost in some mad Teutonic dream of world empire and domination. The other, the mild peering chemist, had taken one turning after another and had come to the dead end. And had saved my life. For what?

There was a tap near the bench, and I soaked my handkerchief at it, and then dabbed away at my shoulder, finally wedging my folded handkerchief against the wound and trying to tighten my shirt and coat over it to keep the handkerchief in position. I had a look at the bench, and found that Rodel had been making a small wooden chest, a sort of toy strong-box, which could be used for keep-sakes. Just an innocent Saturday night hobby, which probably made him feel that he hadn't yet lost all contact with some old, simple, sensible life. I guessed, rightly as it turned out, that he had only slipped across here for a little time and so had probably left some back door of the house unlocked. I made my way slowly across the paved yard, carrying my hat and finding the cold rain refreshing, and didn't take long to discover that unlocked door.

As I expected, there was nobody in the house, and I didn't see why I shouldn't wait in comfort there for its owner. But first I found a wash-place just off the hall, and cleaned my hands and face and brushed my hair. The face in the mirror, white and pinched, didn't seem to belong to me. It had a half-insane look, but though I felt empty and tired and sad, I didn't feel half insane. But there it was. I needed a drink badly, but didn't feel like exploring this man's house to find one, so I sat there in the hall, laboriously filling and lighting a pipe that I found I couldn't enjoy, and waited to hear the colonel's car. After about ten minutes I heard it, and unlocked the front door, then returned to my seat.

Colonel Tarlington, spruce and rosy and fragrantly clouded with cigar smoke, came striding in, and wasn't markedly taken aback when he saw me sitting there. I noticed that he didn't lock the front door after him.

"Well, well, Neyland, isn't it? Where's that fellow of mine?"

"He's out at the back somewhere," I said.

The colonel led the way into a room that was partly a library, and I saw that a door at the back opened into a smaller room, where, I imagine, he spent most of his time. I could see a big desk in there. It was from there, too, that he brought out some drinks. He told me to take off my overcoat, but I refused. When Rodel had fired at me, my overcoat had been wide open, and now I had it carefully buttoned to cover the blood-soaked lapel of my coat underneath. His manner was fairly easy, but he couldn't help treating me as if I were his inferior, and knew it. His very English rosiness, like a kind of bloom, gave him at first a false appearance of warmth, but now I was taking note of the cold pride in his pale blue eyes, which weren't unlike Diana Axton's.

He was, in fact, the elderly male of the same tribe. I refused, with secret reluctance, the drink he offered me, clearly to his surprise. Somebody, probably Diana, had told him I liked a drink. But I wasn't going to drink with him.

"Rather casual, that man of mine," he said, making conversation until we'd settled down. "But a thoroughly good fellow really. Morris—a Welshman. My batman in the last war."

"Lloyd Morris. Late Cardigan Regiment."

"That's right. See you've been talking to him. Queer fellow, of course, not an English type, quite different."

"Colonel Tarlington," I said slowly, "your batman in the last war, Lloyd Morris, died three years ago in the Cardiff Infirmary."

"What are you talking about, Neyland?" It wasn't a man blustering, but a man pretending to bluster. I was watching his eyes. This wasn't going to be easy, and I felt rotten, almost lightheaded, and that shoulder was no joke. "I dare say some Lloyd Morris died in Cardiff Infirmary—probably half a dozen of 'em did—but this one didn't. Damn it, I ought to know the name of my own man-servant."

"You do know his name. It's Felix Rodel."

That hit him hard, but he didn't show too much. "Look here, Neyland, you're talking nonsense, and you're looking queer. I suggest that if you've anything important to say to me, you'd better say it and then get off to bed at once. Touch of 'flu, I'd say. Might be running a temperature."

"I might be. But Felix Rodel's the name, colonel. A member of the Nazi Party in good standing. Engaged over here on espionage. You turned him into Morris."

I heard a noise outside, and I think he heard it too, but he didn't bother about it. He began shouting, apparently in an apoplectic fury, Colonel Blimp full steam ahead, but really still quite cool and wary behind the purpling mask. "My God, man, you must be out of your mind. Coming out here talking that drivel! D'you realize that if I'd a witness here I could take you to court and ask for substantial damages. I could—and—by God, man—I would too. Why, if anybody heard you——"

But at that moment his witness arrived, for there was a light knock on the door, and then in walked Margaret Bauernstern.

"I'm sorry," she said to the colonel, "but I couldn't make any-body hear, and I was so worried that I had to walk in." Then she stared, frowning, at me. "What's the matter?"

I shook my head. "I'll tell you later."

"Where's Otto? I suddenly felt terribly worried, and I had to come out here myself. Where is he?"

"Sit down," I said. "And try to take it easy."

Colonel Tarlington took a pace towards us. "What is all this?" he began, but I managed to check him.

"You sit down too, Colonel. Here's your witness, so you're all set." I turned to Margaret, who was sitting on the edge of her chair, staring at me. "I'm sorry, Margaret. But Otto's dead. That Nazi he was looking for, Rodel, shot him. Then he killed Rodel, and died soon afterwards. He saved my life."

She was white and still. "What about you?"

"I'll be all right. I have to finish this. Don't go."

She nodded. I turned to the colonel, who'd now dropped his blustering act and was sitting rigid, watchful, ice-cold. I had to drive him now until he broke, and I didn't feel I'd much driving power left to do it with, but it had to be done here and now.

"It's no use, Colonel," I began. "You're finished. If you don't listen now, you'll have to listen soon in court. Rodel's dead, out in that stable he used as a workshop. Joe's been arrested, and he's talked. We've let Diana Axton leave the town, for London, just to shadow her."

"All this is very interesting," he said, "but I don't know what it's all about or how it concerns me."

"It was you who told everybody your old batman, Morris, was with you, when, in fact, it was a Nazi, Rodel. But that's only the start of it, Colonel. Take, for instance, our friend Diana Axton——"

"If that's the woman who keeps the shop," he said, "I've been introduced to her, and once or twice she rang me up about vari-ous small matters——"

"Such as my getting a job with the Charters Electrical Com-pany," I said.

"Well, why not? But apart from that, I don't know the woman. I've never spent five minutes alone with her, and I've never set foot in her shop, and I'll defy you to prove the contrary."

"You didn't need to go into the shop," I told him. "When she had a message for you, it was there in the window. It was a nice little set-up. There were you, the local great man, on the Board of the Charters Electrical Company, with Rodel, the real brains of the act, the man who planned it and explained it to you all *in America,* comfortably installed as your man-servant. There was Diana in *Prue's Gift Shop,* and who would ever suspect the kind of woman who keeps that kind of shop? And there was Joe, always the life and soul of any party, in his bar at the *Queen of Clubs,* where the drinks were always moving fast and the Air Force and Army boys couldn't help talking a bit of shop. And then there were always ways of giving you people fresh instructions. This week a female acrobat, Fifine, was using the stage of the Hippodrome as a post office. No, don't tell me you've never exchanged a word with the woman. I know you haven't. It wasn't necessary. But Rodel, who was getting over-confident and careless, couldn't resist having a few drinks last night with an old pal."

"I'm quite fascinated, as you see, Neyland," he said, in a small dry voice, "but where I come into all this nonsense, I simply can't imagine."

"Then I caught you out nicely this morning, colonel," I went on, in an easy bantering tone. "You may remember that I said I'd heard that when Scorson of the Ministry of Supply spoke to you on Wednesday night, he put in a good word for me, for that Charters job, and you said that he had and that it had just made the difference. But——" And I deliberately paused.

He fell for it at once. "There's no question of catching anybody out," he said contemptuously. "You sounded so pleased because you'd heard that Scorson had recommended you to me that night, that of course I pretended he had, out of ordinary politeness. What is there in that?"

"Enough to hang you, Tarlington," I said, dropping the bantering tone, which had served its purpose. "Suppose I tell you now that Scorson *did* recommend me for that job during his talk on Wednesday, where are you? It's quite obvious you don't know where you are about that talk, simply because you never took that personal call yourself. And now I'll tell you why. Olney, of

the Special Branch, who had been put into the Belton-Smith factory as a foreman, came to see you that night, ostensibly to talk
to you about addressing a canteen meeting, but really because
he'd begun to suspect you. He knew something about Rodel—
for there were several references in his notebook to that scar—
but he didn't know he was here in this house with you. And so
you, who'd begun to wonder about Olney, kept Rodel out of the
way. Olney never saw him, and he never saw Olney. That's why,
as soon as Olney left you and you realized that he knew too much
and would have to be killed, you couldn't give Rodel the job of
running Olney down on the road, but had to go and do it yourself. This was awkward because you were expecting a personal
call from Scorson at about quarter to nine. But then you saw that
if Rodel accepted the personal call—and on a long-distance line
any rough imitation of your voice would do—not only could
you go out yourself, but that you were also creating a pretty
good alibi. But you made several mistakes, colonel. You didn't
succeed in persuading the police that Olney had been knocked
down in that part of the town where you finally dumped him.
And, what was more important, when you picked him up and
slung him into your car, not far from the *Queen of Clubs,* you
didn't know that the last thing poor Olney did was to throw away
his notebook. The police found this notebook and I had a good
look through it. Olney was very shrewd and had been on the job
for months. You can imagine," I said, looking him in the eye, for
this was the supreme bluff, "that you had a conspicuous place in
those notes of his."

He was still thinking hard, I could see, but he hadn't a word to
say. I was nearly all in, for my shoulder was bleeding fast again,
and I felt my head singing and whirling. But I had to keep him
retreating and bewildered.

"Then again," I went on, "your first instinct about that
lighter you took out of Olney's pocket was the right one. That
was no ordinary lighter, and you can't buy one anything like it
anywhere." I showed him my own. "Every man in the counter-
espionage service, no matter what branch or department he
comes from, is provided with one of these lighters and a certain
formula of questions and answers. I knew Olney had one of these

lighters because he and I had gone through the usual recognition test that Wednesday afternoon. Now you took that lighter out of his pocket and kept it because you had an instinctive feeling that there was something important about it, perhaps because it obviously wasn't the kind of lighter that a man pretending to be a factory foreman would carry about with him. Then, later that night, when you met Joe, you'd had time to examine the lighter and to decide that it was merely a pretty little gadget, but you didn't want to keep it, because it had belonged to Olney, so you gave it to Joe. And remember," I added, as severely as I could, "we've got Joe now on a murder charge. He's confessed. He's talked."

The room went black for a moment. I heard a cry from Margaret and then discovered that she was standing over me. I made a great effort and managed to steady everything, including myself.

"No, no, just leave me alone for a minute or two," I said to her. "Rodel hit me in the shoulder and it's bleeding hard again, but I can see this through. Sit down, please, Margaret." She didn't, but remained standing just behind me. I looked at the colonel, who was sitting there like a man turned to stone.

"I wouldn't be here, in this condition, telling you all this," I said to him, "if the whole case wasn't in the bag, with all the essential evidence already in the hands of the police. I only came—and stayed on—because I like to round off my own jobs myself. Vanity, if you like. Probably that's my weakness. Yours is pride, Tarlington. You see yourself as a rightly privileged person, quite different from the common crowd, and you're ready to pay a big price to keep your privileges. You hate democracy, and all it means. There's something fundamentally stiff-necked, arrogant, dominating and conceited about you that just can't take it. When Hess flew over here, he was looking for people like you. It isn't that you're pro-German, unpatriotic in the ordinary sense. In the last war, which seemed to you a straightforward nationalistic affair, I've no doubt you did a good job. But this war, which is quite different, was too much for you. I heard you speak the other night. You only said what a lot of people of your kind keep on saying—telling the people to keep in their old place, to fight and work and suffer to maintain something they no longer believe in—and, if you ask me, every word of this stuff is worth another gun or whip to Hitler and his gang. But you're a bit more intelligent and a bit more unscrupulous than most of your kind, and so you realized that to keep all you wanted to keep, it meant that the people mustn't win and that Fascism mustn't lose. So they persuaded you that a Nazi victory only meant that you'd have the sort of England you've always wanted, with yourself and a few others securely on top, and the common people kept in their place for ever. And you went down the old steep way . . . the well-known toboggan run . . . insane pride . . . lies . . . treachery . . . murder. . . . And you've lost, Tarlington, you've lost . . . and if you don't want . . . to be remembered . . . as an English Quisling . . . there's only one way . . . one way . . . out . . ."

I couldn't have added another word, for the whole room was throbbing, between bright dazzling light and blackness, just like my shoulder, but luckily it wasn't necessary. I saw without surprise, like a man in a confused dream, that the door had opened, and that the massive figure of the Superintendent filled the doorway. And I knew, even then, that it only needed that.

"All right, Superintendent," I heard the colonel say. "Just a minute." And he went into the other room.

There was a shot before anybody had a chance to move.

Apparently I was heard to say: "Well, there wasn't any other way of doing it." But I don't remember. I was out.

10

I SPENT the next three days, there in Margaret's house, oscillating between a temperature and a temper. When my temperature came down, my temper rose. This was partly due to the fact that I objected to staying in bed. But the nurse they installed had something to do with it. She may have been a good nurse, but as a companion she was poison. She was a large red-haired woman with a lot of teeth and freckles, and she treated me as if I was a spoilt darling about ten years old. With the least encouragement, she'd have read some jolly tale for the bairns to me. She tried to stop me smoking, but I won that battle. But with the help of Margaret, she did prevent anybody getting in there to see me and offer me a little adult conversation. Then again, Margaret was now just the doctor in charge of the case. We might never have seen each other before. There were times, when the temperature was well up, that I did begin to imagine that I'd dreamt everything that had happened in Gretley, that I never had seen this woman doctor with the severe face and the brilliant eyes before, that I'd been popped into some nursing-home and was simply delirious. So when the temperature came down, I thrashed about and growled, and was told not to be naughty by that red-headed monster.

But on the fourth day, Wednesday, the nurse told me she was leaving. She didn't really think I was fit to be left, but she had another and more urgent case. I said good-bye to her, quite nicely and politely, in the afternoon. Margaret, who was very busy, was out. I wished she'd come back, but, anyhow, it was peaceful without that nurse, and presently I dozed off. When I woke up, the light was on and the curtains had been drawn, there was some tea in the room, and flanking the tea were the Superintendent and Perigo, who now gave the impression of being an experienced comedy team, the one so large, heavy, slow, the other so slight, quick, odd. I was very glad to see them.

"We've been calling all the time, y'know, Neyland," said the Superintendent, "only they wouldn't let us see you."

"I know," I grunted. "Lot of damned nonsense. It was that nurse."

"Oh no, it was Dr. Bauernstern," said the Superintendent. "She put her foot down. Didn't she, Perigo?"

"She was most emphatic," said Perigo. "Flew at me like a fury once. Plenty of character there, y'know, Neyland."

"I'll take your word for it," I grumbled. "She just trots in and out of here with a poker face. Had no talk with her at all. Not that I'd know what to say even if I did have any talk with her. What's happening, for God's sake?"

"Austwick of your department spoke to me on the telephone," said Perigo, grinning, "and I told him you'd had enough of this counter-espionage work. And of course he said Nonsense, you were much too valuable to lose."

"Which is true enough," said the Superintendent. "Look at

this business here. And the joke is—though I can't say it makes me want to laugh much—that if you'd been trained in police work, you'd never ha' brought it off, simply because the evidence was never good enough. Now was it?"

"Good enough? There wasn't any real evidence, half the time," I told him. "Not your kind, anyhow. There was plenty of psychological evidence, though. And that took us where we wanted to go. The rest was luck and impudence. But what did you reply to old Austwick then, Perigo?"

"I repeated to him exactly what you'd said to me. Then he said the department would grant you a good leave, so that you could have a holiday——"

"Holiday! How can anybody have a holiday in the middle of this mess? And where could you go? What could you do?"

"You could follow Mrs. Jesmond," said Perigo. "I hear she's packing, which means, of course, that somebody else is packing for her."

"That woman doesn't fascinate me as she does you," I said. "In fact, I don't want to see her again—except behind a counter, making cocoa for workers on the night shift. And tell Austwick from me that I don't want a holiday. I want work, but my own kind of work from now on. Could he stop me getting a commission in the Sappers?"

"He could and he would," said Perigo. "Besides, aren't you a bit on the old side——"

"Old side!" I shouted, glaring at him. "Good God! Because you find me stuck here in bed—and I'll be up tomorrow, you'll see—you mustn't begin to talk like that. Old side! Why——"

But then Margaret walked in, and this time without her doctor face. I supposed that was because we had company, but I was glad to see her like that again, even if she wasn't doing it for me.

"You shouldn't be shouting like that," she said, but quite human about it.

"He's very cross this afternoon," said Perigo, grinning at her with all his porcelain. "And he says you just trot in and out of here with a poker face."

"They get like that at these times," said the Superintendent, who'd suddenly turned himself now into a medical authority.

She nodded, smiling a little. "We always expect it."

"Don't sit there talking about me as if I were an idiot or something," I said irritably. "If I'm out of temper, it's not because of my physical condition. As a matter of fact, I feel fine. I'll be up to-morrow."

"You won't," she said promptly.

"I will. And of course I'm very grateful indeed for the way you've looked after me, and hope I haven't been too much of a nuisance. But, I repeat, if I'm out of temper——"

"And you are," she said.

"Yes, I am. But it's because—oh, it's because of that old spider, Austwick, and his spy-catching, and this dark wet hole of a place, Gretley, and the bone-headed way we're running this war, muddling and messing in the same old fashion and making the people feel frustrated, and it's because—oh, I need some work to do——"

"You need a thoroughly good rest," she said, promptly again.

Perigo got up, looking at us rather maliciously, I thought, and said: "There are one or two ends in this business I can tie up for you, Neyland. And when I'd finished talking to Austwick, I did try to pull a string or two for you."

"Thanks. Come and see me to-morrow, and tell me all about Diana Axton and Fifine and the rest."

The Superintendent put a hand bigger than a family's weekly allowance of meat on my arm. "Lad," he began surprisingly, "just take notice o' the doctor. I'm not saying you're not clever, 'cos you pulled off stunts that I couldn't have pulled off between now and Christmas, but she's got a lot more sense than you. Now, is there anything you want that we can get you?"

But I couldn't think of anything they could get for me, though I could think of plenty of things I wanted. Margaret went out with them, and I seemed to have ample time in which to think of this and that before she came back. But instead of straightening things out in my more rational mind, I went into a kind of daydream, seeing myself in some fine nameless faraway place, full of light and air, working hard at some sensible big civil engineering job, something that made life easier and fuller and happier for thousands of folk who so far hadn't had much of a chance, and

Margaret was with me there, slogging away all day at her job too, then talking things over with me, outside some mysterious little house of ours, in the cool and quiet of the evening. And I came out of this day-dream to see her sit by my bedside and look at me gravely.

"What were you thinking about?" she asked.

"It doesn't make a lot of sense," I said, "but I might as well tell you." And I did, with rather more detail and colour than I can remember now.

She looked at me with soft bright eyes, her whole face relaxed and lovely. "I understand all that," she said. "But why was I there?"

"Forget it," I said, and looked somewhere else, though God knows where.

"Why should I forget it?" she asked, and then, after a pause: "I think I ought to warn you—that I know much more about you now than I did last Saturday. Mr. Perigo and the Superintendent have told me things about you."

"They don't know much about me," I said. "Not that there's a hell of a lot to know."

"They told me enough to make me understand why you're so—so *sour*, as you call it. I'm rather sour too."

"You're about as sour—as sour—as treacle pudding."

She laughed. "Now that's something. Nobody's ever compared me with treacle pudding before."

"Well, I like treacle pudding. If you've got any treacle, let's have one to-morrow. In the meantime, I know more about you than you'd think. I've thought a lot about you lately. The trouble with you——"

"Oh dear, it begins like that, does it?"

"Yes, it begins like that. The trouble with you is this—and, mind, I'm not going to pull any punches—that out of respect and admiration and veneration and the rest of it, you married a man—yes, all right, a great man, if you like—years older than you, a man who'd had most of his life—and you think that was the grand love-affair, when it probably wasn't any kind of a real love-affair, and now that it's gone, you think you've had most of your life too, and that most of you, the deep feminine part, can be just packed away in ice."

"I see. Now what about you?"

"Me? I'm just unlucky, that's all. I'd better close down."

"I'd much rather you didn't," she said, not smiling at all, but looking at me with those great shining eyes. I dodged them, only to find myself staring at her hand, which I'd noticed before, long-fingered, slight, yet so strong and skilful in its own way. I reached out and touched it, as if to make sure it was really there.

"All right, but you won't like it much," I said slowly. "I've waited for ten years—no, fifteen perhaps—not longer because before that I wouldn't have appreciated you—to meet you. And I've been spending a good part of the last week kidding myself that I didn't know this. But I knew it all right, deep inside. And what good is it now that it's here? What's the use of trying to unpack you out of the ice, or smashing and trampling about——"

She laughed. "I'm sorry, but that's such a good description of you, that smashing and trampling. And yet, of course, you're really very sensitive or you wouldn't know it's like that. I'm sorry. Please go on."

"I only want to say—what's the use of bringing you to life, for that's what it amounts to, emotionally, anyhow, when I haven't anything dependable to offer you. Not a thing. I'm planning even now to go as far away from here as I can, unless, of course, the war really needs me round here. And I don't even write a good letter."

"You mightn't believe it—though you haven't even heard me talk properly yet—but I write very good letters."

"I don't want your very good letters," I growled at her. "I want you. And just because you *are* you—and this time it's real—I know there's no point in grabbing what I want. And why haven't I heard you talk properly yet?"

"Because I was always so terrified."

"You mean, because of Otto and the police and so on?"

"That, partly, and sometimes your manner frightened me. But there was something else, more important to me. You see, I could feel myself beginning to stop thinking the things about myself that you say I think. About having had most of my life. And the ice. There really isn't much ice left."

"Come here, woman," I shouted, for she'd risen and walked away as she spoke the last sentence. "Come here, or I'll leap out of bed."

"You won't," she said quickly, and hurried across to me. And she tried to put back that poker face, but I soon stopped that. Then, after a little time, she said: "I must go down to the hospital. And I'm not going to see you again to-night. I'll send some books up to you. To-morrow we'll try to talk properly. No, I must go, darling."

"Well, for the love of Joshua," I said, "take care of yourself in that blackout."

THE END

Lightning Source UK Ltd.
Milton Keynes UK
UKHW040636141222
413914UK00004B/412